STRANGERS AND SOJOURNERS

STRANGERS AND SOJOURNERS

STORIES FROM THE LOWCOUNTRY

MARY POTTER ENGEL

COUNTERPOINT

A MEMBER OF THE PERSEUS BOOKS GROUP

NEW YORK

Counterpoint books are available at special discounts for bulk
purchases in the United States by corporations, institutions, and
other organizations. For more information, please contact the Special
Markets Department at the Perseus Books Group, 11 Cambridge
Center, Cambridge MA 02142, or call (617) 252-5298, (800) 255-1514
or e-mail special.markets@perseusbooks.com.

Designed by Trish Wilkinson

Library of Congress Cataloging-in-Publication Data
Engel, Mary Potter.
    Strangers and sojourners : stories from the lowcountry / Mary Potter
Engel.
        p.   cm.
    ISBN 1-58243-264-3 (alk. paper)
    1. South Carolina—Social life and customs—Fiction. I. Title.
PS3605.N44S77 2004
813'54—dc22   2003020892

04 05 06 / 10 9 8 7 6 5 4 3 2 1

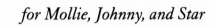

for Mollie, Johnny, and Star

The land shall not be sold in perpetuity,
for the land is Mine; for you are
strangers and sojourners with Me.

—LEVITICUS 25:23

CONTENTS

ACKNOWLEDGMENTS

Many generous spirits contributed to the creation of this book, and I am grateful to each one: first and always—Win, Sam, and Miriam Engel; Mollie Partin, John Partin (z"l), and Star Bennett (z"l), who showed me kindness and love in a dark time, taught me goodness, and made me laugh; Maude Thompson, Lanee Summers, Tammie Caldwell, and Vicky Beals—valiant hearts all; Dianne Probst; the many gracious and vibrant people of the South Carolina Lowcountry; the Lowcountry itself, with its ancient, enduring, and mysterious beauty, at once comforting and unsettling; my sister, Laurie Mills; Cindy Bailey, Stacy Lawson, and Elana Zaiman; Richard Schmitt and Charlene Finn; Monroe Engel; Brenda Engel; Jack Shoemaker; Brenda Gregory Hawkins, dialect queen; Big Mary, Mary Farrell Bednarowski, who taught me to look for the religious imagination outside the academy; Geri Thoma, agent and wise woman; Dawn Seferian, editor and friend, and the others at Counterpoint Press and Perseus Books Group: Patricia E. Boyd and Kay Mariea. "May you find your world in your lifetime" (*Babylonian Talmud, Berachot* 17a).

STRANGERS AND SOJOURNERS

QUEEN ESTHER
COOSAWAW

You want to know how I come by my name. Well, I can tell you that, if you got the time. You thinkin' my mama went fishin' in her Bible with a blind finger and caught a name for me, ain't you? Sure you is. That's what everybody think. But that's not so. Nossir. It weren't my mama or my pawpaw or Old Meme who found my name. The *Maker* give me my name, before I was born. Before my bones was knit, He called out my name and I came flyin' to this earth to do what I was called to do in that very name. And when I'm done livin' out that name, I'll move on. Not a second before, not a second after. The Old Maker do that with everything in this world. Don't call some and somebody else call the rest. He call *everything* alive—the trees and the rivers, the rocks and the dirt. You, too. Well, well, well. Yessir, if you got ears to hear, I can tell you how I come by my name. You got the time, Mister Doctor Reuben? You sure now? I *know* you doctors are real busy.

Before you come here, Pug Padgett was always busy. Some folks didn't like Pug, because he was on pills. They say he sent everybody to get the same operation, too, to fix up the artery on your neck, this one here, and he gave everybody the same medicine, pain medicine. But I'll tell you what: Pug was a prince. He never ask could you pay. He just took care of you and took your two dollars a month or whatever you could give—turnip, sweet potato, croakers. Pug liked croakers. And he never yelled at you like Doctor Calloway does, makin' you feel this high. Pug'd get mad and start stompin' and hollerin' like a preacher, but he never cursed you. He cursed what was ailin' you. "That goddamm arthuritis," he'd yell, stompin' he foot so's the floor shook. "I'd like to shoot that sonofabitch." Lots of folks miss Pug. He's gone on. I don't believe that boy killed heself. I think he just wore heself out helpin' people. I know how that runs. I raised seven head of children and some days I don't want to see a one of 'em anymore. That's why I live by myself.

You think a hundred and fourteen is too old to live by myself. Sure you do, everybody white do. But I don't say I live alone. I got a loudspeaker hooked up to my porch, and if I fall or get myself in a fix, I just call out for help and somebody come. Don't have to be one of my children or grands or great grands or great greats. Whoever hear me come by to do what need to be done. All the people livin' here in Ritter are my children. Different ones come by every day to turn me in my bed, bring me hot rice, read the Bible, or just visit with me, the way you're visitin' with me now, before you start your doctory proddin' and pokin' with those cold hands of yours. First time my niece had you come see me and you had those cold hands goin' thisaway and that on me, lookin' for trouble in my skin, I knew you wasn't from around here. Even Pug took care not to touch us ones. You treatin' me all right comin' by me for my examinations, Mister Doctor Reuben. Yes you are. Next time you come, I'll make you latkes. I make the best latkes in Coosawaw County. Ask anybody. I fry 'em in fresh peanut oil, got to be fresh each time, and I throw in a certain spice don't nobody know. Every Chanukah Mrs. Klein had all her friends in just to show off my latkes. They were that much better than the ones Jestine and Mary and Belle made for their Jewish ladies.

Mrs. Klein was my Jewish lady for many year. She had tzuris, Mrs. Klein. Her husband was a schnorrer. You know what that mean. And she had no people. No mama or pawpaw, no sister or brother or cousin. No children neither. *Ein kind ist von Gott.* That's what she say every time one of my grands born. She was a sickly woman, Mrs. Klein, always takin' medicine and runnin' to this big doctor in Charleston and that one in Savannah. Doctors didn't do her no good. She been gone fifty years, maybe more. And nobody carryin' on her memory. Nobody keepin' her bound up with all that's livin', so she out there driftin' free, lost to the world. If I could reach out my hand and pull her in here with me, I would. But they is some things a body can't do, no matter how strong they made. And I'm *strong.* That's how I know you're goin' give me a good report today, Mister Doctor, because Old Maker made me strong. When I work for Judge Peden Williams, he say I was strong as a horse. What do you think of that? I think he never knowed a horse. He was a city boy. My cousin Mordecai was strong, too. We been through all kind of evils together, Mordecai and me. Here in Coosaw County, but in Shushan, too.

How can I tell you Mordecai? Mordecai was like that red wolf pup they had on Bull's Island. That pup was born wild but they were keepin' him in a pen with he father to study him. He kept jumpin' and jumpin' at that high wire fence until he caught he hind leg and broke it. When they opened the pen to bring it to the doctor, that pup ran clean away. I don't think they seen their prize wolf since. Too smart for 'em.

Not even that old Haman James Upchurch the Fourth could stop Mordecai. When Upchurch tried to make Mordecai step off the sidewalk when he passed him in town, Mordecai could of gone along and stepped aside. Lots did, to save their skin. But Mordecai didn't lower heself, not before a one of God's creatures, specially before a little peep of a man fool enough to think he a mighty alabaster god. I know be trouble when he did that, and sure enough, old Haman got mad. He put Mordecai in the jailhouse. He say Mordecai stole he watch when he workin' in the yard, but all Mordecai took from him was he pride, and that Upchurch boy Number Four didn't deserve none of that to begin with.

I went to visit Mordecai in the jailhouse. They was two jailhouses, then, like you had two waitin' rooms for the doctor. My grands say some of the doctors in town still have it that way. They don't name it what it is, but everybody who come know where he better sit. I sure hope you don't have that at your office, Mister Doctor, 'cause the Maker ain't pleased with that. Well, well, well. When Mordecai was in the jailhouse, he told me, "Esther, you got to help. You got to speak to Judge Williams and tell him what's happenin'." I was *scared*. Judge Williams didn't know I had connection with Mordecai, who was known 'round town for he uppity ways. And just for openin' your mouth in those days—that was right near after World War Number One—just for sayin' anything but "No Ma'am" or "Thank you, sir," they let you go. And once one of them people let you go, wouldn't *nobody* hire you, because you was a troublemaker.

I had five head of children to feed and a husband who went up North to get a job and never come back. I didn't want to speak to Judge Williams. I was scared for my children. I didn't eat or sleep two days. I prayed and I prayed. Then I just got up and did it. I said to myself, "If he fires me, he fires me, but I got to go see him to his face." I didn't wait until the judge come home from the court that day. Nossir. I went down to the courthouse right then. I hid in the hall 'til I saw he secretary leave for the bathroom, and just that minute I slipped into he office. The judge was bent over he desk workin' at papers, and I just walked up to the edge of that big desk and said, "Judge Williams, I got somethin' to say." I surprised him all right. He didn't recognize me there for a time. He never seen me outside he house before. He looked and he *looked* at me. I don't recall breathin' for that while, I was prayin' so heavy. And then I heard a voice—you can believe it or not, it make no difference to me—a voice callin' my name, and just then Judge Williams smile at me, not he politician smile or he kind master smile or he husband smile, but he true kind smile. "Why, Esther," he say, "sit down." I didn't have time to sit. My mouth just opened up and I told him the whole story of Mordecai and Upchurch in one breath. When I stop, the judge stay quiet for a time. The Spirit put a way to he brains to catch on to these things and he was comin' up wise. The judge got heself up and closed the door to he office and told me to go home and not say nothing to nobody, not even Mrs. Williams. He said he'd tell he secretary I come in to ask him to serve papers on my husband up in New York. Well, well, well.

I went straight back to Judge Williams's house. I didn't say nothing to Mrs. Williams. I did the washin' and ironin', made their dinner, laid out their breakfast things, and cleaned up. When I come home late that night, Mordecai was waitin' for me in the kitchen. He was so happy he couldn't sit still. He lifted me up and danced me 'round the room until I thought the children were sure to wake. Later we read in the paper that James Upchurch IV resigned as county administrator. "Personal reasons," the article said. Needed to spend more time on he law practice. A few long year after that, Mordecai ran for a place on the county board and won, first black man Coosawaw County ever had in the government and the onliest one 'til President Lyndon Baines Johnson took the seat. Some claimed Mordecai ran a corrupt election. They gave out that half the people who voted for him didn't have no registration certificate and their votes shouldn't count. But they couldn't get him removed. The whole world was liftin' up, liftin' up. Mordecai served twenty year on that board, every day proud as the first.

We two got married right after my papers come through. That was a sunshine weddin'! Right here in this very house you're sittin' in with your baldy head. Oh, we had us a *time* that day! Yes we did. Mordecai's people smoothed the yard all 'round and raked a fresh pattern in the dirt, a weddin' pattern somebody remembered from the old ways, neat sets of lines makin' long waves endin' in spirals, all of 'em connectin' in a wondrous way. Clear 'round the house that pattern wound, 'cept for one smooth path aimin' straight for the back door and another leadin' out the front. My people wrapped this whole house in muslin, yards and yards of unbleached muslin, windin' it right off the bolt onto the house, 'round and 'round and 'round, swaddlin' this place like it was the baby Moses ready to be put in that basket down the river. They snugged up everything, all the windows and the open front door too, leavin' just a little bit of an openin' at the bottom of the back door for people to duck under. Only one way in and one way out when they was through, that back door hole, and all our family and guests and the preacher come in that way.

After the ceremony and celebration, when Mordecai and I got ready to leave, the preacher shooed everybody out 'cept us. When they was all outside, standin' in the front yard, the preacher led Mordecai and me through the livin' room and stood us at the front door lookin' out through that muslin veil coverin' the entrance. The sun was shinin' through it soft, and we could just make out shadows movin' on the other side, like watchin' a dream of heaven. They was all chatterin' and hushin' each other. Then somebody started singin' "Honey in the Rock." You don't know how that goes, do you? *"Oh, children, one of these mornin's I was walkin' 'long,"* like that. And they all joined in:

> *I saw the grapes was a-hangin' down, Lord,*
> *I pick a bunch and I suck the juice,*
> *It's the sweetest grape that I ever taste.*

STRANGERS AND SOJOURNERS

When they was done with the chorus, *"Honey in the rock, got to feed God's children / Feed every child of God,"* when they reached the end of the singin', it was silent as the grave out there. The preacher took a scissors and made a cut at the bottom of the muslin, right in the center of the entrance. Then he laid the scissors down, grabbed hold of that cloth with he two hands, and ripped it open with a wonderful tearin' like to wake the dead. "Behold the king and queen," he called out. And Mordecai and I stepped into a world of glory.

That's how I come by my name, Queen Esther Coosawaw. Now you know it, Mister Doctor Reuben, you can lay those cold hands of yours on me and give me my report.

YOU GOT TO LEARN HOW
TO READ THINGS RIGHT

Since my baby got Jesus, you can't hardly talk to her. "Thank you, Jesus, Help me, Jesus," is about all that comes out when she opens her mouth. Evelyn'll barely speak to me now without beggin' me to confess my sins and be made whole— just because some preacher says I'm "consortin' with the Devil." I tell her the Devil has nothin' to do with it—I have my own talent.

I don't say I'm better than anybody else. When Evelyn wanted to add "DO NOT COMPARE HER WITH ANY OTHER DIVINER" to my sign, I told her no. I'm no better or worse than anyone else. I am what God made me. I can give out lucky charms, lucky numbers, lucky days; change luck from bad to good; draw out snake poison with sweet spirits of niter; cure the loss of a man's nature; read crystals, cards, palms, bumps on the skull—whatever can be read. It's accordin' to what the customer wants. I do whatever they need. Except for roots. If somebody puts the root on you, sprinkles yellow powder around your house or messes with your food or throws a dead chicken in your yard, you have to go see Old Mary. I don't do roots.

I been readin' things since I was a girl. I came up seein' colors around people's heads that told me if they were lyin' or truthin'. Sometimes their future would open up to me on the edges of my eyes. When I was ten I read the ocean. It was pullin' my baby sister out, down past Edisto Beach, and she was screamin'. I swam out and held on to her, tellin' her, "Don't fight it, don't fight it." I knew the water would kill us both if we didn't bide our time and drift along until it weakened and left us a chance. We just had to be ready when that moment came and we could slip away free. Half a mile down, the tide gave up its hold on us, and I swam for safety, pullin' Grace Ann with me. I hadn't ever heard of a rip tide. I knew all that from readin' the water.

I didn't ask for all those powers—they just came to me. And they brought me my own troubles, too. I thought on account of them, no one would marry me—that's why I never said anything about them to Wayne until he lost his job and I had to hang out my sign. I knew he'd understand the money part and leave the rest alone and he did. That's one thing I'll give Wayne—he never hindered my workin'.

Evelyn was proud of my work 'til this preacher got a hold of her. She's the one designed and painted my new sign a few years back, the one that draws so many people. It says "SISTER GLORIA, DIVINE HEALER AND SPIRIT READER" across the top. In the middle is a peacock, big as life, an eternal eye at the top of each feather. And runnin' down the tail, one word to a feather, is my motto: "HAPPINESS IS YOUR DESTINY DON'T BE SCARED THE SPIRIT WILL SET YOU FREE." Under the feet it says, "Advice on Business, Travel, and Love. $10.00." Ten dollars ain't much for what I give. If a person can't afford but five dollars or two, that's all I ask.

Evelyn and I have always been closer than the bark and the sap. From the time she was a little bit of a thing, Evelyn used to beg me could I help her. Could I see if her kittens were in heaven? Would Easy ask her to the dance? Would she find a rich husband who would love her to death? When Easy left her with two babies, she practically wore my ears off askin' me to tell her where he went, what he was doin', when he'd be comin' back. Course I never told her a thing. You don't read for those close to you. That's too much pain. I told Evelyn over and over there weren't no need for special powers to see that Easy was no good, that she'd be better off without him—anybody could read that right in his face and the way he treated her.

Now that she's taken up with that preacher, Evelyn don't want nothin' to do with my powers. She won't talk to me without a Bible coverin' her heart, protectin' her from me. Soothsayers and neck romancers and murderers like Saul and the Witch of Endor go to Hell, she tells me. "You got to get Jesus. Jesus is burstin' with forgiveness, even for the worst of sinners." When she says "worst of sinners," she looks at me with sorrowful eyes squinty with pain.

"What about that time when I was seven," she asks, "and Daddy made me watch him drown my kittens in a potato sack and then he got sick the next day and went to the hospital for the first time? What happened? What'd you do? God's truth, Mama. 'The truth will set you free.'"

Might as well tell the truth—my Evelyn's easily swayed, especially by men. Always has been. The second time Wayne spent a week in the hospital with the stomach flu, she came home from school cryin' because of a boy's foolishness.

"Will Hamilton said you poisoned Daddy," she said.

"That boy's got a big imagination for a ten-year-old," I said.

"He heard his mama tell her friend that it was clear as day and time somebody did somethin' about it. 'Why else your daddy been losin' weight for months,' he asked me, 'and his color's real bad, but soon as he goes to the hospital he gets better, with no medicine or nothing? Why else it happened just like the last time he got sick, when you was seven?' That's what he asked me. Why, Mama? Why?"

"That's just talk, Baby Girl. Dull-spirited people tryin' to make things out worse than they are. Don't you listen to them. Doctor Calloway says your daddy's got a mean virus. You tell that Will Hamilton to mind his own house before it falls down on him."

When Wayne passed last winter, after another one of those sicknesses came over him, it was Easy who filled Evelyn with fool-headed ideas. He told her she couldn't leave the kids with me anymore because I might do somethin' to them. What am I goin' to do to them but love them, the way I always have, the way I loved Evelyn? But Evelyn was scared, so I told her to go talk to the coroner, the one who came to the house when Wayne was at the funeral parlor. He's so kind, I told her. When he came to the door, he told me right off how sorry he was to bother me in my grief, but that he had to do his duty. Somebody—he couldn't say who—had called and said to check for poison and he hoped I'd understand that when there was any question, he had no choice but to order a toxicology report. Before I could bury my husband, he had to take blood and tissue samples from him, check his hair and fingernails for deposits. He told me not to worry. As far as he could see, nothin' was amiss. Doctor Reuben had shown him Wayne's records from the last months, and Doctor Calloway had sent him records of Wayne's stomach ulcers and bad liver and told him Wayne wouldn't stop drinkin' for anything and that's the reason he refused to treat him anymore. It was just a matter of protocol, the coroner said. He promised to call me the minute the toxicology report came back and let me know everything was OK and he did.

That sweet, young coroner could set Evelyn's mind at ease, but she won't go to him. She wouldn't listen to him when her daddy died, because she was afraid of Easy, and she won't listen to him now, because now she don't mind nobody but Reverend Robert.

"Reverend Robert says Cain went to Hell not for murderin' but for lyin' about it," she says. "Reverend Robert says the Bible says, 'You cannot hide from God; the Spirit will find you out.'"

I quote the Bible right back at her. "'The sad you have always with you.' What about that?" I ask her. "Didn't Jesus say that? And didn't he say, 'Blessed are the happy'? What good's the Bible if you don't know how to read it right? What kind of help can that boy preacher give you? Robert's barely thirty and he hasn't been saved but a year. Just because you got wavy hair, buy yourself a used trailer and call it the Lighthouse Deliverance Temple, and holler at people don't mean you know anything about the Spirit. You can't kill the joy of the Spirit. Anybody who tries can't be trusted—a preacher no different from the rest. 'The Spirit works in mysterious ways.' That's in the Bible, too. Anybody can read it there if they know how to read things right."

Does Evelyn think her preacher and his misery-worshippin' Jesus could have done any better by her that year she turned a woman? After Wayne came home from the hospital that time, she wouldn't even speak to him. He would stand outside her room callin', "Lynnie, Lynnie"—like a puppy that's been punished for wettin' on the floor. But Evelyn wouldn't answer him. For months she just sat in her room in the dark and painted pictures—hundreds of pictures of dark faces floatin' in garbage, two white holes where the eyes should be.

Evelyn's been unhappy most of her life. First her daddy misusin' her, then Easy. Easy disappeared for three years and showed up at her trailer for supper one night like he'd never left. Never has said a word about what he did all that time she was strugglin' to raise those two babies. All Evelyn knows is he won't register to vote, fill out a job application, or get a driver's license. She has to drive him everywhere. Bein' unhappy gives Evelyn the strength to go on. That's why she likes her preacher so much. He tells her God afflicts those he loves, purifies them with tears. He's got Evelyn thinkin' she's a saint.

No one wants to live with a saint, I tell her. They make people nervous. But Evelyn won't give it up. Evelyn can believe whatever she wants and give more money to that preacher than she can afford, but it won't work. That preacher can't hold back the Spirit. Someday the Spirit's going to bust her wide open and she'll be her happy self. She *will* be happy. She's got to accept that. It's as true as her Jesus. Somehow, somewhere, happiness is goin' to sneak up on her and jump her. Maybe one day she'll be gatherin' up the eggs from her Rhode Island Reds and she'll start cluckin' to them. She'll quick look around to make sure no one saw her and hurry into the garden. But when she digs her hands into the ground, she'll start speakin' in tongues to her mustard greens and grinnin' to herself out of sheer joy for the world. She won't be able to help it. Nobody can hide from happiness. Happiness hunts you down, and when it finds you, it cracks you right open, and all those bad feelin's you worked so hard to grow inside, all the smallness of your spirit, all just drips out onto the floor and you slip into that mess and end up laughin' at yourself.

Happiness will get you in the end. Nobody can stop it. Not Evelyn, not her Reverend Robert, not her daddy, not even a man like Pee Wee Gaskins, the one that went all over South Carolina stranglin' women and choppin' off their heads and arms. Right before the authorities electrocuted him, he said he *liked* killin' those women, chokin' off their chance for happiness—it made him feel like *God*. But he was wrong. God's mightier than that. Pee Wee and Wayne and Evelyn and her Reverend Robert can believe they're mightier than God, but they can't hold back the power of happiness. They've got to accept that there are some things it's impossible for a human bein' to do, so you might as well quit tryin'. The Spirit *will* set you free, it *will* make you happy, and there's not a thing you can do about it.

Evelyn says happiness is prideful, that the Lord wants us to be content with our lot, but she's just jealous because I learned all that about happiness in a vision and she hasn't had a vision, even though she's at that church every night prayin' for one. Reverend Robert tells her she might could have one if she keeps at it. But that's not how you get visions, tryin' for them. They got to come to you, find *you* out. That's how I know mine was a vision, and it was just as good as anybody's, even though I hadn't been fastin' and prayin'. Some things cost a lot more than fastin' and prayin'.

Wayne and I were married two years when my vision came. We lived out the far edge of town, by Chessey Bridge Landing, in a little rented house. That spring was colder than usual, with freezes off and on. The camellias all turned brown on the bush, and the redbud and dogwoods couldn't get themselves to bloom into a full display. I had just come back from the hospital, and my neck and ribs were still sore, so I nursed the baby real careful. She was so excited about me bein' back she bit me. I would've cried out if I hadn't been afraid of the pain in those ribs. Wayne had never hit me hard enough to crack anything before. I knew he was sorry and that when his shift was over he'd show up with a bottle of gardenia perfume, a bunch of sweetheart roses, and a pitiful look—none of which we could afford. I shifted Evelyn to the other breast, closed my eyes, and breathed in the scent of her scalp.

Miss Fishburne's peacocks woke me up. They were totterin' through the back yard, headin' to my garden to strip it bare. They were always comin' to my house to eat. They couldn't be satisfied with Miss Fishburne's acres of prize camellias and azaleas. I didn't bother to chase them off. Yellin' would have started my ribs hurtin' again and scared Evelyn awake. And it was no use. Those birds won't budge until they're ready. They just hold their ground, blinkin' their steel-shot criminal eyes, until they decide in their stunted brains it's time to womble off to steal food somewhere else. Useless creatures with draggy tails. Not even pretty, their pinheads nothin' but a mean face endin' in a weapon. I couldn't see why anyone would send all the way to India for creatures like that and pay more for them than I spent on groceries in a year. The only thing those birds were good at was matin'. From March clear through August they kept me awake all night. *Mee-awg*, they'd scream, their voices rippin' open the darkness. *Mee-awg, awg-awg-awg.* The first time I heard them, I thought somebody was bein' tormented. Wayne thought that was funny. "That's peacock love," he said. "You'll get used to it."

I nestled Evelyn into my shoulder and hurried out the back door onto the porch to catch those peafowl at their dirty business. They were rootin' around my collards, titterin' among themselves and diggin' their beaks in the dirt, twistin' them around, leavin' ugly holes in the ground. They ripped my tender greens close to the root, leavin' not one plant with a scarce chance to survive. I headed straight inside for the phone.

"Miss Fishburne," I said, "them birds of yours are eatin' my greens again!"

"Why are you tellin' me?"

"Don't you get my vittles stirred up. You come over here this minute and stop them."

"You must be feedin' them," she said, "or they wouldn't be wanderin' over there."

"The only thing I'll be feedin' them is buckshot," I said and hung up on her.

She knew I would. Right before Evelyn was born, Miss Fishburne called all excited and said there was a snake in her yard set to poison her peafowl. I told her Wayne was off somewheres but I'd be over directly to shoot it, if it wasn't a razorback. I won't kill a razorback. I've stepped real near razorbacks and not one has ever come after me. They just go about their business. Same with a beach rattler. Now a cottonmouth is different. They're just plain mean. They'll run you, chase you down if you half look at them sideways, even if you don't. Miss Fishburne said this one was a cottonmouth, so I went over and shot it for her. Got it once near the head, and when it started crawling toward her, I finished it. Miss Fishburne and her peafowl might be dead if it wasn't for me. You'd think she'd be thankful. But any time I call her 'bout her precious birds thievin' in my yard, she makes like it's my business. I wouldn't anymore feed those birds than I'd serve wine to a buzzard. She knew that for a fact. She knew I'd shoot 'em, too, if I had to.

Before I got three steps from the phone, it rang again.

"If anything happens to those peacocks, you'll pay," Miss Fishburne said. "Those birds are expensive."

"And you can sure afford to feed them, Miss Mighty. Why don't you rip out some of those flowers you're so proud of and plant those birds a breakfast, dinner, supper, and dessert garden of their own?"

I heard her suck in her breath.

"You pen those devils up, Florrie," I said, "or I'm goin' to shoot every one of them."

"That kind of bird is meant to roam," she said.

"So is my baby child! How is she goin' to do that with their mess all over my yard? You come over here and clean up their shit."

I hung up on her and walked to the back door, balancin' Evelyn on my hip. When I opened the door, there was a flutterin' of wings. The porch was covered with birds. Some were roostin' on the railin', some were peckin' at the flakin' paint on the floor, bumpin' into each other as they went. Others stood there lookin' blank, confused. Several had already left their slimy brown-green callin' cards. I stood in the doorway spittin' mad. Evelyn had just started crawlin', and she was jammin' everything in her mouth. Those filthy beasts were goin' to make her sick with their mess. I kicked at them, hollerin', "Get out! Get out!" They started runnin' and flitterin' about, not goin' anywhere, just changin' places with each other. I waved my arm and screamed, "Get yourself gone! Gone!"

One of the cocks jumped off the rail and flew by me into the house, brushin' Evelyn's face and neck with its tail feathers as he passed. She blinked her eyes several times, as if waitin' for it to come back and do it all over again, just to please her. Then all of a sudden, she laughed. Her face stretched to its limit and she shook, just shook, with pleasure. She beat her hands together and burbled to the mess of birds still on the porch, invitin' them to fly inside.

I hugged her to me, pressed her close against my chest. Holdin' her so happy, I felt a lightenin', a tinglin', as if somethin' were burstin' deep inside and bubblin' up under my skin. It spread, quickly, to my nose, cheeks, shoulders, then down through my legs until I could hardly stand still. To steady myself, I leaned harder against the door. It opened wider. The peacocks nearest to me skittered away at first, but then stood still and stared at me and Evelyn. Evelyn beat her hands together and called to them, with cries almost as strange as theirs. Jerkin' their necks, those birds—all thirteen of them—picked their way over the threshold, like so many circus clowns stumblin' along, bumblin' over each other, against invisible rocks, into holes that didn't exist. As they paraded past, I rubbed Evelyn's nose with mine. We couldn't stop grinnin' at each other and I knew right then everything was goin' to be all right. That me and my baby would know from then on how to make things right, her helpin' me and me helpin' her, every day, to see the joy crowdin' around us and inside us, pick it out of the darkness, together. There wasn't nothin' we couldn't raise ourselves out of together. She was my joy. I lifted Evelyn over my head and made her fly around the room, swoopin' her through the natterin' peacocks, both of us laughin', forgettin' everything but each other and our happiness.

It was right after my vision that I cleared Wayne's junk out of the back room, dragged an old table in there, and hung my first sign in the window. It didn't take but a day for the first customer to stop in—a grayish man travelin' back to New Jersey because his gas station in Savannah had gone bankrupt. He was so tickled with what I told him he gave me five dollars and I went right out and ordered my first radio from the Sears catalog. That radio got on Wayne's nerves as much as my singin' did. When we were first married, I used to sing all the time, just make up songs to match my feelin's. If he heard me, he'd sneak up behind me and put his hand over my mouth, or he'd kiss me so hard I couldn't move my mouth. After Evelyn was born, he just hollered if he caught me at it. "Can't a man get any peace in his own house?" When I got the radio, I stopped singin' my own songs and sang along with what they played, but I had to make sure it was off before Wayne came home or he'd pitch a fit and throw it out the window. I lost two radios that way. He just couldn't stand for me to sing.

Some people don't want to be happy. I can tell which ones they are when they come through my door. They act like everybody else, ask Sister Gloria to read the cards or their palms. But they don't fool me. I have an extra sense for that kind of hidin'. I read what they want in their faces, the way their eyes shut out the truth, their mouths work against their smiles. I know they don't want to hear about fallin' in love or everything workin' out fine. They want me to give them somethin' to fuss about, a reason for their unhappiness so they don't have to change what they've been used to and they can live satisfied in their misery. I give my best to people like that. I give them somethin' true—I predict they will be out of their minds happy in the near future. They refuse to believe it. They run out disappointed or mad, like that orange-haired nurse who yelled, "I'm callin' the Better Business Bureau! I know what you're up to!" I'm not up to anything. That nurse can take out an ad in the paper and say whatever she wants, but she's no better than anyone else. She's no different—she can't escape happiness. She'll be happy, too, sometime, some way.

I did my best by Evelyn. I loved her 'til I thought my heart would burst from joy just watchin' her funny ways—the way she painted flowers all over her arms and legs, the way she laid down in the dirt and let those kittens crawl all over her, ticklin' her, the way she flew around the room every time I cried, runnin' and bobbin' her head like those peacocks until I laughed. And I know deep inside her, way below Wayne and Easy and Reverend Robert, she remembers invitin' those birds inside and laughin' and swoopin' with them in the house. I did what I had to do so she wouldn't lose all her happiness. I was careful and bided my time, so they couldn't find it out and take me from her. I had to keep her safe so she wouldn't lose that happiness for good.

Evelyn may think she's got holiness, but it's false spirits she's listenin' to, people who ain't happy and don't want nobody else to be happy. There can't be no holiness without happiness. I know what it means to be happy. When I'm not helpin' customers, I'm singin' my own happiness out with the radio, every minute of the day. Happy people don't need to hurt others with their foolish talk about things they don't know a thing about. That's what I'll tell Evelyn the next time she starts preachin' all over me. I didn't teach you to be unhappy, Baby Girl. You learned that from your daddy. Somewhere along the way, you started lookin' on the gloomy side, believin' whatever nasty thing anybody told you. You got to learn how to read people. People will tell you any old story to get you to be as miserable as they are. You got to learn how to read them right.

Listen to me, I'll tell Evelyn. Listen to me real good this time, and don't you hang up on me, because I don't want to hear about this ever again, from you or Easy or anybody. Was Easy there when your daddy pushed open the back door with his twelve-pack in the middle of the mornin' and found you crawlin' on the kitchen floor in the sunlight playin' with those peacocks and me just sittin' on the floor with my back against the sink, watchin' and laughin'? Was any of those pea-brained gossips Easy listens to there? Did they see Wayne throw his beer against the wall and start kickin' at those birds, all in a fit? Start them screechin' and flyin' away from him as best they could, catchin' their feet in his hair and brushin' him with their wings? Did they smell all that musky smell they stirred up in that room? No. Those people didn't see none of that. They weren't there. And if they weren't there, how could any of them know about you and me and our life and what's right for us? Did your Reverend Robert see Wayne grab for one of the cocks and slip in the droppin's, landin' hard on the linoleum and me still laughin' in spite of my ribs? Did he see Wayne push himself up from the floor and wipe his hands on his pants? Go outside to the truck? Walk back in with his gun and start shootin'—all while I was holdin' you close to me in my arms, coverin' your eyes and your ears as best I could? Did he hear those birds scream, runnin' and flyin' everywhere, trailin' blood across the floor, the counters, the table, your little daisy pajamas? Did he see the one get stuck in the light fixture over the table? See your daddy shoot it and leave it hangin' there? See him walk around the room afterwards and count those bodies, one by one, to make sure they were all dead? Then leave them there for me to bag up and bury so Miss Fishburne wouldn't find out? Leave me to do all that cleanin' and answer to Miss Fishburne when she came to the door wonderin' if we'd heard any shots, seen her birds—him watchin' TV and drinkin' his beer through it all? Was that misery-drunk preacher there when you turned seven and your daddy killed your kittens? When you were ten and he beat you near to death for playin' in the street with Miss Fishburne's latest crop of birds? When you were thirteen and you got sick with his misusin' you and you wouldn't let me watch over you? Did he see me bringin' treats to your room every day and night to cheer you up and you shuttin' me out? Not even talkin' to me? And your daddy goin' about his business? Rap-pin' on the bathroom door when you were showerin', slinkin' around in the middle of the night while those birds screamed their heads off? Did he watch you those long months turn all black and empty inside, like somebody had sucked the life out of you, stolen my sweet baby girl who made all my days so happy? Did your preacher see all that? Did he?

Reverend Robert wasn't there for none of that. He's makin' up stories to make himself important to you, so you'll listen to him about his Jesus. And to make trouble, because some people aren't happy without trouble. It's all they know, all they take comfort in because they don't know anything about happiness; they're scared to death of it. That preacher of yours can talk about Jesus and quote the Bible 'til he's out of breath, but he doesn't know one thing about how the Spirit works. You got to learn how to read things right, Evelyn. If you can't do that, you got nothin'. And nobody can live on nothin'. You got to have some joy. The Spirit sees to that. Don't ever let anybody kill your joy. Anybody who'd try to kill the Spirit ain't worth the air he's breathin'.

ALL THAT WE NEED

Billy Driggers guided his pickup with the license plate declaring JESUS! into a parking space outside Yblansky's Gem and Gift Emporium. "When you go out to spread the Word of God," Reverend Steen taught his students at the Lift Up Thy Voice School of Preaching, "head for the Jew store on the main street. Every town has one."

Billy stepped out of the truck and eased his door closed. "Walker," he said softly, leaning into the open window. "It's time."

Inside the cab, his thirteen-year-old son reached over, cranked up the driver's window as fast as he could, and shoved himself back against the passenger door with a thud.

Billy stooped to pick up a soggy bag of boiled peanut shells from the gutter, gathering the stray shells that had fallen around it, and tossed everything in Yblansky's sidewalk trash bin. It was hours before noon, but already the August air was heavy, pressing everything inward. Sweat stained the underarms of his white short-sleeved shirt and made his khakis sag about his knees. He rapped on the boy's window with his knuckles, wishing he could press his wedding band out with his thumb and click it against the glass, but it had been months since he had worn it. It lay where he had left it the night he came back from Beaufort and worked it over his knuckle with Fels-Naptha—in an empty pickle jar beside the kitchen sink, shining in the morning sun and catching the overhead light at night.

"God's waitin', Walker," Billy said through the glass.

"'For His patience endureth forever,'" the boy said, his voice blurred as if underwater.

"Psalm one thirty-six," Billy said. "Good boy."

Walker flung the door open, forcing Billy back toward the curb, and slid out. The boy's stiff new khakis, white short-sleeved shirt, skinny blue tie, and Marine haircut made him look paler and more angular than he was. Two of his top teeth needed fixing, but since he rarely smiled anymore, no one noticed. He jabbed a stiff palm in front of him and Billy laid a bundle of tracts on it. Walker pressed them down with his thumb so hard his hand shook. Billy reached for the boy's shoulder, but Walker shrugged away.

"Let's get to it then, Walker."

His tenderness was lost on Walker, who shoved past his father toward the sidewalk.

Billy hesitated, hoping to find something funny or easing to say, but nothing came to him.

The boy slouched against Yblansky's display window, the look on his face as hard as that on the jewel-laden, plastic bust behind him.

Billy nodded to him, then clicked the door shut and headed for the back of the truck. He leaped onto the rear bumper, swung his legs one after the other over the tailgate, and stood up. Behind him, the gun rack cut the rear window into three gleaming ribbons of glass. Pulling himself up straight, he planted his feet wide, coughed to clear his phlegm—worse now that he was smoking again—and faced the office of the *Pinesboro Gazette*. Reverend Steen insisted on full volume, always, from every preacher, experienced or new.

"When you preach the Word of God," he taught, "shout. SHOUT! Isaiah says, 'Lift up thy voice like a trumpet.' Pick a point a block away, and project your voice to it. You have to be loud to crack sinners open with the truth."

"THE FLESH OF JESUS CHRIST IS ONE FLESH!" Billy shouted to the *Gazette*.

He was surprised to hear words come out of his mouth. This was his first solo practice after joining Reverend Steen's school two months ago and his first time preaching in his own town. Never much of a talker, he had wanted to fill note cards with Bible verses and sermon outlines to keep in his shirt pocket, so he wouldn't be at a loss, but Reverend Steen had forbidden it. "No need to waste your brain writin' out speeches," he had told Billy. "God can use a lowly car mechanic to spread His Word just like He can use a poor, scared fisherman like Peter. All you got to do is trust the Holy Spirit. He'll give you the words when you need them. See if He don't."

It was that promise that had attracted Billy to Reverend Steen when he first heard him in Beaufort last April. He had gone to Beaufort to find Myra. His friend Emerson called the garage one afternoon to say he had seen Myra strolling the Beaufort dock, arm in arm with a Yankee. "She was wearin' sunglasses and a red straw hat that hid all her hair," Emerson said, "but it was her all right. Couldn't mistake those gorgeous legs that go on forever." Billy left work right away and drove to the coast, not bothering to change his heavy boots and grease-spotted coverall. In Beaufort he searched along the waterfront and in the arty shops on the side streets, but all he found was Reverend Steen and his students hollering on the main street.

The first two times up and down the street, Billy paid the preachers no mind. They were after the rich tourists they called "Lazaruses" and the street vendors in dangly earrings, tight-fitting tops, and tiny shorts—the "whores of Babylon"; he was invisible to them. But as he wound through the line of preachers the third time, peering into alleys and boutiques, investigating the passengers in the horse-drawn carriages that clomped by, one of the preachers called out to him.

"HEAR THE WORD OF GOD, YOU WHO ARE LOST."

Billy continued toward the inn with the wide wraparound porch at the end of the block, planning to stop inside this time, but the voice pursued him.

"'I WILL POUR OUT MY SPIRIT UPON ALL FLESH AND YOUR SONS AND YOUR DAUGHTERS SHALL PROPHESY.'"

He stopped and stared at the sherbet-colored dresses in a shop window, wondering if he should buy one for Myra, to say he was sorry for the way he was, that he wished he could be different, be the kind of man who would know what to say to her to take her sadness away and make everything right. Myra liked wild colors. "They're like friends who stop by just to cheer you up," she said.

"'THE LORD WILL GIVE YOU THE TONGUE OF ANGELS.' YES HE WILL. FIRST CORINTHIANS THIRTEEN."

Billy turned and walked back to the preacher. He was a lumpy boy with a face like a beagle and hair just as short, but he spoke as easily as a deer ran. Billy, his hands in his pockets, head cocked to one side, listened in awe. When Reverend Steen tapped him on the shoulder seconds later and told him he could teach him how to speak in the Spirit, Billy was ready.

"Moses thought *he* couldn't speak," Reverend Steen told him, "and look what God helped him do. How much *more* we can do with *Jesus*. Jesus is the *Word* of *God*. Only believe on the *Word,* and words of *power* will come rushin' out your mouth."

This struck Billy hard. He had never imagined you could change what you were: You were born quiet and that's what you stayed; people took you as you were or left you alone. No one expected a basenji to bark; if you wanted a watchdog, you bought a

Doberman. He hadn't known you could study how to speak, learn words that could fix troubles, turn the world inside out, dismantle it and rebuild it good as new, everything running smoothly again.

Before he left Beaufort that day, he had signed up for Reverend Steen's Lift Up Thy Voice School. He agreed eagerly to read the Bible every morning and night, attend the evening classes held twice a week at Reverend Steen's house in Aiken, bring the first tuition installment of one hundred dollars to the next class, and come to the Saturday practice sessions held up and down the Lowcountry coast. Even though the extra expense, the one-and-a-half-hour drive to Aiken from Pinesboro two times a week, and the long Saturday trips to dens of sinners like Myrtle Beach and Hilton Head had made it hard for him and Walker the last two months, Billy had been faithful.

And just as Reverend Steen had promised, God had rewarded Billy's faithfulness and brought him victory. At the end of eight weeks, he had been made ready to speak in the Spirit, to stand up in his truck on the main street of his town and call out, in a loud and flowing voice, the Word of God to the lost.

"THE FLESH OF JESUS CHRIST IS ONE FLESH," Billy preached outside Yblansky's, hurling his voice across Lucas Street to the *Gazette*. "AND IT SHALL NOT BE PUT ASUNDER."

He was shouting so loud he could feel the strain in his vocal chords, even though he had done all his warm-up exercises and drunk his warm water cut with lemon juice before he left the house and he was taking extra care to preach from his diaphragm, not his throat—all according to instructions. Reverend Steen did not allow his students to begin in a softened or normal voice and work up to the shouting for emphasis; those tricks were for pulpit preachers, the ones seeking money and new brick buildings with towering white columns. In his school, established just last year and growing faster than anything in Coosawaw County, including the loblolly pines the wealthy planted on their extra acres as a quick cash crop, the volume never varied. "Ain't one thing more important than another in God's truth," he told his students. "If your throat bleeds after three or four hours of preaching, well then, think of Jesus bleedin' on the cross."

"JESUS IS ETERNAL GOD BECOME MAN," Billy preached. "ONE FLESH. NOT TWO." He couldn't see anyone inside the *Gazette* office, but he knew they were there behind the blinds. "ONE FLESH. THE LORD JESUS CHRIST. JESUS IS LORD OVER PINESBORO, LORD OVER COOSAWAW COUNTY, LORD OVER THE WHOLE WORLD." He didn't point his finger to the sky or stomp his foot, the way he had seen the TV preachers do. "God don't want no show from anybody," Reverend Steen always reminded them. "God wants us to hear His Word and His Word speaks for itself."

"LET ALL WHO HAVE EARS TO HEAR, HEAR."

Billy turned his head to swallow discreetly and saw Walker hunched near the corner of Yblansky's display window, bobbing his head and working his mouth furiously while watching his reflection in the glass. He was mimicking his preaching and having a good time doing it, but Billy couldn't think what he should say to make him stop. Inside the store, Jacob Yblansky was watching the boy mock Billy, disrespecting his father.

Billy took a deep breath. "HEAR THE WORD OF GOD, ALL YE STIFF-NECKED, REBELLIOUS ONES," he shouted toward Yblansky. He knew if Sol Yblansky, Jacob's father, had still been alive, he would have come out directly and spat on his truck. "Folks will taunt you," Reverend Steen told them. "They'll spit on you, douse you with beer, spray you with a hose. Somebody tried to choke me once. When they despise and reject you, you just remember God's Word can't be silenced and you praise God all the more, for givin' you the privilege of being his sufferin' servant."

Billy didn't expect this Yblansky to come outside and spit: He was too sly. He might call the police, though. Pinesboro's noise ordinance was just as strict as Beaufort's. One complaint from someone as prominent as Yblansky might be enough to get him arrested the way Reverend Steen and the others had been last month. "Don't be afraid to get arrested," Reverend Steen said. "When the apostle Paul went to prison, he said, 'For I am not ashamed of the gospel.'" If it hadn't been for Walker, Billy would have been in jail with them now, planning a defense of free speech with the celebrity attorneys from New York, preaching from his cot to the other prisoners, talking to the papers about the conditions in the jail—overcrowded cells, rats crawling out of the vents, plaster falling from the ceilings—calling for a federal investigation and expensive, mandated improvements. But the afternoon they were planning to get arrested, the school guidance counselor called him at the shop and asked him to come meet with him right away about "a troubling and urgent matter" concerning Walker.

"JESUS IS THE WORD OF GOD MADE FLESH," Billy preached to Yblansky. "JESUS!"

Walker jerked away from his reflection in the window toward the store entrance, where Mr. Yblansky stood behind the glass door, his eyebrows pressed toward his cheekbones and his lips folded inward, as if he were remembering something sad he was afraid of letting out. Walker felt the old man's sadness in his own cheeks and mouth, an involuntary slackening that threatened to unloosen everything and wash him away. He tried to halt it by scrunching his lips tight to one side.

"UNLESS THOU BE WASHED IN THE BLOOD OF JESUS," Billy shouted, "THOU ART LOST, THOU." When he said "THOU" the second time, his right arm pointed at Yblansky, though this was strictly against Reverend Steen's rules.

Mr. Yblansky shrugged at Walker with his face, ending with a smile, as if to say, It's a big joke.

Billy raised himself taller. "THE BLOOD OF JESUS. WASH IN THE BLOOD OF JESUS AND BE CLEAN," he preached, careful not to turn his head midsentence and lose contact with the Jew, "FOR THOU ART DIRTY WITH THY DISOBEDIENCE, DIRTY. 'BELIEVE ON THE LORD JESUS CHRIST AND THOU SHALT BE SAVED, THOU AND THY HOUSE.'"

The sight of his daddy standing in the back of the pickup pointing his arm into the distance reminded Walker of the hunters he and his mama saw parked along country roads every fall. The camouflaged men would stand upright in their truck beds, every muscle tensed in eagerness, legs spread wide, rifles cocked and aimed, ready for the deer their dogs would soon flush out of the woods. For two years he had begged to go with his daddy and his buddies, just once, to stand up with them next to the empty dog cages, their doors hanging open, and wait for the flash of white, the sound of hooves, to try his luck, his aim, but his mama wouldn't let him. "There's enough dying," she said.

"HOW LONG WILT THOU DENY HIM? RETURN, O WHORIN' ISRAEL. RETURN UNTO ME." Billy dropped his arm and gripped his Bible with both hands, holding it like a shield over his heart.

The air conditioner over Walker's head dripped onto the sidewalk, each drop gathering torpidly, then, suddenly, falling headlong to the pavement. It was a lonely sound.

Several of Mr. Yblansky's employees and customers had gathered around him by the entrance to the store, flanking him protectively. Yblansky's long, oval face was blank, but some of the others looked worried or angry.

"JESUS SAID, 'NO ONE COMES TO THE FATHER BUT BY ME.'" Billy was shouting louder now, in spite of himself.

Mr. Yblansky said something to the group, then disappeared into the store. Shaking their heads, the others followed.

"THY REFUSAL IS A STENCH IN THE NOSTRILS OF GOD."

Behind the glass entrance door, a woman appeared, a gigantic purse hanging on one arm, a silver shopping bag on the other, and a large box wrapped in purple foil and dotted with a silver bow held gingerly in front of her. To Walker she looked like a mockingbird: small head cocked to the side, slight, and gray-brown everywhere. She glared at Billy, blinking her eyes rapidly, then flicked her head to the other side and glanced over her shoulder. Mrs. Yblansky hurried toward Camille Boatwright and stood beside her while Jacob Yblansky crossed the store to join them. Yblansky took the gift-wrapped box and shopping bag from Miss Boatwright, opened the door for her, and escorted her to her car. She bobbed along determinedly, her eyes fixed straight ahead.

"RUN, RUN, JUST AS FAST AS YOU CAN," Billy shouted at them, while he gestured impatiently to Walker to hand her a tract. "YOU CAN'T RUN AWAY FROM THE LOVE OF GOD. LOVE!"

Walker pushed himself away from the display window, jumped ahead of the woman and jabbed one of the tracts under her nose. She hesitated, and for a moment it looked as if she might speak to him, reprimand him for his manners, or ask him if his mama didn't have better things for him to do on such a hot day. Sometimes, when his mama wasn't too sad, they would forget his homework and spend the afternoon together, bicycle out to pick scuppernongs or visit her friend Blue's farm. They would bring Blue homemade cookies he called crackers, pick Crowder peas with him, fish in his pond, count his rattlesnake buttons. Walker's daddy didn't like them visiting Blue.

"What do you *do* out there with him?" his daddy asked her once.

"We talk," his mama said.

"You *talk*? How can you *talk*? That fool's deaf. He can't hear a word you say. And he can't speak so as anybody understands him. He talks some kind of deaf talk all mixed up with Gullah and crazy talk—that's what Jimmy in the lumber store says. I asked at the feed store, too, and they told me the same thing. The man can't speak and be heard. He's got to point at what he wants. So you tell me now, how can the two of you *talk*?"

"Blue and I understand all that we need to from each other. The words don't bother us."

"But Blue Hiott's not right in the head. Everybody knows it."

"He's my only friend," his mama said.

Finally his daddy complained so much about Blue that they stopped visiting him. After that, Walker would come home from school and find his mama sitting in the big chair in the living room, in the dark. Or the house would be empty. He would call and call her, but she would be gone, away on one of her "solitude trips," which she took more and more often. When that happened, his daddy would wait a few days, maybe a week—not over a month, like this time—and they would drive to one of her friend's houses in Beaufort or McClellanville, or to the nuns' place up the Ashley River, to bring her home. The closer they got to Pinesboro, the harder she cried. When they arrived, she went straight to her bed in the back room, and she would stay there for days, refusing to respond to anything, even when he brought her toast and instant coffee before catching the bus, or when he leaned over to kiss her good night. Watching her through the window after school, he saw her stare into the distance ahead of her for what seemed like hours, only her eyelids moving—she would be so far away.

"'FOR GOD SO LOVED THE WORLD, THAT HE GAVE HIS ONLY BEGOTTEN SON, THAT WHOSOEVER BELIEVETH IN HIM SHOULD NOT PERISH, BUT HAVE EVERLASTIN' LIFE.'"

Walker jiggled the tract in front of the mockingbird shopper's eyes, almost touching her nose with it. Backing away, the woman raised her chin, pursed her fire-engine red lips, and drew her purse tight across her flank like a shield. The boy leaped toward her again, brandishing the tract. Ignoring Mr. Yblansky, who was motioning her with his head to keep moving, Miss Boatwright came to a full stop and stared at the boy. She drew in a long breath, pulling herself to her full four feet and ten inches.

"Young man," she said in her elocutionary voice, "my great-grandmother was a founding member of the First Baptist Church of Pinesboro. My grandmother played the organ in that church. My mother ran the Ladies' Missionary Circle. And I sing in the choir in that same church every Sunday morning."

Walker glanced at his father in the truck and began chewing his lower lip intently.

Seeing the boy's agitation, Miss Boatwright softened her tone. "Why don't you go on home now," she said. "Let your mama make you a glass of tea."

Walker stiffened and thrust the tract in her face.

She hesitated a moment, then snatched it out of his hand so forcefully the thin pages tore, leaving a remnant in the boy's hand. She stepped past the boy, and Mr. Yblansky quickly followed, making sure he stayed between Miss Boatwright and the boy.

Unable to move, the torn tract burning his hand, Billy watched the woman leave.

As she hurried away from him down the sidewalk, the torn pages in her fist flapped open and shut, like the purified lips of a prophet speaking against her will. "It's not enough," the lips in her hand were saying, "It's not enough." Once, when Walker had come home from school, he had found his mama sitting on the bathroom floor, crying. When he asked, "Are you sick?" she shook her head no. He sat next to her on the cool tile and asked, "What's wrong?" but she didn't answer. They sat together, his hand resting tentatively on her knee, while the sunlight withdrew. When the room was gray, he said, "I love you, Mama." She stared at the dark lines splitting the tiles on the floor and said dully, "I know. I love you, too." She turned to the blank wall ahead of them, her eyes slick with tears that would not fall. "Love's not enough," she said to no one.

"THE LORD LOVES YOU," Billy shouted from the truck bed. "HE DOES, MA'AM."

Up the street, Miss Boatwright settled into the driver's seat of her mint green Crown Victoria. Mr. Yblansky placed the shopping bag and purple gift box on the back seat, spoke to her a moment, then closed the door. As she drove off, he brushed a thread off his blue silk sport coat and walked back to his business, paying no attention to Billy, who was shouting at him, "'RETURN, O ISRAEL, RETURN UNTO ME.'"

Walker bent down to study a small mound of sand on the edge of the sidewalk. Hundreds of fire ants, their tiny, sculpted bodies following hidden patterns, were working there, in oblivion, enlarging their world. Walker rested his thumb lightly on top of their mountain. He held it there until several of them had crossed the bridge to the desert on the back of his hand. He waited patiently until they started biting, then searched out each one and crushed it against his bones. Flicking the dead bodies away, he felt the stinging itch spread in circles across his skin. Soon they would blister and burn, leaving raw patches that nothing but waiting would heal, but now they made him shiver with a chill of shock and pleasure he wished he could prolong.

His mama had been gone longer than ever this time. And she hadn't called once, crying into the phone saying she was sorry, sorry, she didn't know what was wrong, and how much she missed them. After a few weeks, Blue stopped by one afternoon to bring her some honey from his bees and ask where she'd been. When Walker finally made him understand that she wasn't there, he asked if she'd gone to Mexico, and Walker imagined her returning from Mexico tanned and laden with gifts, chocolate and colorful dolls for Blue and an ancient Mayan treasure for him. She would be bursting with stories, and sitting on the tailgate of Blue's truck under the canopy of live oaks that formed his driveway, she would tell the two of them everything, amaze them, make them laugh at her adventures, her foolish wanderings, herself—the way she used to.

"EXCEPT THOU BE WASHED IN THE BLOOD OF JESUS," Billy called after Mr. Yblansky as he disappeared inside his air-conditioned store. "THERE IS NO SALVATION."

"Damn right," Walker said to the clusters of small, white bubbles rising on his hand. "No salvation." He resisted the urge to scratch the ant bites and stared at the broken oyster shells paved into the sidewalk.

"'WASH ME, AND I SHALL BE WHITER THAN SNOW,'" Billy shouted to Yblansky's closed door. "PSALM FIFTY-ONE. GOD PUT THOSE WORDS IN KING DAVID'S MOUTH AFTER HE WENT UNTO BATHSHEBA." Reverend Steen had recommended that psalm in particular and the prophet Hosea to Billy, telling him God had the power to forgive the worst of sins, even fornication, and that God could use a whoring wife and the son of her whoring to make plain the power of His salvation to the world. "Read God's Word in that boy of yours," he would say. But when Billy looked at Walker, he saw only that the boy was strange, overwrought and bookish, underhanded at times—nothing like him or any other Driggers, who were all practical and plain and straight. When he looked at the boy now, rocking back and forth on his arches over the edge of the curb on Lucas Street, his freckles and reddish blond hair, his large ears, even the way the boy held the tracts—as if he weren't sure of his own hands—everything about him seemed a rebuke.

In a scratchy voice, not far off tune, Billy began to sing, *"Whiter than snow, yes, whiter than snow. Oh, wash me—"*

On the *"wash me,"* a woman's voice joined his. It was purer and stronger than his and all but drowned his out. As he turned to find its source, their two voices sang together, *"and I shall be whiter than snow."* Billy stopped at the end of the chorus, but the woman's voice slid into the next verse without stopping. She was standing across the street, in front of Lighthouse Books and Gifts, where *kente* cloth preaching stoles and T-shirts proclaiming "And the Greatest of These is LOVE, I Cor. 13" hung in the window. Though she was about his age, he didn't recognize her from high school. With her yellow, flowered skirt billowing over her black sneakers and the sleeves of her black knitted top pushed up just below her elbows she looked like a stinging bee—except for her gray-streaked, sandy hair, which drifted over her shoulders as her head swayed in song. Her eyes still closed, she finished the chorus and started the third verse, "*Yes, I was drifting far . . .* "

Billy swatted through his Bible while she sang. The sun burned through the thinning hair on the crown of his head. Heat from the black corrugated bed-liner of the truck soaked through his good leather shoes, traveled up his legs toward his chest.

Walker spat in the gutter. He was so hot he didn't know what he hoped for more, that the woman would shut up and leave so his daddy could finish up his test and they could go home before anyone saw them, or that, like the people in Beaufort, she would grow tired of the game and send for the police, and his daddy would be taken away to jail before any of his friends or teachers saw them. He laid the bundle of tracts on the curb and sat next to them with his head between his knees, the backs of his hands resting on the pavement. The woman sang on and on, in a voice sweet but disturbing, full of some kind of longing that made him want to run away or drown it out with screaming or the sound of a brick smashing a plate glass window. If he knew how to sing a song like that to his mama, he thought, maybe he could call her back, from Mexico, from her sadness, from wherever she was, no matter how far.

The wind from a passing car swept three of the tracts into the street. Two landed upright, displaying the cover, "For God So Loved the World . . . " The other lay open, revealing across the top the title " . . . That He Gave His Only Begotten Son."

A Coosawaw County cruiser entered the narrow, one-way street from the courthouse parking lot. As it crawled toward Lighthouse Books and Gifts and Yblansky's, the woman stopped singing. Billy looked up from his Bible.

"REMEMBER SODOM AND GOMORRAH," he preached, louder and more animated than before, in spite of the heat. "REPENT OR BE DAMNED. RETURN TO THE LORD JESUS. HE'S THE AUTHORITY, HE'S THE POWER. HE'S ALL THE LAW WE NEED. EVERYTHING ELSE IS A LIE. A LIE AND A CHEAT." As he shouted, he periodically squeezed the sweat out of his eyes. His wet shirt clung to his back.

As the sheriff drove between the woman and Billy, Deputy Breland, riding in the passenger seat, hung his arm outside the car and raised his index finger in greeting to Mr. Yblansky, who was behind a mannequin peering through his display window. The sheriff nodded out the other side to the woman, winking at her.

"Too hot to be singin', ain't it, Lucy?" the sheriff said cheerfully over Billy's bawling.

To Billy the deputy said tenderly, "Go home, Billy. You don't want no trouble from us. You ain't the only one ever had trouble with a woman."

"'THINK NOT THAT I AM COME TO SEND PEACE ON EARTH: I CAME NOT TO SEND PEACE, BUT A SWORD.' THAT'S THE TRUTH, TRAVIS BRELAND. 'FOR I AM COME TO SET A MAN AT VARIANCE AGAINST HIS FATHER . . . AND A MAN'S FOES SHALL BE THEY OF HIS OWN HOUSEHOLD . . . HE THAT LOVETH SON OR DAUGHTER MORE THAN ME IS NOT WORTHY OF ME. AND HE THAT TAKETH NOT HIS CROSS, AND FOLLOWETH AFTER ME, IS NOT WORTHY OF ME.'"

As Billy preached on, the cruiser inched forward and Deputy Breland said, almost under his breath, "You're not goin' to get any sword from us, Billy Driggers, or any cross either."

"If he wants to be a martyr," the sheriff said to Deputy Breland, "and get thrown in jail so his crazy Yankee wife will pay attention, come home, and see about him, he can damn well do it in some other county. Coosawaw's not as rich as Beaufort County. We can't afford to let ourselves get suckered into a gospel trap the way they did there. We're too smart to give Reverend Steen that satisfaction, and Billy Driggers, too, even if he did grow up here and he's the only honest mechanic in town."

When they had passed Billy's pickup, Deputy Breland settled into his seat, pulled his hat off his head, then replaced it, adjusting it impatiently.

"'HE THAT FINDETH HIS LIFE SHALL LOSE IT: AND HE THAT LOSETH HIS LIFE FOR MY SAKE SHALL FIND IT,'" Billy shouted after them.

"I wouldn't want Billy's trouble," Deputy Breland said to the sheriff.

"It ain't the Lord or anybody else goin' to help him with that wife of his," the sheriff said. "He knew what she was when he married her. We all knew. You can't trust those smart, good-lookin' ones. You saw how she did him when she first came, flirted with every man that came her way, had coffee at Hardee's with Baldwin Peters in broad daylight. Billy's got to cut her loose, find himself a nice country girl who knows how to be satisfied with what we got here."

The cruiser picked up speed, leaving tread marks on the tracts in the street. Lucy, trembling slightly, waited for another car to pass, then crossed the street.

"Hey," she said, staring at Billy from the side of the truck, near the tire well. Her eyes, mud brown, were unblinking.

Billy wiped the sweat off his neck and temples with the back of his wrist, shading his eyes while he watched the patrol car progress up the street. When it turned by the pharmacy, a sigh emptied out of him. He coughed to cover it and said to the woman's composed face, "Didn't expect folks to be so friendly."

"Don't be too disappointed," Lucy said, nodding toward where the patrol car had disappeared. Her tone was firm, but her voice quavered.

Billy cocked his head toward her as if he were trying to make up his mind about something. Out of the corner of his eye, he saw two staff reporters through the blinds of the *Gazette* window. They were smoking and keeping him in their sight.

He threw back his shoulders, raised his diaphragm to his rib cage, and aimed his voice through the smudged glass at their ears. "JESUS SAID, 'BELIEVE ON ME AND THOU SHALT—'"

"'He was despised and rejected,' yes," Lucy said quietly.

Walker stood up, stepped nearer, into the gutter, to hear her better.

"'—BE SAVED.'"

"'But he was man of *sorrows*,'" she continued, raising her voice over Billy's, "'and *acquainted* with grief.'"

Walker leaned closer. The way she said "acquainted with grief" made him think of his mama. Maybe this woman knew something that could help her.

Billy jammed his fingers in his shirt pocket, searching for a cigarette.

"Everybody's got grief enough," Lucy said, more softly, her voice steady now. She paused while he kept searching his empty pocket. "Why create more?"

Billy tried to fend Lucy off with one of Reverend Steen's "gospel" smiles, succeeding only in making his face look like he was in great pain and about to cry. Turning, he saw Walker watching them.

"Pick up those tracts, Walker," he said brusquely. "We can't let the Word of God lay molderin' in the street."

Spreading his legs, Walker dragged his heel across one of the fallen tracts and pulled it toward him in the gutter.

"Getting arrested isn't going to help," she said. "You can't go chasing after your stripes of affliction. That's not how Jesus came to his suffering or how the apostle Paul got put in jail."

She spoke with an uncanny calmness, looking at Billy but not focusing on him. It seemed to Walker she was talking not to his daddy but to herself, or maybe to someone else, someone close by yet far away. Someone who inhabited all her dreams yet whose name and face escaped her. A demon or an angel, or maybe both. Walker stopped pulling the tract across the asphalt and stared, first at his daddy, who looked dazed, then back at the woman.

"I've been in jail." She stood silent for a moment. Her face, smoothed into joy when she had been singing, hung in cavities of sadness around her bones.

Walker took another step closer.

She paid no attention to him as he inched toward the truck and stood beside the driver's door. She was watching Billy's thumbs rub in opposite circles across the top of his Bible. "I thought I could prove to myself I was no good and then . . . " She raised her fist to her mouth and bit the back of it. When she rested her hand on her other arm, the marks of her teeth arched toward each other like two crescent moons trying to form a full one. She stared at the curving depressions, spoke to them. "Then it wouldn't matter that I wasn't loved, because I didn't deserve it anyway. But that doesn't work. Jail's no answer."

Walker leaned his arm on the truck and the hot metal burned him. With a gasp he drew his arm up and looked for the red spot.

"You all right?" Lucy asked the boy, combing her hair from her face with her fingers. Turning to Billy, she said, "Don't go running down trouble. Stay home. Your stripes will find you soon enough. 'Love one another': that's all the gospel we need." She crossed the street and went inside her store, the rope of brass Indian bells on the door handle jingling behind her.

The air grew denser, making it hard to breathe. Walker wished they had brought some Mountain Dew. He would have been willing to drink it warm and tinny, just to clear his head. He looked up the street. Across from the post office stood a tiny plaza with a waterfall, a memorial wall for veterans, and several concrete benches—the town's answer to integration and Vietnam. The crape myrtles rimming the plaza were laden with fresh cones of velvety pink, each one a rebuke to the impatiens along the curb and everything else that had succumbed to the heat. As he had known, there was no drinking fountain. He tried to suck moisture out of his cheeks, but they were dry.

A woman in a tight red tank top and short shorts, her head glistening with cowrie shells, pushed a stroller past the plaza. The small child curved in the sling was practically hidden under a Malcolm X baseball cap.

"THOU SHALT NOT ADORN THYSELVES LIKE THE HEATHEN."

The mother wheeled past Lighthouse Books and Gifts and settled the stroller next door, in front of a clothing store window. She cupped her hands around her eyes and leaned against the glass. Her perfectly proportioned, cane-syrup-colored legs seemed to stretch endlessly from her white shorts to her high-heeled beaded sandals.

His daddy saw her, too.

"PLAY NOT THE HARLOT," Billy shouted at her as she approached. "REPENT. RETURN TO THE LORD AND THOU SHALT BE SAVED, THOU AND THY HOUSE.'"

The child dropped its bottle on the sidewalk, and the mother squatted to retrieve it. Her shorts rode higher up her thighs and the tank top stretched tighter around her breasts, revealing a curve of purple lace under her arm. Resting one hand on the stroller, the woman pretended to drink the juice. The child seized up with delight. The mother tickled it under the arms with the wet nipple until its face darkened with laughter and it struggled to catch its breath.

Walker sucked in quick breaths in rhythm with the little boy, willing the rest of his muscles to keep still, his eyes to stop watering.

"'PUT AWAY THY HARLOTRY . . . FROM THY FACE AND . . . AND THY ADULTERY FROM BETWEEN THY BREASTS.'" Billy stopped and took a long breath. "'ELSE I WILL STRIP THEE . . . NAKED . . . AND LEAVE THEE AS ON THE DAY THOU WERT BORN,' SAYS THE LORD. With "SAYS THE LORD," his voice grew louder, higher, tauter, like a bowstring stretched back in aim. "'I WILL UNCOVER THY SHAME IN THE SIGHT OF THY LOVERS. I WILL SPURN THEE AS THOU HAST SPURNED ME.'"

The mother gave no indication she saw or heard him, not even a quick glance out of the corner of her eyes followed by a mask of indifference. His daddy did not exist to her.

"'THE LORD WILL ROAR LIKE A LION,'" Billy screamed after her, choking the words out of his throat, "'WOE UNTO THEE FOR STRAYIN' FROM ME.'" Still squatting by the stroller, the mother fanned her baby with her hand and bent in to blow cooling air across its face. She rose gracefully and continued down the sidewalk, the baby's tiny leather shoes, impossibly white, kicking happily above the footrest, close to one another, but not touching. Walker wanted to run across the street, grab the little boy's legs in his hands, and pat his feet gently against each other, making him laugh again.

"'VENGEANCE IS MINE,' SAITH THE LORD. 'MY WORD IS A SWORD, THE SWORD OF RIGHTEOUSNESS THAT CUTS TO THE BONE.'"

The mother turned a corner and was gone.

"'RETURN TO THE LORD THY GOD.' PLAY NOT THE HARLOT. PLAY NOT THE WHORE. SINNER! FORNICATOR! WHORE! WH—"

Walker had just jumped into the truck to stop him when Billy broke off crying. By the time the boy reached him, Billy was standing there limp, trembling, not making a sound. Walker backed away. Billy raised his left arm and pushed his eyes down his sleeve, his sweat and tears mingling in the soft cotton.

A man emerged from the *Gazette* office, carrying a boxy camera around his neck and a camera with a giant telescope lens in his hand. Before he was off the sidewalk, the reporter started shooting.

"Excuse me," the man called to Billy.

Billy looked at the reporter without seeing him.

A car stopped to let the reporter cross, then pulled away leaving a trail of oil drops.

"This'll only take a minute," the reporter said.

Billy bit his lip. He stretched his arm up, thrusting his Bible against the cloudless sky, and wiped his nose and eyes on his sleeve.

The reporter clicked another shot from the street, then switched cameras and climbed on the back bumper, positioning himself to catch a better one.

Billy let his Bible hang at his side and stared at the black grooves of the truck's bed-liner, a sea of black plastic troughs between shimmering crests of heat.

The reporter leaned back and to the side and clicked off several rapid shots.

"Sir," the reporter said, "what do you hope to accomplish here in Pinesboro? What is your mission? Are you part of Reverend Steen's school? Do you believe the noise ordinance in Beaufort is constitutional? That the Beaufort businesses have been harassing and persecuting you?" He nodded to Walker. "Is that your son? Are you training him to be a preacher, too?"

Billy raised his eyes to him. He opened his mouth to speak. He licked his lips several times, wiped the wetness with the palm of his hand, and let out a wobbly moan, like a person suffering from a high fever. He ran his tongue across his lips again and parted them, sucking in air and releasing it noisily.

The reporter snapped picture after picture, aiming to capture the moment the tears began.

"Leave him alone," Walker screamed, running toward the reporter.

The reporter jumped down from the bumper, guarding his cameras from the boy, and backed away from the truck into the street.

Walker leaped into the truck and threw his arms around his father, his stringy arms spreading across Billy's damp back and chest.

The reporter fired off several more shots.

"Stop it!" Walker yelled. "Stop it!" He took the Bible from his father and shielded his father's face from the camera with it. With the other hand, he shook his father gently, leaned his face close under his downcast one, searching for his eyes. "Daddy," he said softly. "Let's go home."

His father raised his face toward his. From the corners of his eyes a tight web of blood veins spread across the white surface, cracking it into irregular pieces that fitted together perfectly. The veins grew, reaching for the charcoal rims of the irises, and, touching them, held the ocean-green circles in place around the sinking black holes.

"Maybe she came back," the boy said.

His father closed his eyes and shook his head no.

"She did. I know she did. She promised she would always come back. Let's go home and see."

Billy dropped his forehead, resting it heavily against his son's shoulder.

Walker could feel him trembling. The silence around them frightened the boy and comforted him all at once, so that he didn't know what to do.

Billy drew himself up and let out a loud sigh through his nose. Taking the Bible from Walker with his right hand and laying his other hand on his shoulder, he said, "Come on, Son, let's pick up those tracts and go home."

They climbed down from the truck and combed the street together, gathering the tracts, the crumpled and the flat, the dirty and the clean, Walker running to catch the ones caught by the wind, Billy bending carefully to pull free the ones stuck in the gutter and under parked cars, both of them ignoring the camera's insistent clicking.

LET THEM BIG
ANIMALS COME BACK

I'm waitin' for Rhader T. Avant to come out. You know him? That's his buildin', Rhader T. Avant, General Contractin'. Hnh! I pounded on the big window but he won't come out. He's in there. I seen him. He called the sheriff when I started poundin'. That's why you here. It won't do you no good. Rhader T. Avant owe me and Ricky a hundred dollar and I ain' goin' home until I get it. Don't matter what you or the sheriff or anybody says. I'm waitin' right here 'til he come out. Can't nobody make me move. Ain' no wrong in sittin' in your truck waitin', is it? You know it ain'. It's a parkin' lot here. Anybody use it. How long you been workin' for the sheriff? I never seen you before.

Don't carry no gun in the truck. Somebody steal it. You want to look? Go ahead, look all over. Ain' nothin' in here. Don't have but one gun and that's a deer gun. Ricky use it. Keep it by my bed back at the house.

That gun you got on your hip ain' no good. Too shiny.

My truck's *good*. F-150. Goin' paint it this winter and ask Miss Liles to find me a seat cover at the Walmarket. Trucks today ain' no good. Don't weigh more'n a dime. Ricky and me went down to Mexico in this truck. Ricky crash his car. Can't drive no more. I drove him.

Ricky and me always been together. We had the top room in Mama's house when we was boys. Mama's big house in town *bad* now. Porch and columns fallin' down. Yard all choked up by ivy. Inside dirty, too. I keep my place neat. Loretta come over from Green Pond and clean it.

You ain' from around here, is you? Where you from? Rhode Island? That's a long ways, ain' it? You come here to work for the sheriff? That's good. He *need* help. Sheriff ain' never had no trouble with me. Send him down to the Devil Cat. She in Mama's big house in town. Over by the courthouse, down Chatham Street, yard all choked up with ivy, porch fallin' down. She ain' no sister to me.

The Devil Cat don't care about Mama's house. Let her three boys piss all over it. Let her daughters see men in there. In Sky's room, too. Sky's in the box. That's the way that is.

Ricky and me swing from the live oaks back of Mama's house. Ricky's number four. The Devil Cat, that's Alma, she's number six, the baby one. Number five's name Rain. She ran away. Ain' nobody ever heard from her. Ricky number four. Sky three. Me two. Got it now? The first one's an idiot. Mama kept him tied up inside the fence. He in the box when he twelve. Mama can't do nothin' for him. When the idiot boy went in the box, Sky came swingin' from the live oaks with Ricky and me. Sky's hair long. *Long!* She swing *high* and that woman hair all flyin' out behind her, like a flock of purple martins. One purple martin eat *six thousand* mosquitoes a day. I make gourd houses and string 'em high on a pole. Got sixty-three houses hangin' up there. Purple martins flyin' in my yard every night when the sun go down. *Pretty.*

Sky's in the box.

Mama's in the box, too. Mama showed me and Ricky how to pour gasoline down wasp nests out by the goat shed on her farm. You got to do it after dark, after you seen all the wasps fly into the ground. If you don't get every one of them wasps, they start a new nest right by the old one. You wait 'til they all home and you pour in two cups of gasoline. Two. Then you got to put a jar over each hole. Five, six holes maybe. Put the jar upside down like this, trap 'em. That's the way to do it.

Mama taught me and Ricky to put woman hair on the corn to keep the deer off. Send me and Ricky to the beauty parlor with crocus sacks to collect the woman hair. That hair *smell!* Unh! Why you grinnin'? It's *true.* Some use dog hair, but that ain' no good. You can piss on the corn, too. Me and Ricky done that. But woman hair is the best. Mama learned all that in the orphan house in Charleston. Part Gullah girl, maybe. Name Givens. I like my name. Blue Givens Hiott. Ricky's Riddick Givens Hiott.

Miss Liles tells me all that about Mama. She a friend of Mama's. Helps me with the taxes. With gettin' that money from Mama's lawyer-man, too. Miss Liles don't like Loretta comin' to my place. Says a nigger woman is trouble. She'll get one in the basket and blame me. Take my money. Miss Liles don't like my friend Myra comin' round with her boy Walker either, fishin' and pickin' corn and countin' my rattlesnake buttons. Says Myra got a husband and it don't look right, her and her boy stayin' by me all day like that.

I don't mind Miss Liles. She says my daddy, Mister Hiott, owned the town. Long time ago. Horses in town then, skirts touchin' down to a woman's feet. I seen pictures. Mister Hiott went up to the orphan house in Charleston to get himself a girl to take care of his wife and his big house. Mister Hiott's wife a little bit of a thing. Like one of them China dolls. Break like this, like a snap bean. Easy. Fast. Ain' much good to a man. You got a good woman? That's good. You can't find no good woman nowdays. Mister Hiott's wife sick from havin' one in the basket and when the baby come, she in the box. So Mama took care of Mister Hiott and the baby. Mama can do anythin'. Mister Hiott married Mama directly. She fourteen.

Mama's in the box.

When Mama went in the box, the Devil Cat kicked me and Ricky out of Mama's house. Mama say Ricky and me always stay in the big house together, keep the yard, fix the porches. Mama's Eastatoe man already drowned so he can't bother us no more. Mama took up with that Eastatoe man after Mister Hiott gone. Mister Hiott *old!* Ricky say *Mister Hiott* ain' my daddy. It's a bobcat!

See? You laughin' now. Ricky can make you laugh.

Mama's Eastatoe man catch Ricky and me turnin' somersaults on the bed in the big house and tell Mama to separate us. Mama make me paint a room in the back downstairs and move in there away from Ricky. I don't like that.

Mama's Eastatoe man give me my ears. Me and Ricky washin' dishes and carryin' on and the Eastatoe man hit me on the head. Only hear a little bit after that. Can't talk so good neither. Nobody can make me out. They think I'm an idiot like the first one. Ricky's the only one can hear me good when I talk.

I'm smart. I can read and write. I know all that, too. Been to high school. They think I don't know nothin'. Rhader T. Avant, too. He thinks I don't know you got to pay double for workin' backhoes and bulldozers. He thinks Ricky too drunk on whiskey to know he give us only a hundred dollar. A hundred dollar! Should have been *two*. That's hard work! One hundred for me and one hundred for Ricky. Rhader T. Avant a *thief!* When he come out I'm goin' tell him. Get Ricky's money. That's it.

You know what I'm goin' do? I'm goin' build a concrete gator pit. Eight-by-eight steps goin' up over it. Goin' hang all the rapers and killers and thieves. Throw 'em in the pit. That's what I'm goin' do. I *am*.

I don't work for Rhader T. Avant no more. Me and Ricky quit him. Went to work Mama's farm out Yemassee Highway. Went there when the Devil Cat kicked us out of Mama's big house in town. Didn't have nowhere else to go. Pulled a mattress in the goat shed and slept there. Built ourselves a house.

I don't sleep in the house me and Ricky made. That's for Ricky and his women. I sleep on the porch out the side. Got a warm stove in there.

Ricky and me built the house on Mama's farm ourself. Ain' nobody helped us. Not Rhader T. Avant, not nobody. I can do anythin'. Drive a backhoe, cut a road, dig a pond, dynamite tree stumps. You know all that? I know how to do all that. Me and Ricky, we do all that together. You can't separate Ricky and me.

It's a good house me and Ricky made. No steps. I don't like steps. Could fall down.

Ricky and me used treatin' lumber in our house so it won't never rot. That house be standin' when you're in the box, when your youngins are in the box. Not the Devil Cat's house. Mama's big house in town bad now. *Bad*. The Devil Cat don't care. The Devil Cat kicked me and Ricky out. Stole our inheritance, too. She ain' no sister to Ricky and me. All women is devils. The Old Man goin' tear 'em all up.

I stay clear of the Devil Cat. Her boys and her daughters, too. All of 'em no good. Her boys sleep all day. All her daughters whores. Everybody know it. They wear them two-pieces swimmin' suits. Your woman don't wear one of those, do she? She do? I don't like that mess. I ain' no uncle to them girls of the Devil Cat.

Can't nothin' separate Ricky and me. Our house is out Yemassee Highway, past the rodeo. You come see it. I'll leave the gate open. Bang on the porch window hard, like this, so I hear you.

One room inside all woman's stuff. I don't go in there much. It's Mama's bed from the big house in there and her dolls and mirrors and hairbrushes. We made a room for Sky, too. Big picture window in there. Double glass. Looks out on Ricky's live oak. Sky cracked her back. Mama carried her in the big house and nursed her. In the downstairs bedroom one year. Mama packed cotton around her hips every day. Sky's in the box. That's the way that is.

Ricky's room all cedar. Cedar walls, cedar bed, cedar chest. Smells *good!* He always got women in there, drunk women, crazy. But I don't mind Ricky. Ricky's a good boy. He work hard before the whiskey eat him up. Ricky and me go shrimpin' in the fall. Ricky packs the fish meal into balls, and I stake 'em in the water. Then we cast the nets. We be out all night shrimpin' the creeks. You can't take but forty-eight quarts. Some take the heads off the shrimp and hide 'em under the ones with the heads on. If the game warden catch you, that's five hundred dollar fine and you got to throw the shrimp back. Ricky wants to snap the heads off. Pack the cooler full. Have enough shrimp to sell down to Edisto Beach. But I don't never take the shrimp heads off until we put 'em in the freezer at home. You eat shrimp? I'll bring you some. Show you how to cast the net, too. I can teach you all that.

You come by me Sunday and fish in the big pond. Get 'em with a net, get 'em with a line. You got youngins? Two? You bring 'em along. Miss Liles catch bass in there. Hard work cleanin' out them two ponds. *Hard!* Got to use a tractor to pull out all them weeds. Got three tractors. One nineteen and forty-six, one nineteen and fifty-eight, one nineteen and sixty-five. Two diesels and one gasoline. Fix 'em myself. Lots of fish in them ponds—if folks don't come in the gate and steal 'em while I'm workin'. Two hundred and thirty acres. Work it myself. Ain' nobody helpin' me. I'm sixty-eight, but I'm *strong*. My chest is strong! Ricky's strong, too. Ricky and me cut down the lightnin' trees for Mama and carry 'em off. We tote Mama's johnboat to the creek. Ricky and me shot an alligator in the big pond and ate the tail. *Good!* Tastes like chicken. Can't do that no more. Got to call the game warden if an alligator eatin' our fish now. Can't kill it. Thirty-five hundred dollar fine. *Thirty-five hundred dollar!* It ain' worf it!

Rhader T. Avant can pay it. He got a new truck settin' here and that heavy equipment out back and a house outside town with a swimmin' pool and five bathrooms. *Five!* What he need that for?

They put you to the jailhouse if you kill an alligator. I ain' goin' in the jailhouse. I collect Ricky from the jailhouse. You don't drink whiskey, do you? Just a little bit? You got to watch out for whiskey. I don't never touch whiskey. I don't like bread neither. Don't eat it. Cucumbers and hot dogs, that's what I eat. I'd ride back to Mexico for some of that food me and Ricky got there.

I take care of Mama's camellias real good. People drivin' to the farm every spring to look at Mama's camellias. Them bushes sixty years old! Ricky and me helped Mama plant all those. You got to watch over camellias. Got to pick up all the brown flowers when they fall to the ground. Got to put Epsom salts round the bush when the blooms all done. Got to cut out the ivy with a bush axe so it don't choke 'em. You heard about ivy? First year sleeps, second year creeps, third year reaps. Don't let that mess get in your yard.

The Devil Cat wants Mama's farm. Wants the house me and Ricky built there, too. Says I'm not right, can't take care of things. The Devil Cat won't *never* get Mama's farm. Ricky and me work it. We sell hog corn and deer corn and sweet corn and okra and butter beans and cucumbers and squash and peanuts. That's all in the summer. Later we got turnips, collards, mustard greens. Pecans. Scuppernongs and muscadines, too. We do all right.

I'm goin' make Rhader T. Avant pay me and Ricky that hundred dollar. When he come out, I'm goin' look him in the eye and tell him it ain' right. Rhader T. Avant says I don't make no sense. Calls me Miss Eve's fool child. That's what all them think, 'cept Ricky.

Ricky and me went to Mexico. Drove through Texas. You been to Texas? Jackrabbits big as a bobcat down there. I saw it! Ricky and me caught a bobcat on Mama's farm. I grabbed it by the throat and a front paw. That other paw scratched clear down my arm. See? *Strong! Sharp!* Them hind legs was about to cut my balls off. I kicked it off me, and it run off. A bobcat will stare you right in the eye. You ain' know that, did you? They stare you in the eye and never look away. Don't never fool with a bobcat. You can pick up a rattlesnake by the tail and swing it around and pop it, break its neck, kill it. But don't never fool with a bobcat.

I been to Mexico. I been with a woman before, too. Ricky and me went to a town across that border there. A town with women. Ricky been there before. Ricky got himself a woman in the room and got me two. I got my clothes off, but I put 'em back on and I ran. I'm gone! I ran out of there and Ricky was *laughin'*. Those whores come after me. They was laughin', too. Laughin' and chasin'. Them high heels of theirs was clickety-clacketin' on the street like a rattlesnake. I kept runnin'. Ricky found me in the mornin' and we drove back home. Ricky laugh all the way home. Say I look like a roadrunner tearin' down that street.

Devils is what those women was. All women is devils. The Old Man goin' tear 'em all up. But they was real pretty. Prettier than the women here. Prettier than your woman. May be.

Sky *pretty*. Ricky and me throw a rope over the live oaks in Mama's gardens behind the big house and swing on it. Ricky ridin' on my lap and me ridin' on Ricky's. Ricky *heavy! Strong!* Sky come out with us. Her hands slipped off the rope. Fell down. Broke her two hipbones and her spine. Legs don't work. Mama took care of her one year in the house. Sky went in the hospital and never come home. In the box.

Ricky and me worked that heavy equipment for Rhader T. Avant back when we was buildin' our house on Mama's farm. Dug him canals, cut him roads for all them houses he was buildin'. He didn't pay Ricky and me enough. Said Ricky never work, too drunk. Rhader T. Avant mean as a water turkey. Look here. Water turkey got this shoulder. Didn't want me fishin' the pond. It went over and over me, divin'. I got the gun and shot at it. It dove me good and stuck its beak in my shoulder. *Long* beak! Long as Ricky's knife. Won't never lose that scar. I don't go to no doc. Most things you can over without no doc buttin' in. I fix Ricky up when he come home from fightin'. I help him to the bathroom when he sick and clean him up. I feed him a little bit.

I sew my own self up, too. Chain saw cut my leg, and I sewed it up. Put ice on it. Took a needle and fishin' line. Eight stitches. It don't hurt. It's just skin. You can't do that, can you? Rhader T. Avant can't do that neither.

A bleedin' sore like that water turkey give me, that was nothin'. I was mad, though. I caught that water turkey and wrung its neck. Got the head hangin' in the shed by all Ricky's antlers.

I found a fawn layin' in the back field. Shiverin', like this. Somebody shot its mama. I put it in the goat pen. *Small!* Drank out a bottle. Licked me all over. It liked me. Somebody stole it. Came while I was sleepin' and took it.

I could take Ricky while he's sleepin'. Only a little bit of dirt over him, just this much. Easy diggin'. Fresh dirt. Three days old. Devil Cat stole him out the hospital. Took him before I knew it. Put him in the grave pen in town.

I'll dig Ricky up, put him to work. Too much work on the farm. It ain' worf it. I'm goin' sell it and I'm gone! The Devil Cat can't stop me. Goin' sell everythin' and live in a trailer. Drive it all over. Maybe find a wolf. I ain' never seen a wolf.

I love bees. I been lovin' 'em since I was a boy. They're smart. They have ones to work. They have ones to clean the hive. They throw out the ones without any legs that can't walk. They don't have no hospital.

Bees ain' like wasps. A wasp will sting and sting as long as you're standin' there. A bee sting once. Once it stings, you can grab it and close it up in your mouth, right inside, like this. It won't bother you no more. I can show you that when you come out to me. After a bee stings, it goes in the box. You ain' know that, did you? I like all that.

Bees don't never sting me. I put my arm right in and get the honey. I ain' scared of bees. I'm scared of water now. Water'll get you. Don't go in the deep ocean.

Let me ask you a question. Do the bottom of the ocean move, too? Or just the top? I don't know about that.

I don't swim in the ocean. Swim in the pond. Buck-naked. Not Ricky. Ricky too scared of cottonmouths. He see a cottonmouth and he gone!

Too many weeds in them ponds. Too much work. *Hard* work! And taxes are high. *High!* It ain' worf it, is it? Might as well be in the box.

I'll be in the box before long. Rhader T. Avant, too. You, too. Ain' it?

I don't believe in no church and no Bible. Man wrote the Bible. Don't need all that mess. Here's what it is. The Old Man got three worlds. This one and the one above and the one below. This one goin' be all torn up. Can't recognize nothin', you, me, nothin'. The Old Man goin' turn it all over, tear it all up. People are mean. *Mean.* I seen pictures of all that. Piles of bones. Didn't put 'em in the box. Shoved 'em in a hole with a bulldozer. Hawh! You ever seen that? No coverin' over the women's breasts. Them shakin' in the cold. Bald-headed, all their woman hair cut off. Men like haints they so skinny. I turned the pictures off and went to bed. Make me sick. People are *mean.* The Old Man goin' tear it all up. Let them big animals come back.

I may be in the box when it happen. Don't know what'll happen to me. Maybe tie a cement block to my leg and jump in the ocean.

Might. Go direct to the bottom. Don't know what I'll do. Go where Ricky goes. Ricky run all over. Gets a notion and he gone! In Texas Ricky and me drove two hours to see a twenty-foot snake that eats jackrabbits. *Twenty foot!* Can't find that big snake in South Carolina. The man there let me handle it. Cold! Saw roadrunners at that place, too, me and Ricky. They ain' but this big and the man say they kill a rattlesnake and eat it. They got funny-lookin' tails. *Long!* They was two of them roadrunners there in that pen in Texas. They was runnin' back and forth like this, the two of 'em, together. Ricky fall in the dirt laughin', say, "Beep beep! Beep beep!"

Ricky's a good boy. He work hard. Whiskey ate Ricky up. I stayed with Ricky in the hospital. Weighed less than a bushel of green peanuts.

Everythin' inside him burnin' itself up. That dopey stuff they give him ain' no good. Too much pain. Ricky couldn't hardly talk no more. Couldn't hear me right, neither.

I cried like a woman. Wasn't nothin' I could do.

I'm goin' get Ricky's money for him. Before I go in the box. Before the Old Man tear it all up. You go in there and tell Rhader T. Avant to bring that hundred dollar out here to me. People are *mean*. Rapers and killers. *Thieves.* They ain' supposed to steal. I ain' goin' home 'til I get that hundred dollar. You can't stop me. That's *Ricky's* money, *Ricky's.*

LOWCOUNTRY COLD

My sweater can't beat this cold. And canvas shoes are all I wear now, on account of the swellin'. I had to cut a hole in the toe of the left shoe so it don't pinch. Got to get my coat back from Rebecca. She quit that woman she was workin' for, the one always dressed so particular and who always expected her to notice her children for her while she went out to lunch or shoppin' in Charleston and never paid her a penny extra for it. Mrs. Glenn Murdaugh. Rebecca quit her and started at the motel that Indian family own. "I work for nothin'," she says. "I play grateful when somebody gives me chipped dishes or spotty clothes. But I will not listen to a half-grown woman grieve over the sorry knickknacks that broke when the curio cabinet I was dustin' fell down." My baby's got to walk farther to work now, but the Patels treat her fair, and cleanin' up after motel people is easier than cleanin' for Mrs. Murdaugh. Rebecca says the crust under that woman's kitchen table was hard as Pharaoh's heart.

I'm tired. Hope my legs hold 'til I get to the doctor.

Rebecca don't take rides from white people. She says, "Mama, you know what a woman said to me at the grocery? 'Careful with that cart! This is a thirty-five-thousand-dollar car!'"

That's fine for you, I tell her. You're young, you haven't even been through the Change. And the Spirit's still kickin' in you. But I'm plain tired. I take who God sends me.

Leastwise, that's what I used to tell her.

When I be shufflin' along with my cane, somebody always stop for me. If they white, the first thing I do when I get myself settled inside is I thank 'em, to show I'm one of the sweet ones, and I tell 'em, "I know the *Lord* sent you." They like that. Makes 'em feel good. But it's *truth*. The Lord sends us what we need when we need it. He's never early and He's never late; He's always right on time, *His* time, like sendin' those ravens to feed Elijah right when he was about to starve to death.

If a child be in the car, I always say how pretty it is, even when it's an ugly old thing, dirty and scaredy-lookin'. That's all right. The Lord knows you're not lyin'. It's pretty to the *Lord's* way of seein', ain't it? We're all God's children, and you know parents *always* think their child the smartest and the prettiest one in the whole wide world. That's the natural way. And you got to pay for your ride somehow. If you don't flatter their child, you got to flatter *them*, and that's a *job!*

But I'm done with that job now, praise the Lord, just like Rebecca's done with that Murdaugh woman. I'm *retired* from that job. Since last week, when that too-happy woman picked me up. I was walkin' home from Doctor Inabinett's like I'm used to do, along McDaniel Street. I wasn't too far from the school, right about where I am now. I'd already been to see the doctor, but wasn't nobody there. Had my appointment all set, but when I got there, the place was closed up tighter than a bud that won't bloom and a sign on the door: DOCTOR INABINETT IS OUT OF TOWN. PLEASE CALL AND RESCHEDULE YOUR APPOINTMENT. That happens with Doctor Inabinett from time to time. He's got so many patients and he works so hard takin' care of all of them sick people that sometimes he just needs to rest himself to go on. I don't care what people say about him. They can criticize him all they like. Doctor Inabinett's been a big help to me with my legs and my heart. Well, that day I was walkin' home from his office, I was some tired. My legs were about to give out. And it was a day just as cold as this one here. And right here on McDaniel Street, just a few steps back from where I am now, a little bit of a woman, no bigger than a child herself, stopped and asked me did I want a ride somewhere. Course I did. There was a little boy in the front with her and a little girl in the back who wasn't none too happy about me gettin' in with her. That girl sat back stiff in the seat, crossed her arms over her chest, and set her face hard as stone. I was glad she wasn't lookin' at me, because her eyes could of burned up steel. Well, I thanked the woman kindly and told her them children of hers were real sweet.

When I said, "I know the Lord sent you," that woman smiled bright as angel hosts. "He did," she said. Just like that, "He did," like she was God's own for carryin' me to the doctor's. She's one of them that brags humble, wants everybody to know she drives out of her way to help those in need because the Bible says we got to welcome the stranger and not oppress him.

I ain't in her Bible. I ain't nobody's stranger but God's.

I'm walkin' all the way to the doctor today, cold as it is. And if Doctor Inabinett isn't there, I'll just rest a while until God gives me the strength to go on, and then I'll walk all the way home. I'm tired of payin' for my rides.

WHY

Why'd you do that? Somebody else can give that old woman a ride. Why was she walkin' to the doctor when he wasn't there, anyway? She shoulda called him first to make sure she had an appointment. I'm seven years old and *I* know that. And she shoulda worn proper shoes if she was goin' go walkin' anywhere—her Nikes or her Keds, not those flippy-floppy things. Everybody knows that. And she wasn't cold, either. She just said that. If she was so cold, why wasn't she wearin' her coat instead of that ugly old sweater? You shoulda just given her money, Mrs. Reuben. You got money. I *know* you do. You shoulda given her money for the taxi instead of lettin' her in here with us. We got a taxi here in town. I've seen it, a big old scratchy blue station wagon that smokes out the back. That's what the black people take when they want to get somewhere. Why didn't you just give her money for the taxi? My daddy says you and Doctor Reuben got so much money you could buy our whole country. All the Jews do. He says it's not right that he's got to work his tail off to feed his kids while you're wipin' your babies' bottoms with hundred-dollar bills. And why'd you let that old woman call me her baby? She had no business callin' me that, no business *speakin'* to me. Ellastine doesn't speak to us when she's at our house. She just does whatever we tell her to do and then she goes home. Why'd you have to pick up that nasty old woman and let her in here with us? My mama's goin' be mad at you for lettin' that nasty old thing sit next to me and call me names. And why'd you drive her all the way down that long, bumpety road to her place? You made me sick to my stomach goin' down that road, and when I get home and throw up, my mama's goin' pitch a fit. And why'd you have to take her right up to her fallin'-down house and help her out of the car? You shouldn't have done that, Mrs. Reuben. She's not a *queen*. There wasn't even any grass in her yard, just dirt. Dirt, dirt, dirt, dirt, *dirt*. Now I'll be late gettin' home from school and I'll miss my dance class and my mama'll be mad. She's goin' be hollerin' and screamin' and chasin' and *beatin'* mad. Because of you and that old woman. You're supposed to carry me *straight* home from school. That's the way we do things here. Why'd you have to stop? There are *no* poor people in this town. My mama *told* me. You're crazy, crazy in the head. I don't know why, but you are. My mama's sure goin' be mad at you.

A SOLDIER'S DISEASE

"Does it hurt when I press here?" Doctor Reuben asked.

"Nossir."

The woman's voice was so soft he had to lean toward her mouth to make out what she was saying.

Everything about Lugenia Salley except her lacquered hair was soft—her moist eyes, the downy fuzz on her cheeks, her presence on the table. The ample flesh overflowing the cushioned exam table offered no resistance to his touch; it gave way like an underinflated balloon. Still, he had to press hard through the superfluous tissue to reach her knee joint.

"It doesn't hurt?" he asked.

Looking away from him, her head turned toward the wall, she shook her head no. Her stiffened black hair, brushing against the white paper covering the table, made a scratching noise.

He tapped his index and middle fingers on her left knee and down the leg where her shinbone should be. "Does it hurt when I do this?"

She shook her head again, then resumed staring at the empty wall. When Doctor Reuben first started his practice in Pinesboro, his nurse, Lou, counseled him on how to make the office presentable for his kind of clients. Because he had insisted on renting a space built after integration—so there would be one waiting room rather than two—the only available office was one that had been vacated by a pediatrician who had left town still in debt and exhausted by five years of continuous call. The thousands of mothers and small children the pediatrician had seen had used the office hard—trashed it, Lou said. She had new carpet and chairs installed in the waiting room and spent a weekend painting the walls a soft lilac. Her sons helped buff the floors in the other rooms, which she filled with used furniture and equipment. After removing all the posters of clowns and zoo animals in the halls and exam rooms, she painted those walls a moss green tint. Because there was no money to purchase decorations, every few weeks she would bring a dried flower arrangement or a framed counted cross-stitch from home to warm up the reception area and hallway. The exam room walls were still bare. Once Doctor Reuben came in with his wide, kindly face and intense concentration on figuring out what was wrong with a patient, the bareness didn't matter. But she hated that patients had nothing pretty to look at while they were lying on the table waiting for him.

Doctor Reuben lifted the woman's leg an inch off the exam table. It pulled heavily against his hands and arms, and a scent of Ivory soap rose from the skin where he touched it.

"That hurt?" he asked the woman.

Again a shake of the head.

Holding her foot by the heel and toe, he cautiously rotated her thick ankle.

"Anything now?"

Another shake.

"How about when I do this?" He bent her toes toward her knee, stretching her calf muscles and hamstring. "Does the pain get worse?"

"Uh-uh," she grunted.

He laid her leg gently on the table and consulted the notes his nurse Lou had written on her chart. "It says here, uh," he glanced at the top of the chart and read her name, "Mrs. Salley, that you can't stand for long periods of time, that you have to keep your leg propped up most of the day because of pain, and that you've been having this pain since your automobile accident. Is that right?"

She turned toward him, her eyes not meeting his, and nodded.

"Where do you feel the pain?"

"Everywheres."

"Is it a sharp pain, like stabbing needles, or a dull pain, more like a bruise?"

"Just hurt," she said.

"And the pain doesn't come and go? It's not better at some times and worse at others, maybe worse in the morning, when you first get up, and then it eases, or it's tolerable during the day and then it grows worse in the night, so that it wakes you up?"

"Always there."

He studied her chart again. "Looks like your leg was mangled pretty bad in that accident."

"Yessir." She watched her fingers smooth the white sheet over her left shoulder. The thin cotton gown the nurse had handed her was too small, so she had draped herself on top with an extra sheet.

"Can you stand on it?"

"Nossir."

"It won't support you at all?"

"It give way."

"Have you had it looked at since the surgery?"

"Three doctors."

"What did they tell you?"

The woman looked past him. "They say it wasn't nothin' left for 'em to fix and I should leave it be. It was all in my head."

"Given what you've told me and what I've just seen, I'm not sure I'll be able to do much for you either, Mrs. Salley."

"I heard you was different."

The doctor sighed. He paged through her chart slowly but without letting his eyes focus on the words and numbers. He laid the chart on the counter nearby and leaned back in his chair. Spreading his fingers wide, he made a tent of his hands on his lap and stared into it as he tapped his forefingers against each another. Still tapping, he looked up at her and asked, "Can you tell me anything more about your leg?"

"It hurt."

"What have you been taking for the pain?"

"Doctors wouldn't give me nothin'."

"Did you ask?"

"No cause to waste taxpayer money, one said, Medicaid ruinin' this country."

"He said that?"

She nodded.

"Last one said, make me an addict, like all my people."

The doctor stood up and pulled her chart off the counter. "I'll tell you what, Mrs. Salley," he said, pointing the chart at her with his right hand. "I'll have my nurse, Lou, give you a sample of some pain medication before you leave this morning. It may be that nothing will help, but try the medication for a week or so and let me know how it goes. If it doesn't work, we'll try something else. No sense in your suffering."

Over the next three months, Lugenia dutifully tried five medications. Each time Doctor Reuben examined her and determined that she was ready to try a different drug, he would ask her to wait in the room for Lou to bring her the new sample. Before helping Lugenia off the table and escorting her slowly to the waiting room, Lou would explain how to take the new drug, bundle the colorful pharmaceutical packages in one of the used plastic Wal-Mart or Bi-Lo bags she saved for the office, and hand them to her, saying, "You be sure to call me now if you forget how to take this particular one. Good luck! Maybe this one'll be the charm!" Some of the medications made Lugenia sick to her stomach, some made her dizzy, one made her heart race, and one gave her diarrhea. One gave her no side effects for the first week and then hit her with blinding headaches that lasted for days after she stopped taking it. None eased her pain. She was exhausted, felt worse than ever, and was ready to go back to nothing. But Doctor Reuben wanted to try just one more drug, and she could not disappoint him. He gave her a week to rest and then started her on Neurontin.

At her next visit, he breezed into the room smiling. "How's the leg, Lugenia?" he asked, flipping open her chart. "Is that new medicine still working? The pain hasn't come back, has it?"

"Nossir, Doctor Reuben."

"That's *great* news. I had a hunch Neurontin would do the trick. Let's have a look at that leg, shall we?"

"Doctor Calloway said my pain 'cause I so fat."

"Well, it doesn't look like that's true, does it?" he said, taking her leg in his hands. "Not that losing a little weight wouldn't be good for your heart."

"I won't touch pork."

Her leg rotated easily in its socket and bent smoothly at the joint. Doctor Reuben rested her leg on the table. "Everything looks good," he said, smiling broadly. "My guess is you'll be back to work in two weeks. I may not even have to sign a new disability form for you. Your manager will be glad to hear that. She's called me a few times, you know, to check on your progress. And she always asks about you when my wife drops the kids off. She likes you. She says you're one of the best aides they've ever had at the day care."

"She think I'm lazy. So do Doctor Calloway."

"I'm sure they don't think that."

"Doctor Calloway say so."

"The leg looks good, Lugenia. You just need to walk a little more, to build it back up."

To please Doctor Reuben, Lugenia tried to walk every day the following week. Before breakfast, lunch, and dinner, she stood at the kitchen counter, hands gripping the edge, and let a little weight slip to the leg. Each time, perspiration beaded her forehead and upper lip and formed long ovals on her blouse. Her arms cramped up. But the leg would not support her.

"Still no pain?" Doctor Reuben asked her the next visit.

"Nossir."

"Can you use the leg better now?"

"Nossir. It still give way."

"It's probably just weak from lack of use. We can change that. I'll have Lou make an appointment for you with the physical thera-pist. A few exercises to strengthen these inactive muscles, and you'll be on your way."

"How come it pink?" Lugenia asked, nodding to the troubled leg.

"What?"

"How come it showin' a different color?"

Doctor Reuben turned her left leg toward the light and away from it, shaded it with his hand and removed the shade. The leg had a decidedly pink cast to it. Next to the flat brown of the other leg, it looked as if it had been coated with a transparent color wash.

"Could be a difference in blood circulation. We'll check for clots. It's nothing to worry about. You just keep taking that medi-cine the way you have, and we'll check you again in a week. The important thing is we've managed to control your pain."

Lugenia kept taking the Neurontin, and her pain did not return. With each visit, however, her leg developed a new symptom. One week it had a blue cast, the next it was as gray as an old lead bullet, and the next it appeared much darker than the other leg. One week it would be shinier than the right leg, the next drier; one week thinner than the other, and the next more bloated; one week hot to the touch, and the next as cold as ice. Once, the leg showed up hairless, while the other remained sprinkled with thick, black hairs. Each time Doctor Reuben examined the leg, he discovered a new symptom, benign in itself and painless to Lugenia, yet troubling in its difference from the right leg and in its fleeting presence.

"That's quite the leg you've got there, Lugenia," he told her one day. "It's like a little theater where the scene keeps changing. I just wish I knew what the play was about."

The leg's symptoms and their evanescence were so odd that some days he found himself wondering if Lugenia were encouraging them. When Doctor Reuben had first moved to town, Doctor Calloway and a few other colleagues had warned him about malingering and insurance fraud. The blacks were always falling down in the meat or produce aisle at the Piggly Wiggly, or at the Wal-Mart or in McDonald's, and then suing over wet floors, after they had conned you into documenting their injuries. And it was widely known that they faked car accidents, along with the resulting neck and back injuries, and then hired greedy local attorneys to get them settlements out of court. That was how the ones not on welfare supported themselves and that was why auto insurance was higher in South Carolina than in any other state. He'd see plenty of disability forms, they told him, and he'd get plenty of calls asking him to be deposed or testify as an expert. Doctor Reuben refused to believe it, though he had to admit that since moving to the Lowcountry, he had been asked to sign more depositions and disability forms than he had up North and he had missed more hours of patient contact because of legal business.

The symptoms in Lugenia's leg continued changing over the course of the next year. Each time Doctor Reuben saw her—once a month now—the right leg appeared to be normal and the left leg altered, always differing from the other leg in a new way and always unable to support her. Discovering nothing in the leg or in Lugenia's behavior to confirm his suspicions, he trained his curiosity exclusively on possible medical causes. But as hard as he tried, he found no pattern for the leg's shifting symptoms and, more unsettling, no explanation for the consistent difference in the left leg. He sent her to a neurologist, a dermatologist, an orthopedist, and a physiatrist. She submitted to them all without complaint. Not one of them could find anything wrong with the leg. Their collective failure relieved and disturbed Doctor Reuben. If an army of specialists couldn't discover what was wrong with the leg, then he hadn't missed anything obvious. But if the county's best couldn't determine what was going on, then it was up to him to figure it out.

Lugenia, thinking that the Neurontin was making the leg act up, stopped taking the drug, but the leg continued its drama. The first few days, tremors rolled down the limb in long waves; the next few days, it was as stiff as iron. For a day and a half, purple blotches traveled from her ankle to her hip. When they disappeared, fields of tiny white bumps bloomed across her thigh and calf. The only change she could see in the leg was that her pain now accompanied its displays. After confessing to Doctor Reuben what she had done and reporting her findings to him, she resumed the medication. All this time, she was unable to return to work at the day care center. The second she put any weight on the leg, it buckled under her and she fell in a heap on the floor. Her insurance money ran out. She spent the days circling want ads in the *Voice of the People* and calling folks to see if they needed someone to come in and keep their kids while they worked. She was offered one interview, but as soon as the woman saw her at the door leaning on her cane, she told her she had already found somebody.

Lugenia gave up on the leg. Doctor Reuben would not; he kept after it. Sometimes after he had examined her, he would ask her what she thought was going on with her leg.

"It's sick," she would say.

"But what is it trying to say?" he would ask her. "What does it *mean?*"

"Means I got no job and no money."

One day after he had examined her, while she was still sitting up on the exam table, he said to her, "Lugenia, that leg of yours has me baffled. The injury is long over. The pain is completely under control. But your leg doesn't *know* that. It keeps on thinking something's wrong and it has to react, give you a sign that something's out of whack so we can fix it. We're missing something here, Lugenia. What *is* it?"

"If you can't find it, can't nobody find it."

"Think a minute. Is there anything going on in your life I should know about?"

"What kind of thing?"

"Anything. The other day, I had a patient who came in with chest pain. She thought she was having a heart attack, but it turned out that her dog had just died and her heart was hurting because she was sad. Bodies work like that sometimes."

"You not sayin' it's my mind?"

"No! I know you feel terrible pain in that leg. I'm just trying to understand what's causing that pain and these other symptoms that keep showing up, keeping that leg separate from the other. There's nothing in your life that's upsetting you?"

"My leg."

"I know. But what else? Have you experienced any losses lately?"

"Nossir, Doctor Reuben."

"Any family problems?"

"I love my two daughters, one the same as the other. It's not right they got to watch over a mama just forty years old."

"I just keep wondering why one leg is normal and the other one, even with that old injury, is always so much weaker. There's got to be some reason."

Lugenia reached for her leg and ran her hand up and down the calf, lightly but with great deliberation, as if listening to her skin for an answer.

"*Something* botherin' it," she said quietly. "That's for sure."

"I'm not saying for sure that's what's going on, Lugenia," he said, shaking his head. "It's just a feeling I have."

Lugenia's hand stopped, balled into a fist. "There's nothin' else making my leg act like this? There's got to be somethin' else, Doctor Reuben."

The doctor closed his eyes, reached under his glasses, and pinched the bridge of his nose. The skin between his eyes whitened with the pressure of his fingers. Opening his eyes, he released his grip and adjusted his glasses.

"The only thing I can think of, Lugenia, is what we call RSD, reflex sympathetic dystrophy. Have you ever heard of it?"

She shook her head.

"It's something soldiers experience a lot."

"Something for the mens?"

"RSD can happen to women or men, anybody who's suffered an injury of some sort, but doctors first discovered it in the Civil War. Soldiers would get a bullet wound in their leg and the injury would heal just fine, but for months afterward, they would feel a burning pain in the whole limb that had been wounded, all over, not just at the site of the old injury. It was so horrible they had to wrap wet rags around their limbs and put water in their boots to extinguish the fire so they wouldn't go crazy with the pain."

"I ain't never been in no war."

"I know, I know." He picked up her chart and a pen from the counter and turned back to her. "The point is, Lugenia, those Civil War doctors couldn't figure out how pain spreads from injured nerves to healthy nerves, how hurt carries on in the body long after wounds have healed, far beyond the initial site of the trauma, and we still can't explain it today. It has something to do with the nervous system and we can't cure it, that's all we know. We can help with the pain, but we haven't found a way to get rid of the disease."

"Can you write it on the form?"

"The disability form? I suppose I could—if that's what it is, RSD."

"Could be." She turned her face to him and looked straight at him for the first time since he had known her. "Could be that's what it is keepin' me down."

Tiny beads of perspiration cooled her forehead. Her cheeks, full and smooth, rose into lustrous mounds. Deep creases joined her nose and the corners of her mouth, and the center of her chin was set with a perfectly oval dimple.

Jake Reuben laid down the chart and pen next to her on the exam table. He put his hand on Lugenia's shoulder and met her eyes. "Maybe you're right," he said. He squeezed her shoulder gently. "It's the only thing that makes any sense out of what's happened to you."

She smiled broadly at him, the gold in her teeth shining.

RAT

Well, Doc, this is what I live for! This and my wife's noodles. Nineteen forty-eight Rat Class Harley. Won a lot of prizes. First place at the Sturgis Rally in South Dakota last summer. Canada the year before. This October I'm going to Germany. My wife's going with me. I'll send you a postcard. Never been to Europe. 'Nam's the only place I been. You didn't get drafted, did you? Didn't think so. You look like a man who would pull a high number. Good for you. Damn good. You missed something, though. Most beautiful land I've ever seen. Heaven couldn't be prettier. More greens than God himself could name. Birds singing until your head bursts from pleasure. And everything soft, the earth, the trees, even the sounds, all of it gentled by that watery air. So soft. I wanted to slip into it and flow right with it, like a stick carried down a river. I still dream about it. I went back a few years ago—that's when I met my wife—just to see if all that beauty was a combat dream. It wasn't. It's still there, messing with people's minds.

They have some serious heat there, though, even for a Low-country boy like myself. You think you're dying standing out here in your parking lot, full sun at midday, sweat dripping off your temples and oozing through your lab coat? This is nothin'. There, every time you take a breath, you're drowning. Skin rots off in a couple of hours. Here it takes you at least a day, maybe two, to rot. That's the difference between tropical and subtropical. We got a lot of the same vegetation they have in 'Nam, though—scrub palmettos, pricker vines, swamp bushes, lagoon grasses. That's why they shot the jungle scenes for *Platoon* here.

Get this. Hollywood paid top dollar to a bunch of experts to find them the most Vietnam place in the States, and where did they end up? Right here in the Lowcountry. Hunting Island State Park. They could have saved themselves a lot of time and trouble and asked me—I ride down there about once a week. It's only fifty miles.

Sure, I take my hog. This is my only ride. It goes everywhere I go and I go everywhere it goes. Sometimes I dress it up a little more than what you see here. When I ride it in rallies or parades, I mount my trophies on it, right up here on the front bumper. All my medals are permanent on the back, on the wheel cover here. Welded 'em myself. Go ahead, you can touch 'em if you want. You can't hurt 'em. They're there until Doomsday. The purple heart and the cross and most of the others are mine, but I mixed in a few of my dad's from World War Two, "the Big One," he called it. That star there and this one here are his. Got both our draft cards epoxied next to each other behind the seat here. Edward Kinsey, 1-A. Edward Kinsey the Second, 1-A. And look under here. That's a genuine John Deere carburetor. And those are my mother's dentures. No kidding. Her false teeth, man. She'd take 'em out every night and put 'em in a glass of water by the bathroom sink, and she wouldn't put 'em in until after breakfast. Poured hot milk on corn flakes and let 'em sit until they got soggy enough to eat without her teeth. My whole history's here!

And see this key chain hanging from the handlebar? My buddy Larry from Rosebud made it. Genuine deerskin, and he did all the beading. See the lightning bolt? He gave it to me when I rode out to the reservation to support him in the Sun Dance last summer. About forty guys pierced, one woman. She pierced in the arms, up high by the shoulder. A medicine man pierced in his back. He dragged buffalo skulls around the circle until he broke free. Larry pierced in the chest like the other men. He had to get his wheelchair rolling pretty good back from that tree in the center that they all attach themselves to. Otherwise, he couldn't have got those ropes to snap hard enough to break his skin and rip out the cherry fasteners the medicine man put in his chest. He looked so happy taking his victory lap around the circle with the blood runnin' down his chest over his old piercing scars. Giving your blood for others mends the hoop, Larry says. You'd think he gave enough when he lost his legs, but he doesn't see it that way. Not all of them that pierce do it like Larry, for the people. Some do it to help their brothers or cousins or fathers who are in jail or laid out by drinking. Some do it to say thanks to *Tunkashila,* Grandfather, or *Wakan-Tanka,* Great Mystery, for finding them a job or helping them stop drinking or healing their mother from bad lungs or their kid from cancer. I told Larry, I'm with you, man, power to the people, but don't wait for me to come dance in the hot sun all day with no food or water and tie myself to a tree just so I can break free and bleed. I've had enough bleeding. One thing for sure, though—those Lakota know how to treat vets. About every third drumming song was to honor them. World War Two, Korea, 'Nam—they don't care. They're all warriors, Larry right along with the rest of them. They appreciated my hog out there, too. Called it an Indian bike. I gave the little kids rides when the dancing was over every day. They loved it. During the day, when I was standing in the arbor supporting Larry, I could see them sneaking up to it and running their hands over all my treasures.

Those kids liked this gold locket up here between the handlebars. See it? That's my sister's, from when she was a little bit of a thing. You can see the tooth mark where she bit it. I like to touch it when I'm rolling. It makes me feel like I'm home and Sandra and I are together getting wild, the way we did before she married Horace. I didn't let those kids go inside the seat here. I keep this part locked. My wife's first passport and her naturalization papers are in here. Her name's Mai Nguyen, but everybody around here calls her May Nugent. She works over at the library.

Under Mai's stuff, I keep my girlfriend's picture and the ID bracelet I gave her for her seventeenth birthday. It looks good, doesn't it? No scratches or anything on it. That's her. Lori Simms. She's way more beautiful than this picture. Lori and I went together in high school. We were going together when I left for 'Nam. I got the letters she wrote me in here in a pouch, at the bottom. After a year, she stopped writing to me. Never said why. I signed up for another tour. When I got back, she wouldn't even talk to me. She was for peace. That was the main thing between us. But I was acting crazy, too—drinking, drugs, fights, all that mess—and she didn't like that. It wasn't until I got my first hog that I settled down. Lori never got to see it. She would have liked it if she had seen it. She'd fit just right on the back here. Or she could have gotten her own bike and we could have rode side by side. She was that kind of person: liked to do things on her own, wasn't scared of anything. She was studying to be a nurse, staying alone in one of those apartments by the old hospital. Some guy broke in and strangled her. Raped her. In the middle of the day. Cops never found him. He's out there somewhere, living easy. I used to hope they'd still find him, someway. It can happen.

A couple years ago, a buddy of mine told me about that man from Allentown who got caught for murdering his wife even though it looked like he was going to walk. He told the cops he and his wife went out on the river with their two-year-old son and his stepdaughter and his wife fell out of the boat and drowned before he could get to her. He would've gotten away with it, too, if his wife's parents hadn't heard the stepdaughter saying her bedtime prayers. She asked

Jesus to forgive Bubba for hurting her mother. I guess Bubba thought the court wouldn't pay any mind to a seven-year-old girl with Down's syndrome, but he was wrong. Those detectives put her prayer together with Bubba's habit of knocking his wife around and his buying a big insurance policy a few months before she died, and they figured it out good enough. You know what that woman's father said when the husband was sentenced? He quoted the Bible: "The Lord is known by the judgment He executeth: the wicked is snared in the work of his own hands." You think that's true, Doc? I don't. I wish it was. I guess God or whoever wrote those words didn't figure on how stupid some people can be. He should have asked me, I could have told him. The Pinesboro cops aren't as smart as those Allentown cops. If they had found the motherfucker that killed Lori, I could have taught him something about fear and suffering.

Tell me, I'm always asking Larry, what did Lori give *her* blood for? Some pervert's pleasure? No reason? For nothing? Just her bad luck to be in the way of somebody needing to kill so he didn't explode himself? That should have been my luck in 'Nam, not hers in Pinesboro. How's her sacrifice going to heal this fucking earth? That's what I'd like to know. That's my Great Mystery.

Well, Doc, that's my hog. You wanted to see it. I have to push on now. There's a scholarship named after Lori. You might be interested in it. The money goes to girls from the high school here who want to be nurses and don't have the money. I started it, and I raise money for it showing my hog. If you feel like you want to make a contribution, I'd sure appreciate it. You can do it the next time I come for an appointment, if you want. Or you can give it to me at the Rice Festival Parade this Saturday. Starts on Lucas Street downtown and goes out to the highway. Come on out and see me. I'll be riding my hog at the front of the parade and collecting money for the scholarship. I do every year. Life is good, Doc. My hog rolls great! See ya at the parade!

WHO CALLS EACH
ONE BY NAME

Thursday morning, June 5, 1991

Dear Dr. Calloway,

I know it took many years of training and plain hard work for you to become a doctor and rise above all the other doctors and be named chief of staff at Coosawaw Hospital. When the aide here gave me your name (I'm not going to tell which one she is, so don't bother asking me! You think I want you to fire her, too?), I wondered right away how *you* would feel if the powers that be called you up on the phone and said without any warning, "You are through! Don't come in to work tomorrow!" After my third husband, Remel Waters, died—he died of prostate cancer; my other two, Kardell Bingham and Horace McCall, both had heart attacks. After Remel died, I had a gentleman friend and he told me one of his first jobs was at the slaughterhouse for pigs. He was the one who stood at the belt as the pigs came by. He had a sledgehammer, and just when a pig passed by him, he would hit it on the head, one time, as hard as he could. That's how you'd feel, like you had no more rights than one of those pigs coming down that belt, if you got a call like the one you made to Dr. Reuben. If someone called you out of the blue and told you, "Dr. Calloway, you can't see patients at the nursing home anymore because Dr. Cook is the official nursing home doctor and the only one permitted to see patients there," you'd be mad. I *know* you would. And you'd be the first one to scream about your rights, too, if no one told *you* a good reason why you were fired, if they made *you* leave your job without a warning, if they never gave *you* a chance to inform the people depending on you and your visits to keep them well that you weren't allowed to come see them anymore.

Everyone here's got more aches and troubles than can be tended to by one official doctor who hides in his office all morning and plays golf every afternoon. Most of my aching's in my joints. When I was first married, I worked in Dot's Flowers and had to keep going in that cooler to get out the stems for the arrangements and that's when my trouble began. If you ever showed your face here like the chief of all doctors in the county is supposed to—and the official nursing home doctor, too, but that Dr. Cook has never once stepped foot in my room—you'd see how bent my hands are. They're like one of those metal hooks they give you when you lose your hand. I can still crochet, but I can't do Barbie clothes and baby booties anymore. I have to do big things, things I can handle, like afghans. After Remel died, my joints got so as I couldn't go out in my yard to take care of my sixty-five camellia bushes—I've named many a seedling I started and had the names recorded at the Camellia Society in Charleston, Ruby Lady, Miss Mollie, Lurline, that's just a few. My hands and my hips hurt so bad I had my granddaughter drive up to Blackwell and fill me a bottle of the healing waters there. Lurline swears she filled my bottle from the right spring, from the big one in the middle, the one that's good for legs and joints, and that she didn't go near the smaller springs for heart trouble and bad blood pressure and weak eyes, but that water didn't touch my joints. The aching got so bad I couldn't get out of bed, so she put me in her car and dragged me to Dr. Reuben. He was new in town and from the North and he wasn't a Christian, like you and me—I'm a Methodist, but my first husband was a Catholic, my second was a Baptist, and my third was a Presbyterian, so I can take just about anything. But I don't go for doctors. I'd rather room with Missy Hiers, that devil two halls over, than go see a doctor. We didn't have doctors when I was coming up. My mama helped all the women with birthing, and when I fell off the goat, my daddy set my leg for me. It's good as new. No offense, but a doctor'll kill you if he gets the chance. That's why I stay away.

But Dr. Reuben's different. He was real sweet to me the first time I saw him, and he took care of me real good, especially seeing as how I hate going to the doctor. He offered me some medicine, but he told me I didn't have to take it if I didn't want to and I didn't have to come see him, either. If I had lasted as long as I did and was as well as I was without doctors, he told me, then he saw no reason to start seeing one and ruining everything. Well, that tickled me. I fell in love with him right then, and when I got the shingles—they were so painful I couldn't sit on my bottom or lean back in the chair for weeks—I let Lurline take me to see him again. He couldn't do anything about it more than my mama could have, but he sure cheered me up. So when Remel died and it got hard for me to get around—I don't drive since my accident thirty years ago—my family brought me here to the nursing home and Dr. Reuben started looking in on me here once a month.

Dogwood Manor's a nasty place, you might as well know it, Dr. Calloway. If I had somebody to help me, I'd have myself moved to that new place that black woman Sarah Smalls and her Northern husband built, Apostolic Home. I hear people are friendly there. The aides here at Dogwood Manor are lazy or worn out from working two or three jobs or dim or mental or mean or just angry about how much they're getting paid to wipe up our spittle and slop. If they're not, they're on drugs. One of them spilled coffee on my roommate, burned her crotch, and now she's suing, just like that woman at McDonald's. Dr. Cook told her she was nothing but a copycat and he'd go after her son for insurance fraud, but I say amen to her. There are people dying of thirst in here because no one thinks to fill their water sippers. There are people falling down and no one picks them up. Aides, and nurses, too, walk right by and leave them laying there because they're too busy or they're late for one of Dr. Cook's never-ending meetings. I might as well be in my own house falling down in my own bathroom for all the good it does for me to be here. Except for Dr. Reuben coming to check on me. If he's on call on the weekend and has to check on the sick ones here, he stops in to say hey to me with his little boy or his little girl, and I give those children of his toy balls or Easter baskets I crotchet.

This winter I've had a lot of changes. My bank changed names, WUSC became WPUX, Medicare dropped some of my coverage, Lurline moved to Clemson to go to college, etc. etc. etc. But Dr. Reuben was always there, regular as church. Then yesterday afternoon, he didn't show up for my weekly visit. My thinking went like this—

He's been diagnosed with cancer and has six weeks to live.

He was in a horrible accident and is not expected to live.

He got so stressed from taking care of so many people that he lost his mind.

Maybe this is a church-run home and they got a policy against Jews and those Black Muslims working here and somebody high up just got wind of Dr. Reuben's religious persuasion.

An aide told me she heard you called Dr. Reuben up at his office one day and told him he couldn't see patients here anymore, because this was Dr. Cook's job, you had given the job to him after he got taken off the hospital staff and all the doctors in town understood it was his job and his alone. I told her that was nonsense, even if a kid goofs off and is careless about how he flips hamburgers down at McDonald's, he has to be let go with more dignity than that. "You mean to tell me," I asked her, "that my own doctor, who's been taking care of me all this time before I got in here and who I trust, can't step foot in these doors and take care of me here? That don't sound right." "Dr. Cook's the staff doctor here," she said to me real snippy, "and he's the only one that can see patients in here. That's his job." When she huffed out of my room, I felt like you and Dogwood Manor had put Dr. Reuben on one of those pig belts in the slaughterhouse and he got a sudden hammer blow on the head. And it occurred to me that if you did that to a beautiful professional like Dr. Reuben, that my reality, an eighty-six-year-old Medicare patient stuck in Dogwood Manor, was that I was a pig on that belt too.

Someone told me that there are companies that put people on contract and they have the right to fire them with no warning. I can see where a big hospital corporation could do that with the person who draws the blood, takes the X rays, does the laundry, scrubs the floors, jams pills down my throat every evening to make me behave. But I want you to know that a professional, especially a sweetheart like Dr. Reuben, should never be treated like that. That must have shattered Dr. Reuben to get that call, and it shattered me when I heard what happened to him. I felt like Jesus on the cross when he felt so abandoned. It says in Isaiah—Isaiah 40:26, you can look it up and check me—that God calls each one of us by name, and that when God calls someone to live on this earth, "not one faileth." What that means is that not one of us can fail to do the job he was brought to this earth to do. Now if that's God's plan for this earthly migration, if that's His way, who are we to take a sledgehammer and hit any pig coming down the belt? That's taking the place of God and that is called IDOLATRY and idolatry is SIN, plain and simple, and God punishes SIN. In that same passage in Isaiah it says, "God bringeth princes to nothing, He maketh the judges of the earth as vanity, He blows on them and they wither up and the wind carries them away." You better read that part. Whoever made the rules that it is OK to fire a doctor without giving him fair warning and with no good reason and no chance to attend to the future of his patients or say a proper good-bye to them was wrong. TIME TO CHANGE THOSE RULES.

In Jesus' name,
Athelda Drawdy

PHILOSOPHY
OF EDUCATION

The first time the Smileys got married, they couldn't wait to stand up before their friends, their families, and their God. The two of them had faithfully attended Weight Watchers together for nine months. Jack was down to 229 pounds, and Darlinda weighed in at 164. He grinned in his new European-cut navy suit. She beamed in the fitted yellow satin gown she had sewn, her silk tulle veil crowned with fresh violets cascading behind her. As they stood before the church in their trim glory, Reverend Hill instructed them in the holy trials of married life.

"Jesus doesn't want us to be monks and go live in the desert," he preached. "Celibacy's no challenge. Clement of Alexandria had it right when he said, 'The man who does not have family is in most respects *untried*; the *truly* spiritual man is one who *in the midst of caring for his family* shows himself inseparable from the love of God and rises superior to every temptation which assails him through children or wife or work or possessions.' Marriage is a school of the Spirit, Darlinda and Jack. Rise superior, rise superior."

The Smileys' trials started soon after they returned to Fayetteville, North Carolina, from their honeymoon in Orlando. Late one night, Darlinda heard Jack talking on the phone in the bathroom. When she rapped on the locked door and asked what he was doing, he hollered from inside that he was setting up an important deal with a customer and couldn't afford to be interrupted.

"Go back to bed," he said. "I'll be out in a minute." She knew something wasn't right, so she went to see Reverend Hill.

"People are dissatisfied," Reverend Hill explained, "and they look for something that'll scratch their itch. That's where they make their mistake, because only Jesus can make us happy. Jesus wants us to save those people headed down the wrong path. He teaches us to forgive seventy times seven times. The love of Jesus, Darlinda—that's what'll save your husband from philandering. You have to be the best wife you can be. Love Jack with all your might, and he'll turn from sin and find *true* happiness."

"It's my fault," Darlinda told Jack that night over barbecued spareribs, creamed corn, fried okra, and buttermilk biscuits. "I know I haven't been the best wife to you. I don't always have your shirts ironed on time and I complain about you spending so much time with your friends and coming home late in the night. But from now on, I'm going to be such a good wife you won't need another woman."

Jack forgave his wife, bought her a new Cayman green Taurus sedan, and proposed that they make a fresh start by moving to South Carolina. Darlinda suggested Hilton Head or Beaufort, somewhere where the ocean blew fresh air in every day from the other side of the world, but Jack said he could make better money in a rural county like Coosawaw, where there weren't that many car dealerships and everybody needed a truck. They could save more in a place like that, too, he told her, which meant they could afford to retire on the beach.

"Imagine," he said, "we'll lounge on our balcony every day, sipping tea while we watch pelicans flying past and dolphins trailing the shrimp boats."

Coosawaw County wasn't the coast; it was lowlands and swamp. But compared to Fayetteville's colorless dust flats, it was beautiful. Live oaks, centuries old and lush with resurrection ferns, sprawled across the land, their giant limbs running along the ground and interlacing with one another above to form thick canopies that cooled the sunlight as it filtered down. Spanish moss veiled the ancient oaks, as well as the tupelos and cedars, swamp gums and palmettos, Chinese tallows, sweet gums, chestnuts, pecans, hollies and figs, dogwoods and redbuds, loquats and camellias. Waxy globes of mistletoe hid among the high branches of the cottonwoods. Moss mantled the trunks of the giant bald cypresses. A gentle red carpet of needles covered the acres of sandy soil under the white pines and loblollies. In the mornings, caught in the sunlight, the trees and earth seemed to exhale a fine, steamy mist, and in the evenings, warm fog settled near the ground, softening the landscape further.

"I don't know," Darlinda told Jack during their first visit. "It's pretty, but I might be kind of scared to live here. What kind of people live out here?"

"People like us," Jack said.

"What about that guy who chopped that storekeeper into pieces with a hatchet last year, right in Coosawaw County, and then escaped from the county jail and hid in the swamps?"

"What trash did you read that in?" he asked. "*H is for Hatchet*? You've got to stop reading those murder mysteries of yours."

"A woman at the church told me."

"You're lucky I'm an honest man, Darlinda. You'll believe anything anybody tells you."

They settled on a house miles outside Pinesboro, run-down and only fourteen hundred square feet, but on three acres, with a weed-choked pond, a chicken house, and a goat shed. Darlinda thought she might keep a few goats, for company and milk, but Jack talked her out of it. They were too hard to keep penned, he said, and who would give them their worm shots? Darlinda contented herself with visiting the neighbor's arthritic mare, who came to the fence on the eastern edge of their property to eat. When the farmer on the west side plowed his fields in the spring, she walked the rows collecting arrowheads and bullets and buttons from the Civil War, which she kept in a Mason jar to show the child they would have. Behind their house, near the edge of the pines and cottonwoods, there was a rotting slave cabin with a stone for a front step. She spent hours wondering who had hauled the heavy stone there. The Lowcountry had no rocks; it was flat and sandy. Eons ago, before the Atlantic had receded, the land had been ocean floor. She could dig just below the surface almost anywhere and find sharks' teeth, dusty black wedges with long grooves running down them front and back. Some were as tiny as a fingernail, others over three inches long. Many had been worn smooth, but on some, the two saw edges were still sharp enough to cut your wrist. She knew some were millions, maybe billions of years old, fallen from the mouth of the shark's ancestor, white and brittle at first, but darkening and hardening century after century until they became denser and stronger than death. She would sit on the stone step arranging the teeth she had found in sets of jaws on the ground and imagine those ancient creatures swimming, right where she was sitting, swimming all around her, before Adam and Eve had been created, swimming to the dark below and the light above, through the clear blue offshore and the muddied waters closer in, through storms and calms, through schools of darting fishes and acres of wiggling shrimp, in that silent beginning so long ago. And while she sat there, remembering that time, she would hold a large tooth in her hand until it turned warm. It made her feel good, as if she were part of something older and smarter and truer than this life, something that would carry her beyond herself to goodness.

Within a year of moving to Coosawaw County, Darlinda was up to 222 pounds and Jack was back to 267. Since he was diabetic, it was his sugar they worried about, not his weight. Darlinda had other troubles. She carried a sadness that she blamed on the absence of wind, the sodden air, and the relentless heat. Jack thought it was because she spent too much time alone. They lived so far out, nobody came to visit except pairs of Jehovah's Witnesses and Mormon missionaries. Jack worked late every night, at a Ford dealership thirty miles away in Branchville, and every Friday night he drove to St. George, to eat at Pinckney's Bar-be-cue with the boys from work or customers he was wooing. If you'd just make an effort to get out more, he told her, see people, like I do, you'd be fine.

Their fourth year in Coosawaw County, Darlinda found dirty magazines in Jack's car. She went out to vacuum his car one Saturday morning, to surprise him when he woke up, and discovered the magazines under the driver's seat. She knew they weren't *Playboy* or *Penthouse,* but she couldn't make herself look at them long enough to see what they were. She shoved them back under the seat and finished vacuuming. She didn't say anything to Jack. She was sure the magazines belonged to one of the other salesmen at the dealership, maybe Curt Pellum, who always wore a medallion around his neck and those flashy pink shirts, or Randy Crosby, the new manager from Atlanta. When she looked the next morning, on her way to church, the magazines were gone. A year went by before she found another set, stuffed behind his tools in the garage. She burned those in the trash barrel out back. When she told Jack what she had done with them, he thanked her.

"I know they're no good," he said, "but sometimes I just get curious about how other people live."

"Where'd they come from?"

"That new kid at work, a mechanic just out of high school, he gave them to me, so I wouldn't be a boring old married man."

"You haven't ever, you know, done anything, or wanted to do anything, you know, that you read about in those things?"

"Honey!"

"Why look at them, then?"

"I'm not going to do the things I read about any more than you're going to go out and shoot down a cop or strangle a kid or poison my food because you read it in one of your murder mysteries. I told you: I'm just curious about the kind of people who *would* do such things."

Darlinda believed him. But within months of arriving in Coosawaw County, Jack had started picking up dates. If you were cautious and knew the code, it was easy to find people hungry for the same thing he was. He didn't go looking often, maybe two or three times a year—not so much because he was afraid of being found out in a small town as because it took him a while after each encounter to recover from the guilt. Once a week, to reward himself for his self-restraint, he drove to the unmarked adult bookstore in Branchville to buy his magazines. To those who had no business there, the cement block building behind the feed store, with its peeling green paint, boarded-up windows, and a sag in the roof, looked abandoned. Coosawaw was full of places like that—rusty semitrailers, cut loose from the cab and dumped along the roads, with people living in them; an old, unmarked storage building on Highway 26 that harbored a whites-only roller rink; public schools that to Yankees and other newcomers looked like bombed-out ruins.

After she found magazines in Jack's car a third time—less than a year after she had burned the previous set—Darlinda began spending all her time at the True Church of the Lamb. Every Wednesday night and Sunday morning, she attended worship. The rest of the week, she spent helping out wherever the pastor needed her. When she wasn't at church or praying or reading her Bible or inspirational books from the church lending library, she talked about the pastor. "Pastor Jim says we have to be patient and let God work on people in His own ways. Pastor Jim says God rewards sacrifice. Pastor Jim says God asks us every one of us to give up something in our life to prove our love for Him."

Jack didn't like Pastor Jim. He smiled too much. And he reminded him of the blue-tailed skinks that shot out from the steps and up the walls of the house, smooth-skinned and pretty but poisonous. But he was careful not to say a word against him, knowing how much time Darlinda spent at the church, leaving him free for his own interests.

Darlinda worked tirelessly at the church—setting up and serving the anniversary dinners, decorating the sanctuary for weddings and other special services, delivering food to shut-ins, collecting clothes for missionary families, planting flowers in the yard, painting inside and out. Though she was heavy and her knees were bad, she wasn't sickly or weak. Pastor Jim and the others could always rely on her when there was work to be done for the Lord, especially the hard or dirty jobs that no one else wanted to touch. So when Pastor Jim got the call that Darlinda was in the hospital, he and the church were surprised. The delegation from the Visitation Committee found her on the second floor, recovering from what she called a fainting spell. She told them she had collapsed in the bathroom and Jack had called EMS when he found her.

"It's anemia," she told her visitors. "I'm supposed to eat liver and greens every day."

When Darlinda went home from the hospital, church members took turns dropping off suppers of mustard greens and turnip greens and collard greens, liver and onions, rumaki, chicken liver paté, and liverwurst sandwiches—all with large jugs of sweet tea.

Someone visited with her and prayed with her every day for a month, all of them taking special care to treat her with Christian kindness after they learned the true cause of her suffering. The EMS technician, a nurse told them, had found Darlinda on the floor of her bathroom in a pool of blood, the dead baby she had delivered lying beside her, still attached.

"A six-pound boy, stillborn," the nurse said. "Almost nine months, and she didn't even know she was pregnant! Can you believe that?"

Some of them didn't believe it.

"How can anybody not know she's pregnant?" one churchwoman asked the nurse.

"With all that weight and everything," the nurse said, "I suppose she just can't feel what's going on in her body."

"She'd have to be dead not to know she was *pregnant*," another woman said. "I knew the instant it happened. I felt a tingling."

"Well, good for you," the nurse said. "But not everybody throws up. Not everybody's ankles swell. Not everybody craves certain foods or gains fifty pounds and ends up looking like a blimp. I don't care what the doctors say. Pregnancy's not a disease with textbook symptoms; it's a sign of health. And who notices health?"

To some of Darlinda's women visitors, it didn't seem at all strange that she wouldn't know she was pregnant. Like most married women, Darlinda took more care of her husband's body than her own, spending all her efforts watching his glucose levels, his blood pressure, his cholesterol intake. And in spite of her weight and her love of food, she was more aware of Jack's appetite than hers. Like the rest of them, she had been trained long before marriage to be hypersensitive to his desires. Though she rarely had any idea whether she was hungry or not, she knew in a flash when Jack needed a hamburger, a pizza, a sundae, a breast or something more, and before he even knew what he was craving, she moved in swiftly to satisfy him and forestall disappointment. There was no better way to keep peace in the household.

After three months in bed, Darlinda decided she had had enough crying and enough of people's pity. She got up from her bed one steamy August morning and began to clean the house. For days she cleaned. She threw out plastic yogurt containers and cottage cheese tubs buried in the deep corners of the kitchen cupboards, used plastic sacks—receipts, lists, and other remnants stashed inside—outdated medicines and cosmetics hiding in the bathroom closet, flower baskets and vases crammed in garbage bags in the garage. She emptied the huge chest freezer in the garage, scoured it, and replaced everything according to the type of meal—breakfast to the left, lunch and snack in the middle, dinner to the right, each item clearly labeled. She took down all the curtains, gave them to the Salvation Army, and washed every window. She dragged sacks full of clothes that were too small or too large for her to the church for its missions and donated all her murder mysteries—twenty boxes—to the library for its annual book sale. Jack wouldn't let her touch his closet, but she cleaned everything else. She wanted nothing concealed from her.

In September she enrolled in a basic accounting class at Sangaree, the local branch of the University of South Carolina. She discovered she could set up and balance any account the instructor set before her, even the trickiest ones with hidden funds and dual entries. She would lay everything out before her and rearrange and reorganize it until it made sense to her. With the recommendation from the instructor and the help of a church member, she got a job at the county auditor's office. By Thanksgiving she had made friends with two co-workers, Sally and Jellemma. The three of them would go out to lunch together or drive to the Outlet Mall on Hilton Head on the weekends. Darlinda still attended the True Church of the Lamb, but not as regularly as she had before. If Sally and Jellemma asked her to drive to Hilton Head on a Sunday, to shop and swim, she went along. Now, instead of recapping Pastor Jim's sermons for Jack, she talked about her friends, which relieved Jack greatly. "Sally says I have to get out more," she'd say, or "Jellemma lent me some tapes for the car, Sister Rosetta Tharpe and Koko Taylor." And rather than read in her spare time, she sewed, singing as the needle worked its way in and out, "Precious Memories," "No Room in the Church for Liars," or *I can hold back the lightning with the palm of my hand, I'm a woman, W-O-M-A-N.*"

Jack approved of these changes. He didn't like to think of his wife spending all her time in bed waiting for him to come home so that she could ask about his day, where he'd been, whom he'd talked to. She needed to keep busy, be with other people, he thought. He encouraged her to take the accounting class and never complained about the tuition or her being gone all the time. When she started working full-time and spending her off hours with Sally and Jellemma, he was thrilled; she seemed happy and it kept her from fussing over his health and habits. For several years, things went along better than ever between them. They never spoke about his magazines or her illness and recovery. With both of them working, they were able to save up for an annual trip to Vegas, a twenty-inch TV, and a Bernina sewing machine. They were content.

One April, Jack developed a rash on his foot. At first he and Darlinda dismissed it as a red-ant bite. They rubbed Neosporin on his instep and poured poison on the anthills in the yard. When the rash didn't improve, they decided it was ringworm and rubbed antifungal cream on the irritated area—which had doubled in size—for two weeks. But the dull itchiness and inflammation kept on, spreading across his foot. His whole instep turned pink and the foot felt weird, pebbly and watery right under the surface of the skin, like rubbing your fingers over rocks in a stream. The foot was so tender he had to wear a slipper on it, even to work. Darlinda finally talked Jack into seeing a doctor, the town's new doctor, whom she had met during morning rounds while she was in the hospital.

"That foot's pultaceous, all right," Doctor Reuben told them. "Pulpy."

He put Jack on an antibiotic, which did no more good than their home remedies. Doctor Reuben told them not to worry: Some bacteria fought back harder than others; it was a matter of finding the right antibiotic. It might take a little time, but they'd get to the bottom of it. He had Jack try one antibiotic after another, and when that didn't work, he sent him to a string of specialists—dermatologists, allergists, podiatrists. But the infection wouldn't go away. Because the increasing soreness made it hard for Jack to stand for a long time, he had to cut a few hours off his workday. Some days the antibiotic would make him so tired he couldn't go to work at all. Darlinda felt sorry for him, but she couldn't do much more than help him soak his foot in Epsom salts and soothe his worries.

"If it were cancer, Doctor Reuben would have told us," she told her husband. "He believes in telling his patients the truth. It can't be cancer, or he would have told us."

The rash grew worse, forcing Jack to stay home and rest his foot for extended periods. To pass the time and distract himself from the pain, he bought a computer and set it up in the garage. Soon he was spending all his free time in the garage. Often he would still be working away at the computer when Darlinda got up for work in the morning. She had to coax him out to kiss him goodbye. At first she ignored his infatuation, thinking he was like a kid with a new toy. But when the allure didn't wear off, Darlinda started to worry. She asked Sally and Jellemma what she should do.

"At least he's home for a change," Jellemma said.

"What's he doing in there?" Sally asked.

"I think he's in those chat rooms," Darlinda said.

"White supremacy stuff?" Jellemma asked. "He's not mixed up in those church burnings out by Cottageville, is he?"

"No!"

"You think he could be in some kind of porn ring," Sally asked, "like you read about?"

"He's talking to gay men," Darlinda said. She said it calmly, as if telling them where she was born or how old she was.

"That's all he's doing?" Jellemma asked. "Talking?"

"He says he's lonely," Darlinda said, "but if he's so lonely, why can't he talk to me, spend time with me? Everything was going so good for a while. He was letting me take care of him with that foot, spoil him a little. Now, with this computer, it's like I don't even exist. I know I'm fat and I haven't wanted to be intimate since I was in the hospital, but I'm still his wife."

"Are you sure he's just talking?" Sally asked.

Darlinda nodded. "He says he got into the site by accident, and then once he was there, he started trying to talk them out of it, kind of a ministry."

"You think they're talking about *God?*" Jellemma said. "Girl, you're *crazy!*"

Sally and Jellemma made her promise to go see Doctor Reuben and tell him the whole story, from the dirty magazines on. Doctor Reuben put Darlinda on an antidepressant and suggested she see a counselor, which she didn't do, because the only counselor working in Coosawaw County drove in from Charleston one day a week, saw six cases an hour, and was known for her impatience and chilliness. The only person Darlinda could turn to was Pastor Jim. He was a man who knew the ways of God and the love of God and he had been trained in pastoral counseling; he would know what to do. When she told him she feared her husband was spending time in chat rooms for inappropriate sex—she couldn't bring herself to say the word *homosexual* in front of her pastor—

Pastor Jim took a deep breath and asked her, "What would Jesus do, Darlinda?"

During the time Darlinda's church attendance dropped off, Pastor Jim had discovered the What Would Jesus Do? movement. His church was selling WWJD buttons, pins, key chains, pens, pencils, bumper stickers, T-shirts, and baseball hats to raise money to paint the building.

"Nice, aren't they?" he asked, when he saw her looking at the box of WWJD necklaces on his desk. They were all alike except for the color of the enamel on the letters, some pink and the others white.

She nodded. It was only fair that she make a contribution to his ministry, she thought, given that she was no longer an active member of his congregation. She opened her purse and handed him a twenty-dollar bill.

"Pick any one you like," he said, putting the bill in the desk drawer.

"What *would* Jesus do?" she asked, closing her hand around the necklace in its crackly plastic covering.

"He'd forgive him," Pastor Jim said, "and tell him to go and sin no more."

Darlinda went home, put on the necklace, and thought it over. A week later, when she had finally saved up enough courage to tell Jack she wanted him to stop whatever it was he was doing in the garage, he laughed at her.

"You're paranoid, Darlinda," he said. "It's a good thing Doctor Reuben put you on that medicine."

"I hope you're right," she said.

Darlinda kept taking her Prozac and wearing the necklace, praying morning and night that she was wrong about Jack and that their life would return to normal. Though Jack kept up the frequency and duration of his computer visits, he made an effort to be kind to her. When she came home from work, he would present her with chocolate-iced doughnuts or her favorite Sarah Lee cake and sit with her a few minutes before returning to the garage.

Two months after Pastor Jim had counseled her to forgive Jack and beg him to go and sin no more, Darlinda discovered that Jack was in love with a man in Amsterdam. A travel agent had left a message for Jack at the house with questions about his ticket for Amsterdam. She heard it when she came home from work and immediately called Sally.

"Quick," Sally said, "before Jack comes home, you've got to go check his computer."

"I can't do that! It's *his!*"

"Darlinda, you go in that garage right now and start that computer. I'm not hanging up until you do."

Sally coached Darlinda on how to start up the computer and get into Jack's old e-mail messages. Darlinda read only three messages before she threw up.

She confronted Jack when he walked in from work. He didn't even try to deny it. He told her that he had an "amorous relationship with a special person" in Amsterdam and that he was going there to meet him. He seemed excited, eager to tell her, like someone who can't contain good news about themselves and blurts it out to the first stranger on the street. After making his announcement, he hurried to the garage and locked the door.

Darlinda drove right over to Pastor Jim's house.

Pastor Jim sat on the edge of his chair, horror and satisfaction wrestling on his face. "Homosexuality is an *abomination,*" he said, banging both fists on his desk. "The Bible says so. It's an *abomination* and God will not tolerate it."

"They're only having *computer* sex," she said. "Does that count?"

"What are they *doing?*" Pastor Jim asked.

"It doesn't matter what *they're* doing," she said. "What am *I* going to do? What should I do? I don't know what to do. Tell me what to do. How can I stop him? Save my marriage?"

"The Lord is trying you in a special way, Darlinda, to test your faith and make you stronger. You need to pray with Jack and read God's word with him, help him see these are unnatural acts and that he needs to repent."

"What if he won't listen?"

"God will punish him."

Darlinda drove to Dairyland and had a triple-fudge sundae with pecans and walnuts, methodically lifting each spoonful and savoring the sweet cold in her mouth, bite by bite. When she had scraped the last drop of cream from the bottom of the waxed-paper cup, she drove home. She went straight to the kitchen and knocked on the door to the garage.

"Let me in," she called. "Right this minute. I have something to say."

Jack shuffled across the garage, dragging his sore foot, and stood on the other side of the door.

"What is it?" he asked.

"Let me in and I'll tell you."

"Just tell me through the door."

"If you insist on going to Amsterdam," she shouted, "I'll divorce you."

The week before, she had chanced upon a Dear Abby letter in the Charleston paper, from a woman whose husband was reading pornography and having affairs on his computer. Dear Abby's advice: "Adultery is adultery. Give the guy an ultimatum. Tell him to stop immediately, or you're gone." She hadn't mentioned the letter to Pastor Jim, because she knew he didn't believe in divorce. "God doesn't break his covenant with *His* Beloved, does He?" he would ask during his sermons.

"You don't mean that, Honey," Jack said through the door. "Honey?"

She was silent. Her chest rose and fell rapidly.

"Honey, listen, I know it doesn't make sense, but this is a dream trip for me, the trip of a lifetime. You know I've never been to Europe, never been out of the country, and that I've always wanted to go. I can't help it that I fell in love with this person, can I? But I'm just going to *see* him, just *meet* him once, and then come right home. We're not going to *do* anything. Nothing's changed between you and me, and nothing's going to change. I still love you. Why are you hysterical all of a sudden? Why can't you just let me have this one thing I want? I've lost so much already. I've had to sacrifice so much. All I'm asking for is just this *one* thing. That's all. Let me have just this one thing, and then I'll be all yours forever. I'll do whatever you want. I promise."

The trip was planned for July, four months away. When Darlinda saw that her husband was serious, she went to see Bubba Hagood and filed for divorce. Jack didn't think she'd go through with it, and she almost didn't. If she hadn't promised Sally and Jellemma to call at the first sign of wavering, she might never have done it. The papers arrived the day before Jack left. As soon as she signed them, she took off her wedding ring, slipped it inside the toe of a pair of pantyhose, and stuffed it in the linen closet. The WWJD necklace she threw in the trash under the sink. Though Jack begged her to try to understand his point of view and cajoled and pleaded, she refused to drive him to the airport in Charleston. A taxi came to the house the next morning, and he was gone.

Jack was gone six weeks. What he did during that time Darlinda couldn't guess and didn't want to. And it was a relief not to have to worry every moment over his glucose levels and rash. After the first few days, she seemed happier. She started losing weight. She walked four miles a day before breakfast and cooked herself a healthful supper the nights she was home—boneless chicken breasts steamed with broccoli and served over rice, eggs poached on a bed of greens, fish fillets baked with a potato and drizzled with hot pepper oil.

Sally and Jellemma called her every day and took her out to dinner a couple of times a week. She applied for a promotion at work. She cut her hair, sewed new clothes for herself, and talked about starting a dressmaking business specializing in handmade bridal gowns and veils. She joined the Episcopalian Church downtown. After services one Sunday morning, Earl Owens asked her to go to the rodeo with him and she accepted. She felt lighter and lighter, surprised at how little it took to learn happiness. She stopped taking her Prozac—against Doctor Reuben's recommendation—and after a few weeks, reported to him proudly that she hadn't felt so good since her wedding day.

Then Jack came home. He called from the Comfort Inn on Highway 26 and asked her to meet him for coffee. At first she said no, but when he told her he was sick and he didn't have a car—he had sold his for the trip—and he needed someone to take him to Doctor Reuben, she picked him up and took him to the doctor. She told Sally and Jellemma that night, "If I passed a stranger on the street who was sickly and needed a ride, anybody, dirty or clean, I'd give him one, you know that. You'd do the same."

"Not for somebody who done me like that, I wouldn't," Sally said.

"Even if he was God Himself," Jellemma added, "crying out to me, 'Jellemma, save me!'"

"You would, too," Darlinda said. "Both of you, and you know it."

Jack had lost fifty pounds while in Amsterdam. He had caught a bug while he was there and had become severely dehydrated.

"He's as gaunt as Jesus on the cross," she told her new minister—she couldn't get used to calling him her priest—when he questioned whether her attentiveness to her former husband was good for her. "I'm going to get him back on his feet first. Then we'll talk about what he's going to do and what I'm going to do. For now, all that matters is getting him well."

A general practitioner in Amsterdam had done a stool culture and found a strange parasite, *Cryptosporidium,* that he had treated Jack for, but the medicine hadn't helped. Doctor Reuben told Darlinda and Jack that *Cryptosporidium* normally caused mild gastroenteritis, not persistent diarrhea like Jack's. He took Jack off the medicine for the parasite and started him on an antibiotic. When this had no effect, either, they changed antibiotics again. They tried antibiotic after antibiotic, but not one of them worked. Jack became so weak and dried out, he had to be admitted to the hospital and put on IVs while they kept searching for an effective drug. Nothing helped. Jack continued to lose weight. When the results of the HIV test came back, Doctor Reuben started Jack on AZT immediately, making sure that he and Darlinda both understood that the drug would have little effect, because Jack had end-stage AIDS. He had been infected with HIV for at least fifteen years, and his immunity was practically zero.

"Jack's CD four T-cell count is one," he explained, "and a person's in trouble if it falls under two hundred. All we can do is wait and see."

For the next two months, Jack was mostly in, but occasionally out of, the hospital. When he was able to leave the hospital, he went home with Darlinda. "It's just for a few days," she told Sally and Jellemma. "That's *all.*"

"God don't like anybody outdoing Him in the mercy department," Jellemma said. "'I am a *jealous* God,' it says."

"What do you want me to do? Jack has nowhere else to go. No family, no friends. Even if this is God's punishment on him, how can I turn him away? Did Jesus turn the lepers away? Am I supposed to let him live on the street? Die on the street? Did the Good Samaritan leave that man by the side of the road to die? How could I live with myself if I abandoned my husband like that?"

When Sally reminded her that he wasn't her husband anymore, that she was a free woman, she replied, "How could I abandon *anyone* like that?"

After eight weeks, the AZT kicked in. Jack's immune system rebuilt itself and started fighting off the *Cryptosporidium*. Within no time, he had gained thirty pounds. The hospital pronounced him too well to take up a bed, but he still needed a great deal of care and he had no money. What could he do but throw himself on Darlinda's mercy and ask her to take him back? She said she would, but on one condition: They had to get married first. She wasn't going to live in sin with him. And she'd marry him only if he promised never to have anything to do with men again and stay faithful to her. He agreed.

They got married in the hospital chapel, he in blue-checked cotton pajamas, she in a lavender flannel nightgown and robe, both of them barefoot—to symbolize starting anew, on an equal footing before God. They used their rings from the first wedding. He had never taken his off; she retrieved hers from the linen closet. The chaplain on duty, a Southern Presbyterian, refused to marry them. So did her priest, at first, but after Darlinda talked to him, he relented. One of the custodians served as the witness. Darlinda didn't bother telling Sally and Jellemma she was marrying Jack again. She knew they wouldn't come anyway, and she didn't want them to try to talk her out of it. "Jack's gay and diseased in mind and body," Sally would say, "and you need brain surgery. And you want us to witness *that?*"

A week or so after they got married again, Jack was well enough to leave the hospital. Darlinda took care of him at home. It was a full-time job, so she quit work. She had to watch his fluids, manage all his drugs, help him to the commode, clean him up, do everything for him.

Sally and Jellemma visited her regularly, but they couldn't understand it. Why tie herself to him after she had fought so hard to be free, fighting through all that confusion and lies to a clear act?

She tried to explain it to them, how if she flooded him with love and care, she would cure him of his homosexuality and that this was what God wanted her to do.

"That's why I was born," she said, "to love Jack into goodness. That's what I had to learn, why I've had all these trials. All my life I've been kind of empty, waiting to find out what God wants me to do. And now I know. I wouldn't trade that for anything."

"Nobody can save anybody," Jellemma said. "That's God's job. All we can do is try not to get in God's way. There's nothing more to learn than that. What kind of a stupid-ass God is it who sets up sadistic tests for us so we can learn what we need to? You think God's not smart enough to figure out how to teach us what we need to know without pounding us into the ground, crushing us, damn near killing us, just so we get the point? God's *got* to be more creative than that. If He's not, He should take a course in the philosophy of education. Get a Ph.D. in it. Otherwise, you better get yourself a different God who runs a different kind of school."

"Love *changes* people," Darlinda said. "If I give up hoping Jack will change, I might as well give up living."

"I can hope I won't have to pay taxes come April fifteen, but I will. I can hope I won't ever die, but I will. And I can love myself to death and hope all I want that I'll turn white," Jellemma said, "but it's not going to happen. Some things don't change, Darlinda."

"Jack will never be perfect, I know that. But he'll be better. He already acts different toward me."

"He needs something from you," Jellemma said. "Course he's going to act nice."

"Maybe you can't see it, but he's changed."

"All I know," Sally said, "is I'm *never* getting married again myself, *ever*. Marriage is one of those mysteries that just when you think you've untangled it, you've made a bigger knot."

When Jack's condition deteriorated again, Sally and Jellemma took turns spending nights with Darlinda, to help with Jack's care so that she could sleep. The three of them worked well together. They traded off the cooking, cleaning, and tending, and a hospice nurse came in once a week to check his progress.

When he was conscious, Jack gave Darlinda all his attention. They had breakfast together and did the crossword puzzle together before lunch. While he napped, she designed or sewed, and when he woke, he would go over her designs or admire her handiwork, giving her suggestions on line or color. She read to him every night. They talked all the time, though he never once mentioned Amsterdam, and Darlinda took care not to say or do anything that might remind him of it. She threw away the salty, black licorice and coffee candies she found in his suitcase. If a program on Rembrandt came on, she switched channels. If tulips were on sale at the grocery store, she did not buy them.

"Tired?" Jellemma asked one night when she came to relieve her friend.

"Satisfied," Darlinda said. "Like I've stopped eating things that only make me feel emptier." She looked directly at Jellemma. "All I ever wanted was for him to stop running and let me love him. Now he does."

"Looks like he can't do anything *but.*"

She was right. Jack couldn't do anything but lie in bed in the living room and gaze at her coming and going from him like a dream at the edge of sleep. The seven weeks before Jack died were the best of Darlinda's life. There was a wide stillness around them that made room for everything, disappointment and hope, sorrow and joy, anger and acceptance, and that stillness filled her. Every day until she died, in line at the grocery store or at church, at her sewing machine or out with friends, she would circle her wedding ring around her finger until the gold turned warm and she found herself carried into the silent beginning of the world, before Adam and Eve, where everything that was, was good.

UNNATURAL ACTS

Folks here believe if you move to New York for a time, you come back corrupted: The girls go up virgins and come down trailing two or three babies, and the boys come back addicts, criminals, or otherwise defiled. That's why Lowcountry folks who stay up North for work send their kids home to live with the grandparents—so they can be raised up right. Nobody sends babies down on the train alone anymore, with tags tied on them telling the conductors where to put them off to be collected by relatives, but most still send their kids back down here to grow up. What's the point? If a kid's going to grow up bad, he's going to grow up bad here or in New York. And if he's going to turn out good, it doesn't matter if he's raised North or raised South. Lowcountry folks have been going North to live hundreds of years, and not all come back ruined. Some come home triumphant.

I am not talking about Sarah Smalls. Sarah Smalls isn't the only one who made good in New York. I had my own drumming studio, right in the Village—not the East Village, either, the West Village. I was New York City's best hand-drum maker and Afro-Cuban-Caribbean drumming teacher for more than thirty years. I won every music award the city gives—the Mayor's Award, the

Central Park Festival Award, the New York Magazine Award, and a whole lot more. People here don't even know what that means. Drummers who worked with Coltrane and Miles came to me. Theater people. Julliard students. Gabrielle Roth was always sending people my way. Everybody wanted a drum made by *my* hands, wanted to study drumming with Alfonso Gethers. My name *meant* something. People here are jealous because I had all that in the big world and then came back with money and my own ideas how to spend it. I didn't come home to show off or lord it over anybody. I came home to take care of my Uncle Esau. And just because the only coat I had for winter was a full-length white mink, people started saying I was a disgrace. When I was growing up, I was always careful not to call attention to myself. I never sashayed down Savage Street in a skirt and a wig, like these young boys do today. I was *respectful* of my people. So why, the first time I show up in a coat no one in New York would blink at, do my people abuse me? That kind of mean spirit is the reason why, in all the years I lived in New York, I never came home for more than a weekend at a time and why I spent every hour of that time with my uncle in his place out on the Beaufort Highway. Why mix with those who have made up their minds you're no good? Nothing but a lamb to the slaughter.

If people here want to stay where they're big fish in a little stinking pond, grow up to run funeral parlors or fish shacks or work for the county, fine. Or if they want to be victims—work their whole lives for white people so they can blame them for why nothing good ever happened in their lives—that's fine by me, too. But when an artist like me makes it in the big city and comes back not beholden to anybody, they shouldn't spread lies about him just so they can maintain their world the way they want it: the whites way up over there, where they can keep an eye on them, and all the blacks under Sarah Smalls.

Everybody here's blinded by Sarah Smalls's success. What success? She married a rich man. She and her rich husband ran a nursing home in Brooklyn; they paid people minimum wage to change old folks' diapers and empty their bedpans. Nobody wants to see the feet of clay on that woman. Sarah Smalls is as full of herself as a bumblebee. Her husband struts around wearing those golf shirts and Coogli sweaters. She wears those clingy dresses that stretch too tight across her breasts and her behind. She and her husband take civic groups out on their yacht, miles offshore, where the water's blue, not muddy like it is close in, where all the rest of us have to live. But you never hear anybody saying she's showing off. She fools around, too. I'll bet my reputation she does. But nobody comes after *her* for her unchristian acts. No one in the whole county, black or white, dares challenge Sarah Smalls. Look here. She and her husband don't know the first thing about music, but the minute they say, "Let's hire the Hallelujah Singers to perform in the Pinesboro auditorium" or "Let's bring that African dance troupe from Beaufort to the schools," everyone jumps to it. Just because they're always preaching about black culture and remembering the Lowcountry's connection to West Africa doesn't mean they know anything. I was teaching ancient African rhythms long before Sarah Smalls discovered Africa. Her husband's not even from the Lowcountry. He's from Gary, Indiana. Sarah Smalls may have grown up here and she may have the finest collection of sweetgrass baskets in the world, but she never heard of Sierra Leone and the Ivory Coast rice culture until she saw that show on PBS a few years ago. She didn't know anything about sweetgrass or indigo or Gullah until she gave all that money to the Penn Center and they put her on their board. I bet her relatives never spoke a word of Gullah.

My people, the Gethers *and* the Memmingers, *still* speak Gullah. When my Uncle Esau went to that new doctor here, Reuben, and asked him to cure his "nature," the man couldn't understand a word he said. The doctor had to call in another black patient from the waiting room to translate for him. "His *manhood*," the woman whispered, nodding to my uncle's privates, "he wants you to help him with his *manhood*." When the doctor complimented him on his lilting accent and asked him if he was from the Bahamas, my Uncle Esau put him right. "All-time be from Cherokee Plantation," he told him. Africa's still living in my Uncle Esau's mouth, but has he ever exploited Africa to raise himself in the eyes of others? No. Nor have I. I teach African rhythms not to show off how high and mighty I am, but to keep those traditions alive, hand down those ways of moving through life to the next generation.

New York people know how to appreciate my rhythms. "Fluid and electric," one critic wrote, "simultaneously supple and exploding with energy, a rare harmony of ancient beats and the modern spirit." Folks here criticize my rhythms for not being "authentic" because they don't sound like the six-eight rhythms from Ghana they've heard amateur groups perform here. Some are so ignorant they say my rhythms are devil rhythms, that they move like a snake, smoothing around and striking without warning, so they have to watch out I don't sneak up on their children and molest them. It's Smalls who's sneaky. She and her husband don't go around saying, "Look what we did to keep our black heritage alive and help black folks!" but they make damn sure that every time they do something—give the biggest black donation ever to the Negro College Fund or finance a black political candidate—it gets out among the people, so everyone will come up to them and fall over themselves thanking them so they can blush and pretend it's nothing. Black folks were helping black folks long before Sarah Smalls and that Northern husband of hers needed a tax break. You know it's true. And what kind of help is it they're giving? I don't care if they operate a free clinic and after-school programs for blacks or if they built a black community center and named it the

Denmark Vesey Center after the slave that led the Lowcountry slave rebellion. I don't care if they started their own newspaper, the *Voice of the People,* because the *Pinesboro Gazette* didn't give enough play to the black perspective and the concerns of the black community. All that paper does is give them a cheap way to advertise their businesses and spread their warped ideas all over town. Sarah Smalls goes around saying things like, "The racism in New York is worse than the racism in the Lowcountry, because here people come right out and tell you they don't want to associate with you, whereas in New York they talk like they're your best friend but they don't ever have time for you," and her paper prints it. Sure there's Northern racism and Southern racism. Who doesn't know that? But how can she say it's better here? Those white people living on that fancy resort on John's Island spent a million dollars saving sea turtles last year, but have they ever noticed the black people living right in their back yard on the island, people so poor they have to use the dirt floor in one room of their house for a toilet? If it's so good for blacks here, living and working with the whites, why is Sarah Smalls building her own black empire? I heard she and her husband are going to build a restaurant and a grocery store. What's next? Their own TV and radio station so they can spread their shackled ideas to more people?

Sarah Smalls can shout as loud as she wants to about the importance of establishing and supporting black-owned and -operated businesses, practicing black philanthropy, preserving black culture, encouraging black pride, fostering black values. It ain't nothing but black hypocrisy. She doesn't go to the black doctor in town, Doctor Bruce Inabinett. She and her husband patronize the rich white doctors so they'll get more referrals for Apostolic Home, the nursing home they built. But that's not how folks here tell it. Sarah Smalls, they say, won't patronize a black doctor who joins the white country club—how admirable! Smalls is always giving out that she and her husband are so principled. When her husband goes to the stockyards to buy horses for their plantation, he makes a show of not sitting in the white section directly in front of the auction pit. One time he sits in the cramped section to the right with all the old black men, and the next he sits in the section to the left, where young blacks and whites sit together. It's not about black pride; it's about him and his wife making money and being worshipped for their high morals. I call *that* indecent. I never violated my heritage or my people to make money and get others to bow down to me. I never took advantage of anyone, adult or child.

I'm fed up hearing about Sarah Smalls and what she and her rich husband have done for Lowcountry black folks. You can't go anywhere in Coosawaw County without hearing somebody tell the tale of how she bought the plantation her grandmother was a slave on. How all the time she was in New York she kept her eye on that piece of property, waiting for it to come on the market, and when it did, she was right there with her two million dollars. She and her husband remodeled the antebellum mansion and built one just as big for her two sisters and their families. She lives out there like the Queen of Sheba in her palace, folks say—gold faucets in the bathrooms, marble walls, colored chandeliers, a fountain in the living room, stables and a full-time stable master, an airplane hanger, an eight-car garage, three- and four-wheelers for her nephews and nieces to play on, an Olympic pool, a dock down to the river with a deck for parties and a boathouse for their kayaks, their own barbecue pit. And the way folks talk, you'd think those hundred acres of hers were the Garden of Eden. A quarter-mile canopy of ancient live oaks lining the drive, Spanish moss and resurrection ferns dripping everywhere, cherry trees and cypress trees, hollies and loquats, dogwoods and magnolias and red plums, rhododendrons and azaleas, one of the oldest formal camellia gardens in the Lowcountry, four ponds, and the Edisto River cutting right through the property, all that beautiful black water, some of the purest left in the country, running straight through Sarah Smalls's garden and giving it life. That's the way they tell it. Tell me, what's so sacred about swampy land that's home to cottonmouths and rattlers and alligators and bobcats, where mildew and termites and all other kinds of destruction thrive, just waiting to ruin your house from the inside out? No land is sacred, no matter how beautiful or blood-soaked; it's the way we move through a place that makes it sacred: We can try to learn how to move through this world in beauty, or we can stay stiff and stumble through.

The way folks here tell it, the first thing Sarah Smalls did after she bought Cheecha-Yehossee Plantation was clean up the graveyard where her grandmother is buried. Folks say the grandmother died during Rebel Times and they dug her under a live oak there. Sarah tends that grave and the others right around it like it was a temple to the ancestors. She puts fresh flowers on the stones every day, and from time to time she brings other gifts—a glass of water, a cast net, antlers, drums. People make up all kinds of stories about that graveyard. I've heard folks brag that they steal in there at night just to touch some of the power there and go home with it filling them up, making them feel proud and free. They say it's not just the spirits of those who died in slavery that dwell there, but the spirits of the first Africans brought here too, the ones who killed themselves rather than serve as slaves. Every night all the spirits hold a meeting among those graves, shouting and stomping praise. Sometimes there are so many spirits gathering there, people say, they block the path to the graveyard. The visitors have to shoo them away with their hands and say "whicha whoocha whoocha" to get near enough to the graves to overhear one of the spirit shouts or see one of the steps in the stomp. That way, the visitor can carry it to church the next Sunday and get recognized as some kind of prophet. I heard that Julie Dash or somebody is making a documentary about Sarah Smalls and that graveyard of hers. That's the silliness that feminism and blackism will do. What are they going to call that film? Black Tall Tales? Sarah Smalls and her graveyard are like a story in the Bible: Everybody repeats it as God's truth, no one questions the whys and the wherefores of it, no one stands up and says, "It ain't always 'liable, what you read in the Bible."

Smalls didn't come back to honor her slave grandmother; she came back to show off her rich husband and be a big shot. Just because you marry up don't mean you're above everybody else. In New York she was an ordinary businesswoman cheating her employees. Here she's a "philanthropist." But what is Coosawaw County? Nothing. Now, in *Manhattan,* I *was* somebody. I was a famous artist. People all over the city knew my name. They respected me. I didn't have to come home to reach my heights. I made it there, where it matters. That's what Sarah Smalls and all the people here beholden to her and her husband can't stand.

They all hated it when I fixed up a studio-workshop in the old Jerry's Flower Shop downtown. Why? Because it was the finest place Coosawaw County had ever seen. That studio had *style*—red walls, track lighting, ebony sculptures, black and white checkerboard floor, purple accents on the registration desk. Classy. I wasn't showing off. I wasn't throwing my "lifestyle" in their face. I was just trying to make it nice. I have *style*. But folks here have lived with so much nothing all their lives that when they see something *fine*—not expensive trash like what's in Smalls's mansions but something truly artistic—they piss all over it. Before I even opened, someone painted "FAG DEKOR" on the window. It took me hours to scrape the pink letters off.

Smalls and her husband wanted too much money to run my ad in the *Voice of the People*, so I got the word out myself and a fair number of students signed up. I wasn't getting rich on the fees I set, but I was living and I was teaching. The kids in my school learned authentic rhythms *and* ways to improvise. They caught on fast to my rhythms. They got so good I scheduled them to perform at a high school in Columbia and a Kwanza celebration in Charleston. We were going to do a Ghanaian marriage song, a Nigerian harvest song, a Cuban sugar cane song, and a couple of crowd-pleasing Caribbean numbers for the audience to dance to. They all had their costumes ready. But before we could give our first performance, Sarah Smalls shut me down. She started a rumor—it had to be her, who else could persuade everybody to her side so fast?—that I had been forced to give up my studio in the Village and come home with my tail between my legs because I had been caught performing abominations with one of my students. Once that got out, the *Voice of the People* started printing letters and editorials against me—*Are we going to let animals like him ruin our people? We have a tough enough job protecting our children from whites, God created human nature male and female and all abominations are accursed, Tell Mr. Gethers to go back to Sodom and die with the other diseased perverts there.* I'm thankful that my Uncle Esau wasn't alive to read all that. Most folks did and all my students dropped out except Shamgar and Jamal. Jamal told me the kids at school called him a "bio-sexual" because he associated with me. I had to close the studio down. I gave all the students their money back without question, even though I was hard put to pay out the rest of my lease: I'm a professional and a man of honor.

Running me out of business wasn't enough for Sarah Smalls. She turned the white community against me too—now you tell me, if she didn't do it, who did? Who else has that much power? She's jealous because I know so much more about African culture and I'm an artist who can lead people to the power of their past and I won't play her game. So tell me, who else could have done it?

After I closed my studio, I arranged to teach a night class at Sangaree, our branch university. Demand was so big, there was a waiting list for students. The first session went great, all middle-aged white women desperate for exoticism and excitement. The next day, someone sent the dean copies of recent issues of the *Voice of the People,* and without even checking into my history, without even asking me, he canceled my course. I explained to him that it was illegal to fire somebody on the basis of rumors and that I could file a discrimination suit.

"Our position in the community and the state system is most vulnerable," he told me. "We can't afford even to be *perceived* as approving of wrongdoing."

"Was it Sarah Smalls who sent you the papers?" I asked.

"I'm not at liberty to say," he said.

"But Sarah Smalls is on the board here, isn't she?"

"I don't see what that has to do with it. I'm sorry. I wish I could help, Mister Gethers, but there's nothing I can do."

There's no way I'm ever going to be able to work in Coosawaw County again. I could drive to Charleston or Savannah, but I don't want to spend my life on the road. If my Uncle Esau hadn't left me his place, I'd be on the street. Last month I sold my mink so I could pay the taxes. I came home to take care of my uncle, hoping to live a simple life, minding my own business, and stretch my retirement money. But my life and my ways don't fit into Sarah Smalls's master plan for Coosawaw County. She's the one and only queen who conquered New York and marched home to rule out of love for the people. What she says goes, for the good of the race. And if you don't play along, if you don't work for her or rent from her, buy her paper, beg her for money for ersatz African drum and dance programs, go along with her choices for the artists to bring in to perform, bow before her empire of blackness, or meet her criteria for being black—watch out, she'll bring you down. She wants people to think being gay is a crime against the black people. No one in Africa was ever gay? No slave was ever gay? No gay person ever spoke Gullah, went fishing in the Combahee River in a johnboat, sang "Wade in the Water" in church? One out of ten: The math works the same for black as for white. Sarah Smalls may have lived in New York for twenty-five years and she may pretend she's worldly-wise and cultured, but she's no New Yorker. She and her rich husband are no different from the rest of the small-minded people here who won't admit their sons and brothers and cousins and uncles are gay even when they come home with AIDS to die. "He's got a rare virus," they tell each other. They're not fooling anybody. Sarah Smalls isn't any better than anybody else here in the Lowcountry: They're all scared of me and my success in New York City. Not one of them thinks it's right for a man like me to make good. I'm supposed to be a failure, come crawling home on my knees begging for their mercy. I'm supposed to be punished by God for my "unnatural acts." I guess they figure if God's not going to punish me the way they think He ought to, they'll do it for Him. Who are they to tell God what's natural? Is it natural to hate your brother? Let them go ask Cain and Abel.

One time when I was living in New York, I took the bus down to Memphis to hear Mose Vinson play. Every night for a week, I went to the club where he was. That man beat a *mean* rhythm out of a piano. He had a left hand stronger than God's. Mose was a solo man, but one night he saw I was carrying my *djembe* with me and he called me up to play with him. We did a couple of standard barrelhouse tunes, and then we took off, doing overlays and free work and a call and response that set the room on fire. By the end of our set, there wasn't a still body in the room. Even the bartender and the waitresses had quit serving to dance. Afterward, Mose and I got talking. He grew up in Mississippi, on church music, same as me, so I asked him how he could play the blues like he did, like the Devil himself was steaming in his bones and his blood, making his hands twitch over the keys.

"Some folks do say I'm the Devil's instrument," he told me, "but God put the wisdom in me." Then he looked me in the eye and said, "If you pay attention, son . . . blues . . . all the words are like gospel songs. They got a word to it. You can take a blues song and turn it into a church song. It ain't nothin' but a word. You got a true word in a blues song, you got a true word in a gospel song. That's the way that runs."

I thought about that all the way home and I'm still thinking about it. I try to pay attention. It's my only way of praying now that they've badmouthed me out of Uncle Esau's church. I try to pay attention. And if you pay attention, you see what Mose saw. That *is* the way it runs, with people just the same as music. Some are born in Africa, some in the Lowcountry; some are raised in the North, some in the South; some are capitalists and some are artists; some come gay and others come straight. Ain't but one word, one nature. If you pay attention, you'll hear it. That's all I was teaching those kids in my classes. Drumming and that—nothing else. That's worth just as much as what Sarah Smalls and her husband give to the community, whether people thank me for it or not.

REDEEMING THE DEAD

If it is dark enough, Yetta Kurtz can rest. Long ago every window in her house was sealed against the light. Inside, the shades were pulled and the heavy curtains drawn. Walls of packing cartons and dismantled furniture were stacked against the windows, higher and higher, until they disappeared. Outside, camellias and azaleas were left untended, their wild growth darkening the windows inch by inch until after forty years the plants have hidden them completely from view. And if the southern sun should still seep in, as has been its way since time began, Yetta is safe in bed. This is her secret tactic—to stay awake all night and sleep until day ends. It requires discipline and cunning, but that is how she survives the assault of light. She dozes until she hears Solly's key in the door and his labored breathing, until her head aches from lying down, or until she grows sick from dreaming.

Most afternoons, she dreams she is standing waist deep in a swamp, unable to move, while cottonmouths skim by in the dark licking her arms with their bodies. Between clumps of cypress knees, the snout of an alligator emerges from the water. It glides toward her, molten eyes pulsing, jaws opening wide, then closes in fast.

One afternoon, before the jaws crush her, Yetta is awakened by a shriek. Blood pounding in her chest and ears, every nerve shaking, she reaches for her glasses. Another shriek startles her. Recognizing the doorbell, she tries to remember what she is supposed to do. Get up? Stay put?

The doorbell buzzes again.

She edges off her bed and creeps toward the front hall. If she's quiet, they won't know she's there and they'll go away, like the women from the temple who used to call on her after the baby died. They came once a month, dressed to perfection, their hair just so, to do their duty, visit the sick and walk out better themselves. She could smell how they needed her, how they soaked up her life to wring it out later, in their showy living rooms, at their cozy family dinners, at the Yom Kippur community break fast, where their children crawled under the tables, smearing cream cheese on the linoleum, scattering crumbs of challah, laughing and squealing with delight.

There is a knocking at the door.

Inches away, Yetta stiffens.

"Hello? Anybody home?"

The doorbell buzzes. To stop the jangling in her bones, she reaches for the doorknob. As the door cracks open, her hand flies up to shield her eyes.

"Good afternoon, Ma'am."

She squints into the sun. Two columns, black bottoms rising into white, lean toward her. It's boys, two of them, in black pants, white shirts, and skinny ties, both of them as scrawny as a dog after whelping. The air around them is thick and sweet with the smell of the gardenias she and Solly planted the summer they moved in. Dizzy, seized by nausea, she grips the doorknob so hard her knuckles hurt.

"I'm Elder Beffort," the tall boy says, "and this is Elder Whitmer. We'd like to tell you about the Plan of Salvation."

"You surprised me," she says. Her voice is low and grainy, like the voice of a spirit channeling itself across centuries into the throat of a medium.

"We're asking just a minute of your time, Ma'am," the short one says.

Their smiles are the smiles of the young.

Yetta opens the door wide enough for them to slip in.

Her eyes burning from the light, she shuffles into the living room. "This house is no good," she says. "My spirits dropped when I moved here."

"According to the Plan of Happiness," the tall boy says, following her, "we're all the Spirit offspring of the Heavenly Father."

"For a while I liked flowers," Yetta says. Faded plastic flowers in all colors jam the coffee table and side tables and knickknack stands, sticking out of mayonnaise jars, coffee cans, plastic beach pails. "I fixed them up. It kept me busy."

She sits on the sofa, next to a worn mat that says "KITTY!"

"Sit," she says, pointing to the chairs across from her. A stuffed toy dog is propped up in a child's rocker between the chairs. A brown fedora, once dapper, sits at an angle on the dog's head.

"I call him Mister Solly," Yetta says, nodding to the toy, "because he always wears a hat. My husband is afraid if he uncovers his head God will punish him."

"The Heavenly Father wants us to share His exaltation," the tall one says.

She unfastens the pink rubber curler in her bangs and places it beside a clump of dust-coated roses on the end table. Methodically she rubs down the bump of hair that springs from her forehead.

The tall one nudges the short one. "That's the message we want to share with you today, Ma'am," the short one says.

Yetta removes a cigarette from the pocket of her housecoat. She lights it and begins to smoke.

The short boy coughs. The other one gives him a look to quiet him.

She swings her cigarette toward the dining room, stacked high with sealed cardboard boxes and piles of newspapers, some bundled with twine, most of them loose. A small mattress and the slatted pieces of a crib frame stand on end between the sideboard and a wall of boxes.

"Solly and I were going to move to Florida to be by my sister, but Solly wouldn't leave his store. His father used to have a big store on Lucas Street, for hides and all kinds of dry goods. Solly wouldn't give it up." She takes a long drag on her cigarette and blows the smoke toward the dining room. "I don't remember what's in all those boxes. Nothing I need. I've got my cigarettes and my TV right here."

"We all have the power to achieve divinity in this life," the tall one says. "But we have to work for it."

"I worked. On Wall Street. Before I moved here. My girlfriends and I would race to catch the train, first to Manhattan, then home to Brooklyn. We used to go to a deli that served chopped liver sandwiches four inches thick! Imagine that. Four inches thick."

"It's our responsibility to better ourselves," the tall one continues, "by choosing good and not evil. Every one of us has to choose: Will you do good, or will you do evil?"

"Only those who die in infancy are free from the responsibility to do good," the short one chimes in. "They're the lucky ones. They're saved by the atonement of Jesus."

Yetta sucks the menthol smoke through her saliva to freshen it. "Solly's Jekyll and Hyde, but he brings me my food. Dinner from Dairyland or Angelo's. Breakfast from Shoney's. Used to be Hardee's, but they kicked him out. He took too many things—cream tubs, sugar packets, napkins, straws. Come and see," she says, rising.

"Maybe we should come back another time," the short boy says, getting up and shouldering his backpack, "when you're feeling better."

The tall one grabs the dangling strap of his partner's pack to keep him from inching to the door. "Yes, Ma'am," he says to Yetta.

The missionaries follow her through the tangle of boxes to the kitchen. The chairs, the table, the counters, and the stove burners are hidden under piles of napkins and folded paper bags, each scribbled with phone messages, grocery lists, reminders to change the litter box. A stockpile of cereals and bottled juices, jammed into makeshift shelving, obscures the window that opens onto the back porch.

"I shouldn't show you," she says, opening the refrigerator. "See?" Individual serving packets of ketchup, relish, lemon juice, taco sauce, tartar sauce, and soy sauce, all advertising restaurants, cram the interior and the shelves of the door. They spill around cottage cheese containers, yogurt cartons, fruit, pickle jars, packages of lunch meat, cans of apricot nectar and prune juice—everything packed tightly, so that nothing falls out. "I don't lack for anything. Solly does the shopping. I don't go out. I never know what to wear." With her free hand, Yetta pulls her housecoat away from her body, then releases it, letting the slack cloth fall against her gaunt frame.

"This mortal life is an opportunity to learn things we can only learn in a physical body," the tall one recites, "so we can reunite our physical and spiritual bodies."

"I have a cat," she says, closing the refrigerator. She steps from the kitchen to the back porch. "Here, Pepper!" she yells. Protecting her eyes against the light, she searches among musty cushions and heaps of stuffed animals.

"Pepper!" she calls out the closed door into the yard. After a few more tries, she gives up. "Pepper keeps me company. I used to raise schnauzers, but the city made me get rid of them. Do you boys want some cookies? Pepper likes vanilla wafers."

"No thank you, Ma'am."

"Let me show you Solly's den. Oh, I shouldn't. You'll think I'm awful."

"I'm sorry, Ma'am," the short one says, "but we can't stay any longer. We have to witness elsewhere."

"That's right," the tall one agrees. He holds up his *Book of Mormon,* the blue cover too bright in the crowded, dark kitchen. "'The Church of Jesus Christ of the Latter-Day Saints has three missions: to proclaim the gospel to those who have not yet heard it, to perfect the saints, and to redeem the dead.' We must get on with our work."

"Don't leave," Yetta says. "Not yet. I'll listen."

She leads them through a dim hallway, where the air is fragrant with mildew and where water stains blotch the ceiling.

She stops in the doorway to a small, paneled room, where a recliner faces a television. "A mess. Everything's a mess."

"It's very orderly," the tall boy says, peeking in. "Everything in its place."

"Do you think so?" Yetta asks. She stares at his face, wondering if he has already learned how to cover judgment with lies.

"Where'd all these alligators come from?" the short one asks, stepping past Yetta to examine the hide laid out on top of the widescreen Japanese TV, claws spread, teeth ready. A larger hide serves as a rug between the easy chair and the TV. Several smaller ones are tacked to the paneling, between yellowed cartoons ripped from newspapers.

"Solly bought them. At first he bought them. From whoever was selling them cheap. When hides got too expensive, he started raising alligators in the pond out back, under the live oak. He loves that tree. Says it's so old it's been here since creation."

"I seen alligators in the Combahee," the short one says, excited now. "When I was fishing with my daddy. I even seen one carry her baby in her mouth from the bank down to the water."

"Solly fed them scrap fish and dog food. They killed my best schnauzer. Drowned it and ate it. I begged him, Get rid of them before they kill something else. But to him they were money, hundreds for one hide. He didn't care. He left me alone with them, always flying to New York, selling, selling, selling, hides in the summer, furs in the winter. Always alone! That's no family!" She looks at the tall boy. "That's no family, is it?" Her voice is trembling, about to break.

The boy grips his *Book of Mormon* to his stomach. "In our church, the family is sacred," he says. "Parents are sacred because they give the earthly bodies to the spirit children of the Heavenly Father, and children are sacred—"

"It wasn't me!" she pleads loudly. "The doctor said it wasn't me! It wasn't my smoking or worrying that made her die. It was Sol—"

The tall elder backs away from her, pulling his partner by the back pocket. "Thank you for receiving us, Ma'am," he says. "But we have to go."

"Tell me more," Yetta says, following them into the living room. "Do you know more? What about saints? You didn't tell me about perfecting the saints. You didn't tell me about redeeming the dead."

"We have to go, Ma'am," the tall one says as the boys open the door and scramble down the steps toward their bicycles in the driveway.

She follows them outside. "Don't tell anyone about this place," she says, calm again.

"No, Ma'am, we surely won't."

"They'll blame *me.*"

She watches as they fasten their bicycle helmets under their chins. Before they have mounted their bikes, Solly turns into the driveway in his new red Isuzu truck. Why so early? she wonders. Now he'll ruin it: confuse her about what happened with the baby. He drives up to the boys and rolls down his window.

"What you doing here? We don't need you here."

"Nice tomatoes, sir," the tall one says, walking his bike to the street and nodding at the five-gallon buckets nurturing staked plants.

"Real nice," the short one says, close behind him.

"I like my farm," Solly says. "I like everything I do."

"Your farm stinks!" Yetta growls.

"Shut up, Yetta. You don't like nothin'."

Yetta walks toward the row of plants, her slippers flopping. She picks a ripe tomato.

"Hey!" Solly gets out of the truck and walks over to her. "Whatcha doing?"

"Giving those boys some tomatoes."

"What for? Hating you and your religion?"

"What are *you* going to do with them? Sell them to pay for your trip to Israel?"

"I asked you to go! You don't want to do nothin', Yetta. Stop!" Solly yells so hard he has to grip the tailgate to stabilize himself and wait for his breath to return.

The missionaries tear down the street, standing on their pedals.

Yetta picks a few more tomatoes and drops them into a pocket she has formed by raising the hem of her housecoat to her waist.

"Stupid woman. You don't know nothin'." Solly swats his hand toward her.

"Who went to college? *I* went to college and *I* know."

"You think I don't know?" he yells. "I know Talmud. That's what *my* family taught *me*. *Bikkur holim,* caring for the sick, will bear fruit in this life and in the life to come."

"I know why you won't take off your hat. You're scared, scared of being punished for keeping me in this hole." She raises her fingers toward his head. "Maybe I'll just take off your holy hat for you!" She reaches for the brim but has to lower her hand to reach it. Solly has shrunk without her noticing. Everything is shrinking.

"Damn you!" Solly slams his hat on tight. "Your fancy ways ain't so great. Look what they did for you and your sis—" A cough grips him and he grabs the truck to steady himself.

"I never should have moved to South Carolina. Nothing would have happened."

"The trouble with you, Yetta, is you don't think positive. New York, South Carolina, Florida, what does it matter?"

"Snakes! Ignorant people!"

"You could have adjusted. If you wanted. That's what the doctors said. You're not the only one ever lost a baby."

The cat runs over to Yetta and rubs itself against the back of her legs, purring softly.

"Hungry, Pepper?" Yetta asks, her voice pulled into a knot of sweetness. "I'll get you some milk."

"Damn cat. Get rid of it. If I catch it around me again, I'll skin it. You know what the Cossacks did with cats, Yetta? They sewed them up inside the bellies of pregnant Jews. Cut the baby out and sewed a cat up inside."

"Pepper helps me."

"No one can help you, Yetta. I should know."

Yetta lets go of her hem and the tomatoes thump on the ground, scattering around her feet.

For weeks after the missionaries' visit, summer hangs on. The air is thick in the night; during the day the sun is merciless. The live oak sheltering the pond out back barely stirs. Its branches spread wide, opening to receive word of a breeze; they sprawl across the moist ground seeking the coolness of the water bound in the black dirt. From the fissured bark spill resurrection ferns, each green bouquet preternaturally inert. The leaves, thousands of green slippers that in a breath of wind would shuffle and thwut-thwut against each other in a potent lullaby, hang still. Even the mockingbirds and wrens taking refuge in the canopy above have been silenced by the heat. The only thing moving is the light; it travels from the heavens through the thick growth of the branches to the duckweed on the pond, creating a pattern of soft green against the shadow.

Inside, the cat, grown heavy and sluggish, sleeps all day and most of the night, occasionally stirring to roam the house, traveling slowly along the back of the sofa and the walls of boxes in an endless circuit.

Solly has grown lethargic, too. Every day he comes home from his store a little earlier. And when he walks in—he has started to shuffle—he doesn't speak. He drops the food on the kitchen table, grabs the edge of the table to steady himself until he stops coughing, then scuffs to his den, where he sits, barely moving, in the flickering grayness until he pulls himself to his bedroom. He has abandoned his farm. The plants have withered, the tomatoes on the vine bursting their skins in the steam heat, the others rotting where they have fallen.

In the morning, instead of stopping for breakfast, he buys coffee at McDonald's drive-through window on his way downtown. Then he locks himself in his store, leaving the CLOSED sign hanging in the door. This is the way he has worked for years, and everyone has respected it; shoppers, the other Jewish merchants downtown, the men who hang around the Red Dot liquor store across the alley— they've all left him in peace. But now when he's at his store, he takes greater care: He doesn't turn on the lights or roll up the bamboo shades protecting the display windows and the door. Sunlight slants through the bamboo and the gaps between the shades and the windows, but all the light he needs comes from the ten-inch TV mounted behind the counter. Solly stands in front of its gray light for hours, leaning on the counter, sipping the cold coffee, smoking, and watching the stock market reports silently scroll up the screen.

One morning in early September, a rap on the door rouses him from his dozing. A black man is pressing his face against the glass in the gap between the shade and a display window. He raps on the glass again. Solly waves him away, returns to the stock prices scrolling up his TV screen.

"Open up," the man says. "I need to buy somethin'."

"Closed," Solly says without turning from his TV.

The man turns the handle of the door again. He rattles it.

Solly walks to the door and pulls aside the shade. "What you want?" he asks through the glass.

"I want to buy that knife," the man says, nodding toward a display window.

Solly opens the door and the man stumbles in. He smells of whiskey and orange peels.

"Which one?" Solly asks.

The man points to the right-hand display window, near the door. The bare wood platform is heaped with things—a set of mugs on a wooden tree, yo-yos, hammers, dish towels, baby dolls from China in crinkled plastic wrappers. Several packaged jack-knives hang from nails in the door molding along the side of the display. Below them, a used skinning knife lies crowded between a used pair of cowboy boots and a whisk broom.

"That long one," the man says, pointing to the unwrapped knife.

Solly picks up the knife. Grime has collected in the depressions of the handle. The blade is scratched and discolored, but the edge is clean and true.

"How much you want for it?" the man asks.

He reaches in his pocket, pulls out a fist, and opens his palm to show Solly a few crumpled dollars and coins. A penny drops to the floor.

Solly stoops to pick it up and hands it back to him.

"Take it," Solly says, handing him the knife and waving him out of the store.

The man stuffs his money back in his pocket, rolls up his pant leg and slides the knife into his boot.

"I heard you was a rich man," he says, rising.

"Be careful what you hear."

"I heard you was like that rich man who let the dogs lick Lazarus's sores. When the rich man got to heaven he called out, 'Father Abraham, have mercy on my soul, and send Lazarus to dip the end of his finger in water and cool my tongue, for I am anguishin' in these flames.' That's Luke sixteen. I know all the stories from the Bible. That's my business. I'm a preacher."

"Your Bible don't have nothin' to do with mine."

"God is God."

"Maybe so," Solly says. "But people ain't always people."

The man cocks his head at Solly and is silent for a moment. "You're right there. I'll be goin' now. I thank you for the knife."

That afternoon, Solly comes home so early he surprises Yetta in the kitchen, searching for her breakfast. Breathing hard, he drags himself into his den and drops into his chair. The TV blares on, scraping the inside of Yetta's skull. If she doesn't eat soon, her head will burst. She checks the counters and table again for a Styrofoam box of pancakes and syrup. She opens the refrigerator hoping for yogurt or an orange, but there is only a quart of tomato juice with a tinny smell. Solly hasn't bought groceries in a week. She finds a small package of saltines on the windowsill and takes it to her bedroom. In bed, she nibbles the crackers slowly, careful to catch the crumbs and lick them off her palm.

Through the night, Yetta spies on Solly, sleeping in his chair. He breathes loudly. The gray light of the TV screen flickers over his sunken face.

Toward dawn, Yetta stands in the doorway of his den, pinching the loose skin above her eyebrow. Solly is sleeping with his head thrown back, his hat askew. His chest heaves erratically. The TV blips and fuzzes. Everything's off the air. What will happen to her? She needs someone to bring milk from the store, take her to the doctor to see about the shimmering in her eyes.

She wanders to the front door, wondering if Solly has left the food for her in his truck. If it is not too light yet, she will go and look. On the porch, atop an overturned bucket, she finds a small package wrapped in blue and white tissue. Clumps of long, red pine needles have all but buried it, and the ink of the greeting, "Happy Rosh Hashanah! From Temple Israel," has run. She hurries inside and unwraps the honeycake at the kitchen table. When she opens the foil, a dark fragrance of orange oil and spice greets her.

The cat leaps onto the table mewing loudly. She tries to catch it, but it jumps to the door of the den.

"Here, Pepper," she whispers, stooping to pick up the cat. "Mister Solly doesn't want you."

The cat screeches and scrapes its claws down her shin until she lets it go. It runs off, leaving her bent in the doorway, whimpering.

"What the hell," Solly mumbles from his chair.

Trembling, Yetta rubs her three middle fingers in the slippery blood on her shin.

"Can't you do . . . anything . . . right?" Solly rasps. "Look at you. Can't take you . . . to doctor . . . now. Ah, doctors too rough on you any—" Coughing wracks his body, the vinyl of the recliner squeaking every time his back hits it.

Yetta stands up, stiffens. "You frightened Pepper," she says. Walking to the back porch, she finds the cat nestled between the wall and a mattress stained with mildew.

"Pepper." She reaches in, but the cat hisses at her and she withdraws her hand. She bends in to try again. "I'm not going to hurt you."

In the early morning light, she sees Pepper licking something. She squints at the glistening lump. Kittens. Adjusting her glasses, she counts four, five of them.

"What day is it?" Solly asks. He is standing in the doorway between his den and the kitchen, both hands gripping the frame, his head naked. The dome of his skull shines, as if rubbed with a polishing cloth.

"Wednesday. No. It's almost morning, so it's Thursday."

"Yom Kippur's almost over then." He works at his breath a few minutes.

"You want a cigarette?" she asks.

He waves the offer away and, steadying himself against the refrigerator, shifts toward the table, landing in a chair.

Yetta removes a stack of calendars from the other chair and sits too, her thumb and finger pinching her cheek, working the skin against itself.

"Break . . . my fast . . . with that," Solly says, nodding to the honeycake between them.

Yetta peels back the foil from the honeycake. The top is darkly furrowed, the sides smooth and golden.

Solly sags in his chair, rests his elbow on a pile of paper towels.

He smells. Like urine. Like the baby. Like death. Yetta pinches her cheek harder.

Solly reaches for the honeycake, but his hand drops to the table.

Yetta's fingers keep pinching her flesh. Tomorrow, a red bruise the size of an egg will mark the place she has worried.

Solly grasps the cake and breaks off a piece, then pushes the loaf toward Yetta.

She pinches off a bite and raises it to her mouth.

He covers his head with his left hand and squints at her. "A good, sweet year, Yetta," he says, then closes his dry lips around the moist sweetness.

Yetta stares at her piece, her stomach active and alert. "A good, sweet year, Solly." She puts it in her mouth. The strong coffee-and-spice flavor is almost bitter.

"Yom Kippur, Day of Atonement," Solly says, taking a breath between each word. "The Talmud says: 'Atone for sins . . . against people first . . . then go to God.'" He breathes. "Yetta, the baby . . . wasn't nobody's fault. Not mine . . . not yours."

Yetta rocks back and forth.

Solly rests his forehead on the heels of his hands. After at time, he lifts his head to her.

"Maybe I should have let you . . . move to Florida after it died."

Yetta stands up. "There's something new. A surprise. I'll show you."

She breaks off a small piece of honeycake and walks to the back porch. "Pepper, a little treat for you." She places the cake on the threshold. As soon as the cat leaves its nest to eat, she removes one of the kittens. She cups it in her palm and pets it with one finger, barely touching its moist fur.

"Look," she says, carrying it to the table.

Solly has slumped down, his head resting on his forearm, his eyes closed.

She presses a fingertip into his forearm, against the bone.

He opens his eyes, pulls hard for air. His lungs wheeze and rattle.

Yetta starts to shake.

"Call . . . nine-one-one."

She glances at the phone, then at him.

"Call."

Careful to hold the kitten securely, she dials.

"He can't breathe," she says. "My hands won't stop shaking. Come right away, right away. Solly and I got out of order. Twenty-one Fairview."

When she hangs up, Solly's head has slipped off his arm onto the table. His glasses are askew. She touches his arm, calls his name.

"They'll blame me, Solly. They'll send me away. They'll say that I was never a good housekeeper. I know. I've got that much of a piece of brain left. Oh, something's wrong, something's terribly wrong."

She lets go of Solly and brings her right hand under her left to cradle the kitten at her chest. Her head drops to it and she stands there, rocking back and forth.

"Sarah," she says. "Sarah."

She closes her eyes and rocks the kitten harder, her mouth and cheek pressed against its wet body.

"Nineteen hundred and fifty-three! What's that? I can't remember, I can't remember!"

The kitten squirms in her hands, its eyes barely open, its mouth searching for milk. She carries it to the back porch, looking for its mother. As she approaches, Pepper runs out the door. Yetta follows, pushing the aluminum door open with her hip. Standing on the top step, propping the door open with her body and squinting against the sun, she calls, "Pepper! Pepper! Come feed your baby." But Pepper has disappeared. All Yetta can see is the pond and the tree embracing it. The leaves are shuddering against one another, humming a song she can almost remember. Several fall, twirling down until they glide onto the soft duckweed. The breeze stirs around her, cooling her forehead and tickling the hair on her arms. She bends down to the kitten in her hands and kisses its hungry mouth. "Don't worry," she whispers. "I won't let you die."

TONGUES OF ANGELS

"You can't draw a yin-yang," Jacquelyn said to Michal, who was drawing in her notebook while the rest of the class finished their addition and subtraction sheets.

Jacquelyn's desk was smack up against Michal's, facing the same direction. She didn't have to lean a hairbreadth to see what her neighbor was doing. She could scoot her eyes over without anyone being the wiser.

"I'm an artist," Michal said without interrupting her work. "I can do anything."

"Yin-yang is wrong."

"No, I did it right. I put a white dot in the black and a black dot in the white. My karate teacher showed me."

"It's wrong. People are all good or all bad. You can't mix them up."

"It's just a picture," Michal said.

Jacquelyn looked across the room to where Mrs. Benton was correcting papers, her breakfast Diet Coke in her hand. Every day, while Mrs. Thiboudeau, their regular teacher, went across the hall to teach reading and social studies, Mrs. Benton came to their room to drill them in math and science. Mrs. Thiboudeau's class liked to catch Mrs. Benton cupping her hands under her breasts and adjusting them in her bra when she thought no one was looking. Michal could imitate her perfectly and packs of kids congregated around her at recess, begging her to show them.

"You have a funny name," Jacquelyn said to Michal. "Nobody can say it."

"Mrs. Thiboudeau can."

"Mrs. Benton can't."

"I like it," Michal said.

She finished filling in the black of the yang and began sketching a peace sign with colored markers.

Jacquelyn watched while she carefully surrounded the image with a rainbow circle. "You can't draw a peace sign, either," she said.

Antoine stopped erasing and studied Michal's drawing. His desk and Ferrabee's butted up against Michal's and Jacquelyn's, facing them. Mrs. Benton had grouped Antoine with the three girls so that they could tutor him and help keep him out of trouble.

"You ain't her mama, girl," he said to Jacquelyn. "You can't tell her what to draw."

Jacquelyn folded her arms over her chest and snorted. "It's the *Devil's* sign," she said. "You want her to call the Devil in here to slap us silly? Yank our tongues out with a pliers? Grab our hair and twist it burning tight against our heads and drag us across the room by it 'til we scream our eyes out of our head and say we're sorry?"

Propping himself on both forearms, Antoine leaned across the huddled desks and stuck his face in Jacquelyn's, so close his long, black lashes almost brushed her cheeks. "It's nothing but an old *peace* sign," he said, "same as you see on stuff at Wal-Mart." He gave her book bag a kick under the desks and sat back in his seat before Mrs. Benton could catch him.

"How do you know?" Jacquelyn sneered. "You can't even read."

"Can too."

Jacquelyn pointed to Michal's peace sign. "See those two lines at the bottom? They're pointing down. See? They're pointing straight to the Devil. I *told* you."

"What about this big one growing out of them?" Michal asked, pointing with her red marker. "It's pointing *up, to God.*"

"How do you know?" Jacquelyn asked. "You're *Chanukah* people."

"My mama knows Chanukah," Antoine said. "She's from New York. She likes latkes."

"Me too," Michal said, outlining the rainbow in black.

"You don't eat our food," Jacquelyn said to Michal, "and you don't believe in Jesus."

"Jesus is my brother," Michal said, shrugging her shoulders as if she were letting her know her family drove a Ford instead of a Chevy.

"You're not even Jewish," Jacquelyn said.

"I am *too* Jewish," Michal said. "Look at my earrings!" She pulled her hair back to expose the brass Stars of David suspended from tiny blue beads.

"No you're not," Jacquelyn said. "My father says *we're* the real Jews. We're the *true* Israel. You had your chance, and now it's our turn. You killed Jesus, so you have to pay. But we're going to be saved, because we love Jesus. And we're going to save all the unborn babies for Jesus, too, even if we have to hurt people to do it."

"Your dad doesn't know anything," Michal said.

"He's a certified public accountant, he knows *everything*. And he's famous, too. He's been on the news for witnessing at the murder clinic. Mrs. Benton's seen him. She goes to our church, and she told me she saw him on TV."

"That don't make him good," Antoine said.

"He's better than *her* father," Jacquelyn said.

"My dad's a doctor," Michal said.

"No decent people go to your father, because he sees abominations in his office. He shouldn't be helping them. He should leave
those sick AIDS people to God's punishment, like the other doctors
here do."

"Do you know Hebrew?" Michal asked. *"I* know Hebrew."

"I'll prove you're not a real Jew," Jacquelyn said. She pulled a
sheaf of scrolled papers out of her desk and untied the white satin
ribbon.

"What's that?" Antoine asked. He, Ferrabee, and Michal
watched as she unrolled the papers.

"The Ten Commandments. My father typed them on the computer. See the fancy lettering? It's just like in the Bible. I'm supposed to wait until recess and take them outside and give everybody
a copy to study and then test them. But I'm going to give *her* the test
now."

"I'll read them to you," she said to Michal, "and you say them
back to me, if you can. 'I am the Lord thy God which brought thee
out of—"

"She don't have to take no test from you," Antoine said.

"Do you want to go to H-E-double-hockey-stick?" Jacquelyn
asked Michal.

"No."

"Then you have to take the test."

"I won't."

"I'll tell Mrs. Benton your earrings are too long, and she'll send
you to the office."

"They are *not* too long," Antoine said. "Ask Miz Singleton."
Miss Singleton, the guidance counselor, wore African earrings that
brushed her shoulders—painted bone, fancy beadwork, etched
brass hoops.

"Kids aren't allowed to wear danglies to school, stupid," Jacquelyn said. "They're not safe. Somebody might rip one out of

your ear at recess. Come right up to you and yank it out and there'd be blood all over and a long, bumpy scar where the two parts of your ear grew back together and you'd never be able to wear earrings again."

"She wears those earrings every day," Antoine said, "and ain't nothin' ever happened."

"I wish I had pierced ears like Michal," Ferrabee said softly.

"God won't stand for girls piercing their ears," Jacquelyn said. "He wants His girls pure. Girls aren't allowed to cut their hair short, either." She grabbed the hair that fell to her waist, flicked it over her head, and let it cascade down. "And boys," she said, inspecting Antoine's fuzzy head, "have to keep their hair *real* short."

"Why?" Antoine asked, sorry that his mama had just cut his hair.

"Because God made men and women different. That's why I always wear a dress."

"God don't care about dresses," Antoine said.

"He cares about *everything*," Jacquelyn said, "even when you lose one of those long eyelashes of yours."

"God's wack then," Antoine said.

Jacquelyn smiled. "See?" she said. "The Devil already took over your mouth. I told you she'd call Him in here with that drawing of hers. Better watch out."

"That's a lie!" Antoine said.

Jacquelyn turned to Michal. "If you don't take this test," she said, "I'll tell the teacher you and Antoine cursed God and kicked me under the desk and Antoine will have to go shiver in the principal's igloo office all day again holding his pee until he turns yellow and he won't pass second grade again and you'll get detention and your father will be really mad at you and whip you and tie you to a tree in the backyard in your underwear so the mosquitoes can eat you all night."

"My dad wouldn't ever do that to me!"

"Then he's bad. All fathers have to chastise their children when they stray. It's their job. They have to teach us what's right, too. That's why my father's making us learn the Ten Commandments."

"You stole the Ten Commandments from us," Michal said.

"They belong to me. I'm Jewish and you're not."

Antoine widened his eyes at Jacquelyn and shook his head. "You crazy, girl."

Jacquelyn rolled up the tests, tied them with the ribbon, and zipped them in her backpack. She reached in her desk and took out the WWJD pencil case her father had given her. She stood up, set the case on the floor, raised her right foot, and stomped on it. The brittle plastic gave way at once. It separated into pointed shards that clung together, exposing the pencils and erasers inside. She picked up the case, sat down at her desk, and scratched her fingernails down her arm. Streaks of blood appeared, starting at the elbow and slowly creeping to the wrist, like fire descending from heaven to light the altar of the prophet of the true God. The red shone against her blue-white skin. Clutching her pencil case to her heart, she started to cry, quietly at first, then louder, until she was sobbing.

"What's going on over there?" Mrs. Benton asked, getting up from her desk. "What happened?" She walked over and stood by Jacquelyn's desk. "Jacquelyn? Are you all right?"

Jacquelyn raised her wet face to her and shook her head yes, her lower lip quivering.

"Why are you crying? What's wrong?"

"Nothing," Jacquelyn said. She hung her head and clutched the pencil case closer to her chest.

Mrs. Benton knelt by Jacquelyn. "It's OK, Jacquelyn. You can tell me."

Jacquelyn glanced at the others, as if afraid, then met Mrs. Benton's eyes. "I was doing my worksheet like you told us, and Antoine took my pencil case and stepped on it. I didn't do anything to him. He just reached over and took it and broke it. And then he gave it to me and said, 'You dropped your pencil case, you' . . . I can't tell you the name he called me. My father told me never to say that word.'"

She held out the smashed case to the teacher.

Mrs. Benton snatched the pencil case from her. "That's no recess and a week of after-school detention for you, Antoine," she said, pointing the case at him. "I warned you. Put your head down on your desk until I tell you to pick it up. I'm going to the office to call your mother at work and have her pick you up in the principal's office. She won't be happy about that, will she?"

Mrs. Benton put her hand on Jacquelyn's shoulder. "You don't have to keep quiet, Jacquelyn. If someone hurts you, you should tell me. That's not tattling. That's justice."

"I raised my hand to tell you, Mrs. Benton, but Michal pulled my arm down and scratched me."

She twisted in her seat to show the teacher the red stripes on her pale arm.

Mrs. Benton looked at Michal, who was biting her lip, trying to decide whether to argue with the teacher and be punished for it or remain silent.

"I found this note she wrote, too." Jacquelyn pulled a carefully folded packet from her pocket and handed it to the teacher.

Mrs. Benton unfolded the lined paper and read, DEAR FERRABEE, JACQUELYNS DAD IS MEAN MEAN MEAN. HE'S A SON OF A BITCH AND I HOPE HE ROTS IN HELL. MICHAL. When she saw the drawing below the signature, a pentagram with a smiley-faced horned devil in the center, she quickly folded the paper and clenched it in her hand. Her heart beat fast and her breathing leapt to its pace. She opened the note again, checked the signature to make sure, and then carefully folded the paper over itself five times and put it in her pocket, to hide the desecration from the others in the room.

"Michal Reuben," she said after a few moments, her voice trembling with fear. She paused to gain control of herself. "I don't know what they teach you at home—I'm not familiar with your people's customs—but we don't talk like that here, you understand? We don't say bad things about people's parents and we certainly don't use that kind of language, *ever*. It's not Christian."

"Excuse me? Mrs. Benton?" Ferrabee said, squeezing her left hand hard so she would keep talking. "Michal didn't—"

"It's not polite to interrupt, Ferrabee," the teacher said.

"But it was Jacquelyn's daddy who was writing notes," Antoine said. "He gave her tests to give us. Look." He reached for Jacquelyn's book bag under her desk, but Jacquelyn kicked it away from him.

"Do you have something from your father in there, Jacquelyn?" the teacher asked.

"It's the Ten Commandments, Mrs. Benton," Jacquelyn said, smiling. "Everybody should know them."

"That's true, but you'd better let me see."

Jacquelyn lifted her bag on top of her desk and opened it for the teacher.

Mrs. Benton pulled out one of the scrolls, untied the ribbon, and read.

"Her daddy wrote them," Antoine said. "She was gonna pass them out at recess and give us all a test. She can't do that at school, can she?"

"Quiet, Antoine," the teacher said, rolling the scroll up. "Jacquelyn, will you please hand me the rest of those?"

Jacquelyn dug them out of her bag one by one and handed them to Mrs. Benton, who kept the bundle secure in two hands.

When the last scroll had been handed over, Mrs. Benton said to Jacquelyn, "I'm going to keep these safe for you. Come to my room right after school, and I'll give them back to you. Don't worry about your father. I'll call him at lunch and tell him you weren't disobedient, that you did your best, but we have certain limitations in public school, even for children, even at recess. We might not like it, but that's the way it is right now. He'll understand. Don't you worry." The teacher smiled at Jacquelyn and, straightening up, turned to Michal. "Michal, I'm going to show your note to Mrs. Thiboudeau first chance I get. I'm sure she'll want to talk to your parents about it. Now," she said, raising her voice and waving the bundle of scrolls toward the foursome, "get back to work, all of you. You've caused enough fuss for one day. This isn't a playground; it's a *school*."

WHAT ADDIE
WANTS

I did you proud, Addie. You and the boys. Kenneth's mighty proud. Grayson and Wiltz don't know for sure it was me who did it, but they're proud, too. I showed 'em I could do somethin'.

The sheriff won't catch me. He's lookin' at Lonnie Ackerman and them other big mouths always talkin' about nigger churches and the spawn of the Devil. Went down to Horace Turner's and Billy Bishop's yesterday, askin' where they was Tuesday night and could he check their garages and their trucks. I heard it at the Dixie Kitchen this mornin', standin' in line for my biscuits while they was havin' their coffee. They was all thinkin' Lonnie done it, and they was mad he didn't ask 'em along. Lonnie just grinned, let 'em think it was him had the guts to do it.

Not a one of them's goin' to come lookin' for me. Didn't I always tell you it was a good thing to keep to yourself and keep your mouth shut? And they won't find me out sideways, neither, because I did it real quick, without help from nobody. You didn't think I was that clever, did you? That I could do somethin' without you.

I knew that snake Reuben was no good from the beginnin'. I told you not to go to him. What's a Jew doin' down here, anyway? You ever think of that? Runnin' from somethin'.

I don't care what Doc Craven said about Reuben bein' so smart. Doc Craven just wanted to get rid of you because you took up too much of his time with all your troubles and because you was on Medicaid. Now he moved to them fancy offices, he don't take no Medicaid patients, not even the white ones. That ain't right. You been seein' Doc Craven all these years. He had no business handin' you over to somebody who don't even belong here. What's *he* know about people like us?

You didn't like goin' to see that Reuben much, remember? That old woman in the waitin' room, unwrappin' a towel under your nose 'til you almost fainted, showin' you the big old mud cat she caught for the good doctor's supper? And ridin' the van to his office with those people every month? You didn't say nothin', but I knew it hurt your pride. What they got to pity *you* for?

You didn't like the way that Reuben started in on you right away, neither. Don't you recall? Why didn't you eat right and take exercise? Why'd you let your sugar get the best of you the last twenty years? If you'd of watched out for yourself, you might not of lost the feelin' in your legs. What are you tryin' to do, kill yourself? Remember how he talked to you?

You told him it was Doc Craven put you in the wheelchair, but he wouldn't listen.

"You're only forty-nine," he said. "You have a lot of livin' ahead of you. You have to start takin' care of yourself, so you'll be around for your grandchildren."

That was no way to treat you. He should've shut his mouth and give you the pills you asked for, like Doc Craven always done. That's his job—to get you better, not tell you what to do. He's not God. I don't care how many people call him a miracle worker and praise him because he treats 'em so kindly and gives 'em free medicines. He don't know what God wants you to do. Maybe God wants you in a wheelchair, to keep you close by, for some kind of blessin' to somebody. That Reuben don't know. It could've been *God* took the strength out of your legs, didn't have nothin' to do with your sugar. Made you numb so you wouldn't feel no pain and you'd be happy some way. You never said you was in pain. That's somethin' in life.

Grayson told him that when he called the house last month, askin' why wasn't anyone takin' care of you. Grayson told him you never complained.

"Your mother has bed sores," Reuben told him.

Grayson said he hadn't seen 'em.

"There's no excuse for bed sores," the man said.

Who's he to tell us about excuses and how to do for you? Bet he got a nigger maid and a cook over to his house. People like us can't afford excuses like his. We have to do what we can do by ourselves and let the rest go.

Grayson told the man he didn't know nothing about bed sores.

"Don't you move your mother periodically?" Reuben asked him.

Now, Addie, you know how hard it was to move you, on account of your weight, and that's what Grayson had to tell Reuben. He meant no disrespect to you. He had to tell what was.

"If you don't start doing something for your mother," that doctor said, "it's going to get worse. She needs to be taken out of her wheelchair regularly. And someone has to get up every few hours at night to turn her in bed."

Grayson didn't tell him you slept in your wheelchair. It was the only place you could rest, you said, because when you were in that chair, nobody would get after you to do for 'em. My vacation home, you called it.

Well, after that insulting phone call, we tried, Addie, you know we did. I brought you those Krispy Kremes you like so much, remember? I even called Crissy to see could she come look in on you. But the next thing we knowed, you was in the hospital. The mornin' you took the van in for your regular appointment, that Reuben calls me and Grayson in for a "family conference."

"It's urgent," he said. "Your wife is in intensive care."

"She's been there before and didn't nobody tell me to come in."

"Your wife is dying, Mister Abel. We need to decide what to do."

"*God*'ll decide what to do. Your job's to keep her alive."

I didn't have time to change my T-shirt or shave, Addie. If you'd of been there to help me, I would've looked better. I just went over like I was. Grayson came and got me. Crissy drove over too.

Reuben was waitin' for us at the hospital, in a meetin' room with all his buddies, nurses and social workers and I don't know who all. Tried to shake my hand, but you don't shake hands with the Devil. Grayson shook it and he's sorry now.

"Mister Abel," Reuben said, "your wife is dying. She came to my office this morning complaining of a fever—"

"She never told me she didn't feel good."

"We found a seven-inch-wide sore across her buttocks and—"

"My wife never wanted me to undress her for bed. She's a private woman."

"It was an infected bedsore. When we uncovered it, Mister Abel, the stench was horrible. The sore had been neglected so long it had reached her bone and the infection spread to her bones. From there it traveled to her lungs in little bursts, like a pulmonary embolism, only lots of them. When we X-rayed her lungs, they were shot through with pneumonia, cannonballs of infection everywhere."

"Mama's had pneumonia before," Grayson said. "The penicillin always knocks it out of her."

"I'm not sure antibiotics can help this time. The infection's too far gone. You have to understand: This is like cancer, and it has already spread."

"But it's not cancer, right?" Grayson asked.

"I'm afraid the outcome is inevitable."

"We'll carry her to Charleston," I said, "where they got real doctors."

"Can we do that?" Grayson asked.

"Even if you get her to the best infectious-disease specialists and she gets on the right antibiotic, it would still take a miracle for her to survive this."

"I don't know, Daddy," Crissy said. "Maybe we should keep her here, not put her through any more. You know Mama always wants to just leave things be."

"Addie's not goin' to die. He's just tryin' to scare us so we'll do what he wants."

"Mister Abel, I give your wife a one percent chance of surviving, under the best of circumstances. And even if she does survive, the quality of her life isn't going to change. You have to think about that."

"We done the best by her we could."

"Nobody bothered to take her to my office this morning."

"Like to see you do better with a woman stubborn as she is."

"We'll carry Mama to Charleston, Daddy," Crissy said. "She'll do it for me."

"I don't think Addie would want that, Miz Abel."

"What do you know about what my wife wants? You think she wants to just give up and die? Leave us all alone like that?"

"I think at this point, I know her better than you do. This is her preference."

"You got papers she signed? You got to have papers. I know that."

"Let me be straight with you, Mister Abel. We don't think anyone should be beating on her chest, giving her cardioversions, or hooking her up to a ventilator."

"We're not goin' to do what you say just because we don't know any better, because you got a lot of big shots sittin' here noddin' their heads at you."

"Mister Abel, prolonging your wife's life would be going against her wishes. The quality of Addie's life has been terrible. Nobody's taken care of her up to now, and she doesn't expect anybody to start. Let your wife die with dignity, Mister Abel."

"You don't know what's supposed to happen to us. You don't know *nothin'* about us."

"Mister Abel, I know you've depended on your wife for a great deal and that it's going to be hard for you to do without her, but you have to accept this. The situation is hopeless. Nothing is going to make any difference; it would just be wasted effort."

"Doc Craven wouldn't let this happen."

"Be honest, Mister Abel. You and your family don't intend to do anything for Addie yourselves. You want someone else to take care of her."

"We're her *family*," Grayson said, "and if we say she goes to Charleston, she goes."

"I'll agree to send her to Charleston, but only if you get a doctor there to take her. If you can find another doctor, I'll sign the release. But I'm telling you, there's nothing they can do there differently than I've done here."

"You ain't done nothin' here but lie," I said.

"How do we get a doctor in Charleston, Doctor Reuben?"

"Don't ask him nothin', Grayson. He don't want to help. He's sick of Addie and her troubles. She's not a moneymaker for him anymore. If we were niggers, he'd feel sorry for us and keep her on so he could show everybody what a big heart he has, a regular Bobby Kennedy."

Grayson and me went home and had supper. Wiltz came by. Crissy and Kenneth, too. They brought some beer and we talked it over. Crissy said maybe you were tired of livin' and give up, but Kenneth set her straight. All Mama ever wanted was to be with us, he told her.

Grayson couldn't find no doctors in Charleston to call, and by the time we got back to see you the next day, you were gone. We done what we could, Addie.

It's no secret where that Reuben lives. He's in the phone book. I called a few times in the night and hung up, like a guilty conscience wakin' him up. But then I got to thinkin'. He took you away from me, Addie. It was wrong, plain wrong. Things like that don't happen to people like us. God don't let it. And I went out back, to that pile where you used to get after me to clean it all up, and I took out some of those fence posts and hammered 'em into a cross. Kenneth and I wrapped it in those flowery sheets you always liked and slid it in his buddy's truck, along with a can of gas. Drove up Reuben's street without the lights on and parked in the woods down a ways. Everybody was asleep. The whole neighborhood. Sleepin' sound. Ain't nobody come and take their wives away from *them* people, leavin' 'em without a helpmeet. Quiet as the End of Days. Just an owl singin', Who, who, who cooks for you? That cross was so heavy, Kenneth had to carry it on his back to get it all the way to Reuben's yard. The ground was real soft after the rain, and it went in easy, like it wanted to be there. I lit it. You should have seen it blaze, Addie. Tall and bright, like that pillar of fire you was always talkin' about, the one that led the Israelites in the wilderness, so they wouldn't feel so alone in the dark.

M TO F

People can all treat you like you're Jezebel, but that doesn't make you Jezebel if you're the Virgin Mary, does it? Look at you. You don't look old enough to be a social worker. You look about fourteen. I bet cops pull you over all the time to check your license because they're sure you're a kid taking her daddy's car for a joyride. I'm right, aren't I? See?

Well, no matter what anybody else thinks—I don't care if it's a shrink or God or the pope himself—I'm Samantha. I was born Samantha. So what if it says Sam on my birth certificate? Lots of parents name girls after male relatives, especially when they don't get the boy they were hoping for. Jo for Joe, Alana for Alan, Georgina for George, Maconette for Macon. Your parents named you Roeburn, for God's sake. Does that make you a man? I bet your parents still wish you were a boy. I bet they're mad that you turned out a girl. Think about it. You know what I heard yesterday when I was touring the halls in my chair? I heard some guy yelling at his wife for having another girl baby. He was screaming at her, "Where's my *son*? When you goin' to give me a *son*?" That's how people are. Not just here in the South. Up North, too. Especially in Chester, Ohio, where I'm from.

Did Doctor Reuben tell you I was gang-raped up in Chester? It's true. Five boys picked me up and drove me across the New York line and used me all night, then dumped me in the woods. That's how I got here to Coosawaw County. After the trial, the FBI had to relocate me and give me a new identity, to protect me. You should have seen that trial. The FBI brought in experts to say I had post-traumatic stress disorder and irreversible physical and mental damage. But I was the prime witness, and I did a damn fine job on the stand. Oscar material. Everybody said so. And it worked. Every one of those boys is doing time. I hope they're all getting theirs in prison. I'm sorry if that shocks you and your oh-so-feminine sensibility, Roeburn, but there has to be some justice, doesn't there? Trouble is, there are too many people in the world like those boys that came after me that night yelling, "You want to be a girl? We'll show you what it means to be a girl." Gridheads, I call them: people with no imagination, who want to carve up the world in straight lines so nothing in one square touches anything in another square, everything as separate as hell. It drives those people crazy to see someone rubbing out the lines. What about you, Roeburn? You like to color inside the lines? Looking at the way you dress, that pretty little blouse buttoned just so and those gold knot earrings, I'd say you do. I could be wrong, but I don't think so. I'd like to see what you'd be wearing now if you'd been washed in the wrong hormones while you were in the womb. Probably an eighteen-piece Brooks Brothers suit, navy blue, with a white shirt and a diagonally striped tie with a little silver and lavender in it. I got it right, didn't I?

Sure I did hormone therapy. So what? Taking all those hormones didn't change me any more than breast augmentation changes a woman. You ever think about having that done, Roeburn? Yours look smaller than mine. See how nice mine stand up? Jealous, aren't you? It wasn't hormones that gave me these pretties. Hormones didn't make me Samantha. I *am* Samantha, I *was*

Samantha, I will always *be* Samantha—therapy or no therapy. All those hormones did for me was give me a blood clot in my leg. I had to have an operation to remove it. Here's what upsets Doctor Reuben about me: He wants to know why I underwent such extensive hormone therapy yet elected not to have the surgery to remove the wrong part and give me the right one, "finalize the transformation," as they say. Once, when Doctor Reuben was consulting the chronicles of my operations, he said to me, "I don't understand your resistance to this. You're obviously not a person who's afraid of surgery." I don't need the surgery for me, I told him, and I'm not doing it for anybody else. Would you have elective surgery just to make your wife comfortable with who you are? He wouldn't answer that.

Doctor Reuben likes to be helpful. He thinks he knows me because he's been to a transgender conference in Boston and he reads articles about F to Ms and M to Fs. He says it's been proven that M to Fs suffer more depression—because they lose status with the change. That's a lot of crap. Are you depressed because you're a woman and not a man? Of course not! If you're depressed it's because you're a little bit of a tight-ass. You ought to loosen up more, Roeburn, have a little fun—spice up that dull hair, paint your nails, get yourself a pair of five-inch mules and a thong and a glitter bra. Do you wonders, trust me. I can see you like being a woman, though, the little-girl ways you have of making people feel like they want to take care of you, because you're so helpless and charming and it makes them feel so strong and needed and noble to come to your aid. It's a kick to be a woman and feel so powerful, isn't it? Those experts can't study or measure that kick-ass feeling of luring people to do for you and enjoy doing it, can they? I had a feeling you'd understand that, Roeburn, you and that soft little mouth of yours and the way you talk so quiet and look down at your notes when I'm talking to you.

Research, research, research. People today think they're so advanced, but it's the same old shit, people trying to cut the world up in bite-size chunks so they can chew it and digest it, when life's got to be swallowed whole, like a snake ingesting a rat. I'm not F to M, M to F, X to Y, or Why to Why Not. I'm not anything to anything. I'm Samantha Foscoli and nobody else. I never changed. I am who I always was. It's the people looking at me who keep changing.

I keep trying to explain it to Doctor Reuben. I told him about that EMT I met one time when the ambulance took me to the hospital, nice gal, a mom working a volunteer shift. Cheryl Bennett. You don't know her? Cheryl told me she went out to Cherry Point on a call one night because a man had been thrown from a horse. He was unconscious when they got there. Cerebral spinal fluid was pouring out of his ears. She figured he was a goner. They got him to the hospital in Charleston, and the next week the medical university transferred him to a nursing home. Everyone gave him up for a vegetable. But after a few days, he woke up perfectly fine, same as always, not a thing wrong with him. So his family came and took him home. Only thing was, before he fell, he was a shy man, a real introvert, never bothered anybody. But when he came home, he was a flaming extrovert, a nonstop talker, couldn't stand to be alone for a second and couldn't shut up. He annoyed the hell out of his family until they weren't sure if they were glad he had survived the fall or not.

I to E, now that's a change, I tell Doctor Reuben. You may be a doctor, but you aren't fooling anybody with your M to F. I'm F, always have been. F to sexier F. Try that on! If you and the other doctors want to cut off your own toes to try and make your foot fit the glass slipper, be my guest. But don't start cutting anyone else's feet to fit the glass slipper you think they should be wearing. I'm no stepsister, I tell Doctor Reuben, I'm Cinderella: I know there's a shoe that fits only me. Most people settle for less than they're worth, but not me: I'll get my prince and my castle, complete with servants. You ought to hold out for what you're worth, too, Roeburn. You deserve it, as nice and as pretty as you are. Don't let any man con you, not even someone as charming and smart and well-off as Doctor Reuben. Hold out for your truth, Sweet Thing.

Just because I have to set Doctor Reuben straight sometimes doesn't mean he's not a good man. He's handsome, too, don't you think, in an ethnic kind of way? You know what they say, don't you? The bigger the nose, the bigger the equipment. I bet you'd like to take a whirl with Doctor Reuben, wouldn't you? Sure you would. Who wouldn't? Well, he's as kind as he is good-looking. I can vouch for that. I think that's why so many of the nurses here are in love with him, because he treats them gently and respectfully, not like those other doctors who are always throwing tantrums and calling them cretins. The staff here thinks Doctor Reuben's a saint. The saint of Pinesboro! Maybe they're right. When I call Doctor Reuben with a suicide attempt, he doesn't argue. He doesn't ask me if I'm making it up or if I have the wounds or the drug levels in my blood to prove it. Why would anyone lie about that? I have no reason to lie, Roeburn, not about my hair color, my teats, my ass, anything. Even if I did, I wouldn't. The truth's too important to me, the whole truth, not the half- and quarter-truths people go around living. When I tell Doctor Reuben I'm suicidal, he *knows* I am; he calls the ambulance and tells them to admit me to the hospital right away and keep me under observation. He doesn't dink around asking me lots of questions to see if I'm really psycho or I'm just after a little R and R in the hospital. He doesn't fight me on the antibiotics and pain medication I need, either, like other doctors do, wanting to know if I'm really sick or just after drugs. I can just call Doctor Reuben up whenever and tell him I'm having another urinary tract infection and he calls in the prescription for me without making me come in for a test. "That's a waste of your time and mine, not to mention the state's money," he says. "Your urine's always scrotty from your self-caths, so nothing's going to show up anyway."

I end up in the emergency room a lot because of bladder infections. I'm susceptible to urinary tract infections. You can look that up in my medical records. It's because of my cath. I have to catheterize myself because of my injuries from my fall. When I was living in New York, someone pushed me out of a three-story window. Jealousy. Some people see you being yourself and getting all the attention and they just get mad. They get mad at you because they don't have the guts to be who they are and claim attention for themselves. Does that make any sense? That fall is what paralyzed me. It's a miracle I survived, don't you think? But I'm a survivor. *"I will survive, I will survive, I'm not that chained-up little girl who's still in love with you."*

Ever since that fall, I've been in the wheelchair, though. The paralysis comes and goes. Sometimes I can walk into my doctor's appointment, but most times I can't. People don't understand it. They think I'm lying. You don't think I'm lying, do you? You're too smart for that, Roeburn. I could see that right away. One of the physical therapists up in New York told me I was faking it and refused to work with me. There was talk of sending in some doctor to grill me to see if I had Munchausen syndrome, but they knew they couldn't prove anything. I mean, all these medical problems in me can't be denied and they know it. They're as real as anybody's pain. I got scars everywhere, inside and out. Ask Doctor Reuben. He's seen all my charts and X rays and examined me over and over for this, that, and the other thing, and he's a smart doctor. You can't fool him too easy. He doesn't like to be conned for drugs. Everybody knows that. But he doesn't like discrimination, either. Did any of the staff here tell you how mad Doctor Reuben gets at them when they complain about me? He's got a way of seeing other people's suffering. Must be the Jew in him, don't you think? Unless he's really an F, too, and hasn't realized it yet. Don't look so surprised, Roeburn. Stranger things have happened. Once, when I suspected Doctor Reuben was wondering if I was telling him the truth about my bladder infections and that fall out the window, I looked him right in the eye and asked him, "Tell me, why would anybody want to be in a wheelchair if they didn't have to be?"

"Because they like being pushed around?" he said.

"Funny, funny," I said.

Do you know what he said then? "I don't know why you're in a wheelchair, Samantha. Sometimes I think I know what people want, what they need, what's good for them, but I don't. We've all got hidden reasons for what we do, hidden from ourselves as much as from others. You tell me what I'm doing in this godforsaken place beating my head against one quandary after another and I'll tell you why you're in a wheelchair." I swear that's what he said, Roeburn. If you don't believe me, ask him.

It's not important who pushed me out that window or why or how. I'm not one to point the finger or hold grudges. It poisons the soul, don't you think? I'd rather focus on the positive. It's better for your heart and your complexion. Since my fall, I've had to spend a lot more time in the hospital. And just between you and me, Roeburn, I like it that way. I never had a room by myself at home, and it's nice having a TV you can control without having to ask a bunch of other people's opinions.

I'm not saying it's nirvana here. The food stinks. They can't figure out what to do for my wheat allergy. All they give me is potatoes, potatoes, potatoes, or rice, rice, rice. I'm damn sick of it. A trained nutritionist can't come up with something more tantalizing to a sick person who needs to eat for her strength? The nurses are OK, though. Usually one of them will make up my face for me if I'm too weak, or shave my legs when they get too itchy. There's somebody to help you do whatever you need. They'll even come help me sip out of my cup if I can't reach it. Now that's service. I can't do much for myself anymore.

When I'm not in the hospital, I have to be in a halfway house or a boarding home, where I can be taken care of properly. But it looks like I'll be here a while this time, even though the hospital wants me out. "You can't stay here any longer," the administrator told me yesterday. "The insurance companies are running the show, not us, and according to their rules, you should have been sent home weeks ago." Doctor Reuben got him to agree to keep me here until he can find me a place to go. "We can't have you living on the street again," he said to me. "I don't think the hospital wants to be liable for discharging you onto the street."

He called Bilton's first, the last boarding home I was in. But those pricks won't take me back. They said I swore too much at the other residents and hit them and it was no use trying to sue them because they were not required to keep anybody with a temper like mine. A bunch of sissy Baptists running that place. Nobody in New York gets upset about a little yelling or a friendly pop to somebody's arm or head. They don't even notice if you call someone an *assholemotherofafuck* or slip in a *jesusfuckingmaryandjoseph* once in a while. People up North have more important things on their mind, like global warming and genetic engineering of animals. You don't think they should alter our sheep like that, Roeburn, do you? Clone them? Now *that's* scary. We've got enough cloned minds in the world; we don't need cloned bodies, too. The people at Bilton are all cloneheads. I told Doctor Reuben I wouldn't go back there even if they agreed to take me, so now he's trying to get me into a nursing home. He's called every nursing home in Coosawaw County, and not one will take me, not even that stinkhole Dogwood Manor.

They all say they can't find a room for me. They can't put me in a room with another woman, because I have a penis. And they can't put me in a room with a man, because I dress like a woman. And they can't give me a private room, because the state won't pay for a private room. People in the South have no imagination, Roeburn—yourself excluded, of course. That's no prejudice; that's the truth.

So it looks like I'm stuck here for a while. Stuck with round-the-clock nurses caring for all my wants and needs and Doctor Reuben coming to see me every morning on his rounds to see how I'm feeling and if the staff is treating me right and if I have everything I need. The best part is: There's nothing you or anybody else can do about it. Cinderella never had it better. Take notes, Roeburn. If you want to be as happy as I am in your life, without anybody telling you who to be and what to do, without anybody selling you short, everybody serving *your* truth, take notes.

A BETTER MAN

The Harts had been going to Pug Padgett all their lives, an arrangement that worked well for everyone. Pug prescribed Mrs. Hart all the pain medication she wanted for her headaches and sore neck, no questions asked, provided that, on her way home from the pharmacy, she slipped him exactly half the number of pills he had ordered for her. Mr. Hart went to see Pug once a month for his pain shot, the same shot Pug gave everybody who came for an appointment, whether they mentioned having pain or not. When the Hart boys, Lloyd and James, were thirteen and fourteen, he started them on pain shots, too. Both boys worked with their father painting houses, and they had already developed the same chronic lower back pain he had. A general practitioner, Pug didn't discriminate between adults and children: He treated everyone the same, give or take a dosage adjustment here and there for the frail and the obese. "A body's a body," he would say. When Lloyd or James called him between shots, complaining of pain and asking for medication, he prescribed pain pills for them, even though he knew Mrs. Hart made them call and forced them to turn over the pills to her the minute the prescription had been filled. He still got his share from her, same as always, and who was he to say how much pain a person could bear? If Lydia Hart said she needed more medicine to help her endure the pain of her life, then she did.

This happy understanding between the Harts and Pug Padgett continued undisturbed until Pug gave himself too much morphine with his nightly fifth of bourbon and died, leaving Lydia, now fifty-seven and a widow, Lloyd, forty-one, and James, thirty-nine, to find another doctor. That was a challenge in Pinesboro. All three of them, because of disability, were on Medicaid and received Supplemental Security Income, and most doctors in town—with the exception of Pug and a young doctor for the blacks, Bruce Inabinett—did not accept patients on either of those government plans, just as they refused to take any new patients who were on Medicare. This restrictive professional policy had nothing to do with not loving their neighbor; it was strictly a question of business: Doctors offered a service for a fee. If every doctor did the job of a missionary, gave away his expertise to the chronically poor, malingerers, and addicts, the whole system would fall apart and no one would get the help they needed, and that certainly wasn't what Jesus had in mind when he called men to follow him. And there was no harm done, after all: People like the Harts and other sorry sorts always managed to find some way to get along.

The Harts saw their opportunity to get the medical care they needed when Doctor Reuben moved to town and opened an office in a small building on Highway 26 near the new hospital. A stranger to the community and in need of establishing his practice without benefit of family or social ties, Doctor Reuben took anyone who walked in the door or landed in the hospital during his shift on call—no questions asked. All three Harts set up appointments immediately.

Lydia lasted one appointment. Complaining of debilitating neck pain, she asked Doctor Reuben to prescribe Lortab 7.5s for her, the extra-strength ones, the only thing she had found that took even the tiniest edge off her pain. When he called in the prescription, the pharmacist informed him that in the last week he had received calls from two other doctors, one in Varnville and one in Orangeburg, for the same medication for Mrs. Hart. Doctor Reuben called Lydia immediately and told her in his kindest and most apologetic voice that he was sorry, but he couldn't keep her as a patient, because he couldn't trust her and he had to be able to trust a patient if he was going to prescribe a controlled substance. In fact, without trust, he couldn't help anyone. Lydia found a compatible doctor in Charleston, an hour away.

Lloyd hung on several months. When his monthly supply of Lortab 7.5s ran out a week early, he called the office, impersonating his brother, James, and convinced Doctor Reuben to prescribe a refill. The minute he hung up the phone, he drove to the new Eckerd pharmacy to pick up the prescription. James figured out what had happened two days later, when he called the office asking for an early refill for his Lortab 7.5 supply. The nurse told him that he would have to wait at least three and a half weeks before Doctor Reuben would even consider another refill, no matter what had happened to the refill they had just phoned in for him forty-eight hours ago—lost in the garbage, eaten by the dog, or stolen by haints. James drove right over to his brother's house. He and Lloyd fought.

"If I can't trust you," James said, "you can't see the same doctor I'm seein'. Reuben's *mine*. You find somebody else, or I'll release certain information to certain Drug Enforcement Administration officials."

Lloyd found a doctor in Beaufort, an hour and fifteen minutes away. Two years later, without any help from James, the DEA sent him to prison.

James got along well with Doctor Reuben from the beginning, so well that he brought his wife, Patty Joyce, to see him, too. Both

James and Patty Joyce showed up for their appointments dirty and smelling unpleasant, but they were always regular and prompt, and they often brought their six-year-old with them, a little girl who was immaculately cared for and who charmed the entire office staff and everyone in the waiting room besides. Patty Joyce needed Lortab 7.5s for her headaches and Xanax for her anxiety. James needed Lortab 7.5s for his back pain. Doctor Reuben prescribed Patty's pills as needed and James's in month-long supplies. James had already undergone three back surgeries to relieve his pain. The surgeons had told him there was nothing more they could do for him.

"They cut me loose," he told Doctor Reuben. "You're all I got now."

The first two months James got by on his supply, though Doctor Reuben suspected he was supplementing with Patty Joyce's pills. From then on, James had a habit of calling the office a week before the end of his month and asking for a new month's supply. He always had a good reason for running out—he left his pills in his car and somebody stole them; his mother came over to see her granddaughter, found where he had stashed his pills, and took them; his brother had sneaked into his house while he was working and taken them; James had taken a short-term job in pest control so that he and Patty Joyce could make ends meet, and hauling tanks of chemicals all day had made the pain worse, so he had had to double up on his pills to keep working. For months, Doctor Reuben complied, but the fourth or fifth time it happened, he called James into the office.

"James," he said, "I can't prove it, but I think you're taking too much of this narcotic."

"It's the only thing that helps my pain," James said. "I've tried everythin' else—chiropractors, herbs, prayin', speakin' in tongues."

"I don't doubt Lortab is easing your pain, but it's making me uncomfortable."

"You're goin' to stop givin' it to me?"

"I'm not going to ask you to suffer unnecessarily. If you say you're in pain, you are. The Talmud, that's Jewish law, says if a hundred doctors say a patient doesn't need something, and the patient says he does, the attending doctor is obligated to give the patient what he needs. I wouldn't be a very good doctor if I didn't trust you about how much pain you can bear, would I?"

"So you're not goin' to stop givin' me the Lortabs?"

"I want you to quit smoking and drinking. That's the first thing. We'll have to talk about that. The second thing I want you to do is be very careful about how you use the medicine I give you. Take a look at this."

Doctor Reuben set a document in front of James. "I want you to read this. If you agree to this treatment plan and sign it, then we can continue working together, as long as you keep your end of the bargain."

James pored over the paper, squinting, biting his lip, and using his finger to keep his place.

Doctor Reuben, watching the finger crawl back and forth through the words, controlled an urge to snatch the paper from under the man's hand and read it to him. When James finally looked up, he asked him, "Do you agree to everything there?"

"I think I do," James said.

"Let's review it together," the doctor said. "One"—the doctor's thumb sprang out from his fist—"you promise to show up at my office for regular visits; two"—his index finger went up—"you promise to vigilantly maintain the security of your Lortab 7.5 supply; three"—the third finger—"you promise to take only *your* Lortabs and *no one else's*; four"—the ring finger—"you promise to notify me if you receive *any* other medication from *any* other doctor; and five"—the pinky went up, completing the doctor's stubby hand—"you acknowledge that you understand that if you fail to keep any one of these promises, I will immediately stop prescribing pain medication of any sort for you. Immediately, without warning. Do you understand?"

James signed the agreement.

"You're a good man, Doctor Reuben," he said, accepting his copy of the plan and shaking the doctor's hand.

Four years went by. During those years, James showed up at Doctor Reuben's every third Wednesday without fail. He adhered faithfully to the other conditions of their contract as well. Several times each year, however, he would call the office before the end of the month saying he was working another painting job and had to take extra pills to keep going, so he needed his prescription refilled a little early. Doctor Reuben called in the prescription for him every time—though not without giving him a lecture about managing his medication wisely. About once a year James would call Doctor Reuben at two or three in the morning, drunk, asking for more Lortab 7.5s.

Angry, Doctor Reuben would tell him, "James, you know you shouldn't call me like this. You *know* I can't do anything about this situation now. Come see me at the office in the morning."

"Tomorrow," James would repeat, but half the time he wouldn't show up the next day.

That annoyed Doctor Reuben even more, and invariably, at James's next regular appointment, he would chastise him as if he were a little boy.

"James, what are you *doing*? I thought you were going to quit drinking. How can I help you if you won't do anything to help yourself? I can't give you any more pain medication than I'm already giving you. I don't know any other way to help you."

James never took offense. "I'm sorry, Doctor Reuben," he would say, lowering his head and hiding his face. "I don't mean to make you mad."

Sometimes James would get so desperate he would call Emergency Medical Services in the middle of the night and say he was having an asthma attack and an ambulance would take him to the emergency room, where the doctor on call would admit him. No sooner would he be settled in his bed than he would request injectable pain medication for his back, which the staff doctor would approve and the nurses would administer. When Doctor Reuben made his rounds the next morning, he didn't spare James his fury.

"If you gave up smoking and took care of yourself, you wouldn't be in here," he would say, or, "I have to admit, James, it's hard for me not to believe you're faking these asthma attacks." Once he stuck his head in the door, said, "I thought we had an agreement, but I guess it's not important to some people to honor their word," and left.

In spite of this, James remained loyal to Doctor Reuben. He spoke highly of him wherever he went. He sent all his friends, most of whom suffered chronic pain and were users like himself, to see his doctor. Reuben treated them all, all more or less successfully, depending on the standards by which improvement is measured.

One May, James scheduled an extra appointment, after he had already made his regular monthly visit and received his standard refill. Doctor Reuben walked in the exam room to find him sitting in the consultation chair, his forehead in his hand, his elbow resting on his knee. He stood up and shook the doctor's hand.

"What can I do for you, James?" the doctor asked, looking through James's chart for the date of his last refill. "Don't bother asking me for any more pills. I won't give them to you today, no matter what story you tell me."

"I'm leavin'," James said.

Doctor Reuben looked up from the chart.

"We're movin' in with Patty Joyce's sister in Aiken."

Reuben let out his breath, hoping the man wouldn't detect his relief at losing the burden of a difficult patient's care.

"You've been good to me," James said, "real fair, real straight, so I didn't want to leave without sayin' somethin'."

"That's OK," Doctor Reuben said, closing the chart and making a mental note to tell Lou, his nurse, to label it inactive. "You don't have to say anything." He offered his hand and said, "Good luck, James. If there's anything I can do to help you find another doctor, just let me know. I'd be happy to help."

James didn't take the doctor's hand. After a nervous moment, the doctor hid both of his hands in the pockets of his lab coat and met James's gaze.

"I know I haven't been easy," James said. Gripping his waist with his thumb, he rubbed the soreness in his back with his fingers. "But I want you to know . . . I'm doin' the best I can."

"Sure you are," Doctor Reuben said. "That's all anybody can do. None of us is perfect. Just last week I missed a patient's bacterial endocarditis, thinking it was arthritis or vascular inflammation. She might have died if she hadn't seen a specialist on her own—a doctor more attentive than I was—and been put on antibiotics right away."

"No," James said. "Not like that." He stopped massaging his back and took a deep breath, like someone taking in enough air to last him through a noxious tunnel. Staring at the stethoscope around Doctor Reuben's neck, he said, "When I was a boy, my daddy used to beat me with a two-by-four on my legs and my back. He beat me so bad I couldn't walk some days. If I could get to school, the teachers would bandage me up. He beat my mother, too. When she was carryin' my younger brother, he beat her so bad he was born dead. His grave's out by Ritter, in a little cemetery there. I visit two, three times a week, whenever I'm able."

He looked up to his doctor's face. Behind his horn-rimmed glasses, the doctor's eyes were squinched in discomfort.

Doctor Reuben folded his hands over his chest, pressing the stethoscope hard against his sternum. He glanced furtively at his watch. The next patient was waiting. Out of respect for the patients, he and his staff worked hard to run an efficient office. Any second, Lou would be poking her head in, telling him everything was ready for him in the next exam room. He met James's gaze again, ready to thank him and send him on his way.

"I know I'm not a perfect man," James said. "And I can understand how you'd be mad at me and think I'm no good, just another redneck loser livin' out here in the middle of nowhere, a man just about your own age, the way I figure it, but with nothin' to show for himself, not like you."

Reuben shook his head vigorously. "I never—"

"But I'm a better man than my father. I've always treated my wife and my daughter well." James pressed his lips together, inhaled deeply, then puffed out his breath. "You're a good man, Doctor Reuben. You've been like a father to me." He began to cry. He paused but made no effort to hide or stop the tears bathing his face. "I'll never forget you," he said after a moment. He stepped forward and hugged Doctor Reuben, a firm embrace with no guile in it. "I love you," he said.

He let go of the doctor and walked out, leaving Jake Reuben alone in the room. He was still standing where James had left him when Lou peeked in a minute later. "Here you are!" she said. "Mrs. Strickland's waiting across the hall. Better smile going in. She's having one of her bad days."

WHAT WE OUGHT TO BE

After Bud died, the boys decided it would do me good to have some place to go to every day. Somebody to talk to—that's what I miss. My credentials were dusty but still in order, so I applied for a job with that new doctor who was startin' up a practice here at the time, Doctor Reuben.

It took me some time to get used to workin' for that man. First, he's a Northerner—I don't have to explain to you what that means. Then there's all his other strange habits—not goin' to church, not touchin' the shrimp I brought him, not eatin' meat and milk together, runnin' from crackers and ketchup and Coke durin' Passover. He had foolish ideas about settin' up the office, too. I told him it was no use puttin' in fancy chairs with cushions in the waitin' room. The old people were just goin' to urinate on them. We should have put in fiberglass ones, but he wouldn't hear of it. Same thing with the carpet. Why did he need to put in that expensive carpet when I *told* him the blacks were just goin' to set their sacks of croakers down on it and let their kids slobber all over it? "You're not from here," I told him. "You think you know, but you don't. What goes up North doesn't go down here. I have experience with these people."

The man wouldn't listen, so what do we have now? A nice carpet trashed by his patients, just like I told him. He wouldn't listen 'bout curbin' some of the patients, either. The first time he had to tell a black family their mother was going to die, I told him, "Don't tell them here in the office. Get you a conference room at the hospital and tell them there, because they are goin' to carry on somethin' awful and it'll put off your other patients." He didn't believe me. He went right ahead and told that family in his office. And sure enough, most of them fainted to the floor and stayed there till we could revive them, but one of the girls ran straight out the office and stood in the parkin' lot jumpin' and tearin' her hair and screamin', "Doctor say my mama goin' to *die!* Doctor say my mama goin' to *die!*" Eh Lor'. This world and the next.

Those patients of his—God Almighty, I've never seen anything like it. Seems like not a one of them is what they ought to be. The rich ones, few and far between as they are, storm in demandin' to be seen right away when anybody with one eye can see the waitin' room is burstin'. The poor ones bring every last person and animal related to them and crowd the whole office with their mess. The crossovers make a racket adjustin' their skirts and diggin' in their makeup satchels and makin' up their faces; they cause a stir no matter what they do.

Some of the patients are just plain off their heads, like Leland Biggers. Leland lives in his car and drives all over town with a big old aluminum extension ladder strapped to the top of his car. Never takes that ladder off his roof. He wants to be ready, he told me, to climb up to God when he sees Him. Leland never takes off a stitch of his clothes, either. No matter how hot it gets—and it gets hotter than I-can't-say-what here in the Lowcountry—he always wears everything he owns, one thing layered over another. Doctor Reuben has to work his way under all those clothes just to hear his heart beat or check his prostate. One time Leland had off all his clothes for a full checkup, and Doctor Reuben couldn't get him to stop talking and get dressed. He kep' wanderin' out the room with one shirt or another half buttoned and ask me or Christine, our other nurse, to help him. We'd tell him no, we were too busy, but he wouldn't stop talkin' and botherin' us. He'd go back in the room and come out with another shirt or pair of trousers unbuttoned. It was near closin' time and we were all tired as old mules. Doctor Reuben was fit to be tied. "Lou," he said to me, "will you see if you can get Leland to leave? You know I can't ask him." I went right to the room where he was talking to himself and fiddling with his clothes and told him, "Leland, we got to close up and go home. If you're not put together and out the door in *five minutes,* we're going to lock you up in here for the night." Don't you know he was dressed, coats and all, and out the door in four minutes, leaving only his odor behind. Leland does smell now. Christine won't have anything to do with Leland because of the smell. I used to wear heavy perfume on the days Leland was scheduled, but Doctor Reuben asked me to stop because it set off the asthma patients. Now I just spray that citrus deodorizer in the waitin' room and the exam rooms before he comes. Leland's sweet as he can be, though, no matter what mind troubles he has.

Can't say that about all our patients, most assuredly not "Samantha." Samantha's one of Doctor Reuben's crossovers. He bamboozled somebody up North into payin' for a load of hormones to be pumped into his body so he has an excuse to act like a woman. He's always dressed to the nines and always makin' a scene. "You got to watch that one," I warned Doctor Reuben when Samantha first started comin' to us. "He's always dyin' and always lyin'—a real user." Samantha claims he can't walk and it's no wonder: He sports heels so high and skinny a half-starved girl couldn't stand up on them. He's nasty mouthed, too, and bad tempered. I pray and take extra care when I draw blood from him so he won't cuss me like a bailiff or jam one of those spiky heels down on my arch.

The Lord knows I try to accommodate Doctor Reuben. He's doin' the Lord's work with these people. When he first started seein' HIV-infected patients, I drew the line. Nobody else in Coosawaw County would see those patients, so they all came to us, about four or five them at first, black and white. Now, you know I felt sorry for those people; sick as they are, it's a hardship for them to get all the way to Charleston to see a doctor and get their blood work done. But the doctors and nurses in Charleston got more experience with that kind of thing, more ways to protect themselves. "Get Christine to draw those people's blood," I told Doctor Reuben. "She's not married. I may be a widow, but I'm a *grandma,*" I said, holdin' up my arm and shakin' my wrist so my bracelet with the danglin' picture-charms of my nine grandbabies jingled in his face. Doctor Reuben drew the blood on those patients himself. Never said a word against me or Christine. And wouldn't you know it, it wasn't long before he talked me into helpin', scared as I was. "It scares me, too," he told me, "but we'll take every precaution. And Lou, remember, we have to 'be kind to the stranger, for we were strangers in Egypt.'" I'm a sucker for people quotin' the Bible. My middle son's a tent preacher, and he can get me to do just about anything. I told Doctor Reuben he could go on back to his doctorin' business and I would prep the HIV patients for him like I did all the others.

You know what the worst part is? All those HIV patients just die on you. Some faster, some slower, but they all die. That's what's hard, gettin' to know them and seein' the life drain out of them a little more each day all the while their family members are pretendin' they don't know what's goin' on, though anyone with half a brain who watches the news could figure it out. "He's got a bad flu," they'll say when they bring them in. Or, "Livin' up North just weakened him." I know they have their families to protect and they want their children to have a Christian burial, but do they for one second think I'm that big of a fool? If they're worried about me blabbin' their business outside the office, they have the wrong woman. I see how they treat their sick sons and daughters when they come in here, lookin' the other way, denyin' them. They'll stare at two-year-old magazines, our ratty carpet, the fake dracaena in the corner, a sweaty Wendy's drink cup, their hangnails, the legs and the outfits of the crossovers, my bosoms, and Christine's rear end—but they will not look in the face of their own child sufferin'. And do I run to my church or my hairdresser and accuse these parents of havin' faith without works, bein' dead in the spirit? No I do not. I keep my mouth shut. "The tongue is a fire, a world of iniquity that defileth the whole body of Christ," James teaches, "an unruly evil, full of deadly poison." I want my tongue to be a tongue of blessin', not a tongue of cursin'. That's why I try to cheer up the HIV patients while they're here, and most of them are real grateful for that.

One in particular was always real grateful: Terri. Terri had bottle-dyed red hair and the best collection of pocketbooks I've ever seen—a new one every time she came for her appointment—but otherwise she was ordinary lookin', average height, medium build. She said she got HIV from a blood transfusion. She had more than her share of surgery, I can tell you that, but I don't know about that transfusion business. I think she engaged in a lot of risky behavior when she lived up North, if you know what I mean. One thing's for sure: After she came back home to live with her mother out in Round O, she didn't do one thing she wasn't supposed to. If she had blown her nose too loud, her mother would have gotten out of her sickbed and strangled her with a bed sheet, so you *know* she wasn't out foolin' around. Terri was afraid of her mother. That's the reason her blood pressure and heart rate were always so high. Terri told Doctor Reuben she used to be Terry with a Y and that after she finished the hormone therapy and the sex change operation when she was livin' up North, she changed to Terri with an I. I overheard her explainin' it to him when I was puttin' up a new chart outside the exam room.

Doctor Reuben's no dummy: He can smell a drug con a mile away. Any fraud who calls, desperate because he supposedly forgot to refill his prescription before he leaves on vacation or because someone stole his pills the third month in a row, and beggin' for another hundred or fifty or twenty right now, better find himself another doctor. Same with any liar who comes in with a headache or back pain and asks for a prescription for Percodan or Darvocet or Vicodin because that's the *only* thing that'll work. Doctor Reuben's always on to them. He's gullible about some things, though. Sometimes he gets kind of susceptible to a patient's sufferin' and then he'll do most anything for them without questionin' their wild stories. Last week, for instance, there was a foreign girl in here with her mother—some kind of Arabs, I think—askin' for an exam to certify that her hymen was intact. Can you imagine? I wanted to laugh so bad my sides hurt. Well, Doctor Reuben sent the mother out of the room so he could examine the girl and he found out that she was takin' birth control pills and that she and her boyfriend were sexually active. The girl insisted, though—naturally—that she and her boyfriend had never had intercourse. Doctor Reuben gave her a pelvic exam and found nothin'. He called the mother back in and explained that the results of the exam didn't mean anything, that the hymen sometimes ruptures all on its own, when the girl's quite young, or that insertin' a tampon can break it. But that wasn't good enough for those two. The mother insisted that the daughter was pure and that the hymen *had* to be there; he had just "by mistake" missed it. "Please, sir," she said, "you will check again." What could he do? He looked again, and he "found" it. They went home with a letter certifyin' everything was intact, both mother and daughter practically in giggles.

"Did you know that girl was lyin'?" I asked Doctor Reuben later.

"Who am I to say that girl's not pure?" he said.

"But she was *lyin'!*"

"Sometimes," he said, "people have to lie to tell the truth about themselves."

That's the kind of doctor he is. With Terri, though, I don't think Doctor Reuben caught the lie, though it was plain enough to me because I'm a woman. The problem with Terri was she had gigantic bosoms, way too big to pop out because of hormones. I've seen the chests of some of these crossovers, that nasty Samantha's, for instance, and they're nothin' to brag about—a little swellin' like what you'd see in a fat old man. Not Terri's. Terri's bosoms were about as big as mine, and she carried them like they were dear friends; she didn't need to stick them out like Samantha does, to prove to herself she's got them. I don't mean this unkindly, but Terri didn't get those bosoms from takin' a few pills and shots. She was *born* a woman. I don't know why she made up that story about the hormones and the sex change operation. Could be she was ashamed to be a woman. That's natural enough, seein' as how her mother made her feel bad for just livin'. Could be she was afraid of bein' a woman, plain and simple; Lord knows things happen to us because we're women, things we all just have to work hard to heal from. I know somebody hurt Terri bad when she was little, but every time we got close to talkin' about it, she'd clam up. I don't know why she needed to believe she was a man who chose to be a woman instead of just a woman straight out and that's fine with me. And I don't care about the facts of the matter either, whatever they might be. It's Terri's body and she's the only one can tell the truth about it—no doctor, no nurse, no medical examiner. If she *says* she's a man who became a woman, then that's who she *is*. No doctor, no matter how smart, can tell a body where they hurt. And no doctor, not even one wise as King Solomon himself, can tell a person what their pain means to them. Doctors may act like they know us better than we know ourselves, but they don't.

I didn't used to feel that way. When Terri first started comin' to us, I used to ask Doctor Reuben, "Why don't you examine her? See if she's got an artificial vagina?" But he wouldn't do it. He said there was no need for him to give her a pelvic exam. It wasn't any of his business. She had a urologist *and* a gynecologist who did that.

Ooh, Terri hated that urologist. Doctor Cline Douglas. I don't like Doctor Douglas much myself—too full of himself, and I can't stand a man in a bow tie. Bud, my husband, wore the most beautiful ties you ever saw. He ordered them from New York, silk ones in all colors and patterns, so beautiful they put the lilies of the valley to shame. When Bud died, the boys wanted his ties, but I hung on to all of them. Who knows? I might make a quilt out of them one day. That Doctor Bow Tie was ungentlemanly and *unchristian* to Terri. He *insisted* on referrin' to her as "he," on the phone to me and Doctor Reuben, and in front of Terri herself. But Terri had to go to Bow Tie: He's the only urologist in the county.

And wouldn't you know, Terri had constant urinary problems. She claimed she had fistula scarrin' between her vagina and rectum— I saw it on her chart—but Doctor Reuben never had occasion to check that. She did have more urinary tract infections than a harem. She had so many that the doctors up North gave her a divertin' colostomy just to try to cut down the number of episodes. But then, because of complications from that surgery, they had to undo her colostomy and she got all those urinary tract and bladder infections right back. I used to slip her Macrobid samples, so she wouldn't have to see Doctor Bow Tie. Macrobid is what works fastest for me. Terri was real grateful. When she got to feelin' better, she would bring me chocolates or take me out to lunch to show her appreciation.

Lots of times, though, the Macrobid didn't work and then she had to be hospitalized. The nurses over at Coosawaw Regional were always complainin' that Terri asked for an IV with pain medicine the minute she got into the bed. They would call me up and say she asked for too much in the drip and she used it too fast and Doctor Reuben better do somethin' about her. But they liked Terri just the same. She was the nicest patient they could ever hope for. She complimented them on their hair and nails and smiles and children, gave them beautiful thank-you cards, brought them presents— knew how to do just the thing their heart needed to keep on goin' in that God-forsaken hospital, where they pay you nothin' and expect you to do the work of three people. Terri gave Doctor Reuben a framed needlepoint she made for his kitchen. It says "This is a Kosher kitchen" in Hebrew. It's still hangin' in his house. Terri was devoted, *devoted,* to the people who were good to her. That's how she was. Everybody loved her. Everybody except her mother. She went up North because of her mother. "To my mother I'm an oyster toadfish," she told me once when I was takin' her weight—which kep' fallin' no matter what she ate—and complimentin' her on her good nature. "When I was a kid she would call me in from playin' and yell at me, 'I can see who you are. *You.* And you are *covered* with slime. You're nothin' but a trash fish, not fit to eat, not even good enough to be hacked up for bait or thrown to the dogs.'"

"Every one of us is a child of God," I said, "but don't some people just act like dogs?"

"I don't know what I am," Terri said, "but I'm not what she thinks I am."

When Terri came home from up North, she ended up livin' with her mother again. And do you know that woman had the gall to try and throw her out? Here her daughter quit her good-payin' job and came home to take care of her when there was nobody else who would do it, and all that mangy old woman could do was throw a fit. But the Lord stayed her hand, and Terri didn't get forced out. That mother should count her blessin's. Terri did a you-know-what good job of carin' for her mother, when she wasn't in the hospital herself. She had to change all the beddin', give her shots, everything. I've never seen such an attentive nurse. She always had a glass of cool water by the bedside and a vase of fresh-cut camellias from the yard. I'd be proud to have such a daughter, HIV or no HIV, but God saw fit to give me only sons. I'm not complainin', but you know once a son gets married, he goes with the wife and *her* mother. You know how it is. The boys came and visited more after Bud died—they were real dutiful about it—but once I got back on my feet, they tapered off again. A daughter's different. She'll call you in the mornin' just to tell you she's happy or to ask for your tomato jam recipe. She'll sit by you when you're dyin', not sayin' a word—knowin' that's what you want—just holdin' your hand. Terri's devoted to her mother, but that woman—you know what I'd like to call her—would die before she'd treat Terri right. Do you know she wouldn't let Terri eat off her plates? Her own daughter. That's no mother; that's a sick and twisted heart. Terri had to buy herself a nice set of china, and every night she set the table beautifully for two, her mother's dishes on one side, hers on the other, the candles and the homemade pasta or meat loaf between them. That mother would just sit there chewin' her food without sayin' a word, starin' at her daughter, while Terri had to do her best to keep up a lively and positive conversation.

"Why don't you move out?" I asked Terri once, while I was drawin' her blood for one of those never-endin' white-cell counts. "How can you stand bein' in her presence when you know how much she hates you? The thought of all that hatred oozin' out of her and pointin' itself right at you gives me the creeps. If it were me, I wouldn't even want to come near her, let alone touch her."

"I can't," Terri said.

"Why?"

"She's my mother."

"The Bible says we have to *honor* our father and mother, not sacrifice ourselves to them."

"I love her."

"Would you love a scorpion if you happened to find it in your bed?"

"Probably." She grinned when she said that, her thin lips stretchin' over her pretty teeth.

One day Terri came in the office cryin'. She didn't have an appointment. When I asked her what was wrong, she said her heart hurt. Myocardial inflammation, I thought. You don't run up on that condition much, but I just had a feeling that's what it was, so I took her blood pressure and Doctor Reuben tested her and we got her started on antibiotics. She was supposed to take rest and I knew she wasn't goin' to get any rest with her mother around, so I offered to let her stay with me. She wouldn't at first.

"You need somebody to take care of you," I said. "What if you faint in the middle of the night and fall down and split your head open?"

She wasn't any better after a few days, so I just drove myself over to her house after work and knocked on the door.

"Get the door!" the old mother screamed.

It took a long time for Terri to open the door. When she did, she was deathly pale.

"Who is that?" her mother screamed from the back room, the rage in her voice sickenin' me. "Who *is* it? Tell me!"

"A friend, Mother," Terri said. "Go back to sleep."

"*Friend? Freak!* What kind of *friend?*"

"You're comin' home with me, and don't argue," I whispered to Terri. "Don't worry about your mother. I'll arrange for home health care for her."

She was too weak to say no. We went to her room, and while Terri lay on her bed and her mother screamed in the other room— "I'm bein' robbed! Police! Police! Get out, you filth!"—I packed Terri's belongin's. I wrapped her china in newspaper and carried it out in grocery sacks. Eh Lor'. This world and the next.

Terri and I lived together two years. I cooked all my best soups for her, made hoppin' John with field peas, greens, corn patties, boiled peanuts. She would sit in bed with a bowl of warm peanuts in her lap, shellin' them and suckin' them while she watched TV or we chatted. Somebody to talk to—that's what I miss. My preacher son used to come to my house for Sunday dinner with his wife and children once a month, but while Terri was there, he refused to step foot in the house. He wouldn't let me come to his house, either, or meet me for coffee downtown. I thought he was just scared of gettin' infected, but that's not what he was worryin' himself about.

"It's an abomination," he said.

"Her or the fact that she's here?" I asked.

"An abomination," was all he would say. Still, I was never happier in my life—after Bud died, I mean—than in those days. Terri and I used to take long rides in the car, to Rum Gully to see the Christmas lights, to the Sweatman's in Holly Hill for barbecue, to Edisto Beach to buy shrimp and sit on the dock. At night I'd read to her until she fell asleep, sometimes an Oprah book, sometimes *People* magazine, sometimes poetry, sometimes her Bible. She liked Ezekiel and the Psalms. Ezekiel 12 was her favorite: "Therefore, son of man, prepare for yourself an exile's baggage, and go into exile by day in their sight; you shall go like an exile from your place in their sight. Perhaps they will understand, though they are a rebellious house." I had to read that passage over and over to her, her whisperin' the words along with me.

At the end Terri didn't have to leave our house. I set up a hospital bed in the livin' room and made everything as cozy as can be. Doctor Reuben came by every few days to check on her. The last few weeks, he stopped in every day, on his way home from work. He gave us the morphine prescription. I did all the hospice care. Terri died a natural death, the coroner said. Congestive heart failure, the paper said. Nothin' but AIDS, the gossips said. Could be. But I think sometimes your exile's baggage gets too heavy and no matter how loud the Lord commands you to keep carryin' it, in order to go on, you just have to set it down.

DIS ALITER VISUM

Arthur has it good here. He won't find another job as rewarding as this one. He has the opportunity in our establishment to interact with intelligent people, people of taste and culture who know how to treat him with the respect he deserves. And he won't find an employer in the whole Lowcountry, Jew or Gentile, black or white, who will treat him as well as Celia and I do. We've given him raises right along, good benefits, and generous discounts; we taught him merchandising and gemology, let him take time off whenever he needed it, no questions asked, and promoted him. He works side by side with me. He locks up as many nights as I do, takes the diamonds out of the window and puts them in the safe. I leave him in charge for weeks at a time when Celia and I go on vacation. What other proprietor is going to let him do all that?

Arthur's worked for us his whole life. I hired him as an inventory clerk the day he got out of high school. Today everybody employs blacks, but in 1968, no one hired—pardon my language—"niggers." Celia and I felt an obligation to use our position to stand up for justice and social change. We know what it's like to be discriminated against. Celia was never invited to join the Pinesboro Cotillion—because of her religious persuasion—even though every one of her society friends was on the membership committee. She's still mad about that. I'll never forget driving to St. Simons Island in the fifties and seeing on the road into Sea Pines a sign that said "NO JEWS, NIGGERS, OR DOGS ALLOWED." To this day we will not patronize that resort.

The moment I hired Arthur, I could see he was a real asset—Celia tells me I'm the best judge of character she's ever seen—and within a year I moved him from the back room to sales. That's when the trouble started. The first day Arthur worked the floor, my mother called me at the store to tell me her friend Eugenia Beeson had seen a "nigger" salesman.

"Mrs. Beeson is lying, Mother."

"Jacob!"

"Mrs. Beeson never sets foot in our store, you know that. She shops at her cousin's jewelry store in Charleston. She didn't see anything. It's hearsay. Ignore her."

"Yblansky's has always been a *quality* store, Jacob," my mother said. "Remember that before you ruin the business your father and I worked so hard to establish."

That evening, she demanded that my father get rid of the boy first thing in the morning.

"Jacob runs the store now," Isadore—may his memory be for a blessing—told her. "Not us."

There were other complaints about Arthur, of course, and we lost a few customers over him, but Celia and I stood by what was right and kept him on the floor.

Isadore and I taught Arthur how to wait on customers the old-fashioned way, with honesty and integrity: Never try to sell a customer something he doesn't want or can't afford, and never try to sell a lady a jewelry item that doesn't look good on her. We want our customers to trust us to tell them the truth—tactfully, of course, not with the gruffness Sheldon Rosen uses at Rose's Auto Supply, or with his mother's foolishness. One of my customers told me that when he ordered a water pump at Rose's, Edyth Rosen told him he'd do better to buy a new car than throw good money away on junk. Sheldon had the good sense to reprimand his mother in front of the customer, but they still lost that sale. Truth with diplomacy—that's my motto.

It wasn't long after he started working the floor that I let Arthur take charge of the gift department. Sheldon warned me not to let him manage. "They steal," he said. But Arthur was different. And he had a real talent for helping customers pick just the right gift. That may not seem important now, when gift certificates and checks pass for thoughtfulness, but the first years Arthur worked for us, the world was still civilized. Arthur knew the kind of goods that would attract a better clientele, too. He kept the silver baby cups, engraved graduation steins, Wedgewood wedding china, and Hummel figurines in stock—those are still our bread and butter—but he slowly added art pieces to attract the Northern retirees living on their plantations or out at Hilton Head. He ordered Lladro porcelain figurines and signed Val Saint-Lambert paperweights and vases from exclusive European distributors. Our customers didn't fight over our figurines and vases like the ladies in Karesh's Department Store fought over the latest shipments of New York– and New Orleans–designed hats, but these buyers made sure they got here in time to make a good selection. We'd sell out a shipment of Lladro limited-edition pieces in less than twenty-four hours. To this day we make more money in fine porcelain and art glass than all the stores in Charleston and Savannah put together. That's all Arthur's doing. He has impeccable taste.

Over the years, he's built up our pearl line, too, and that does very well for us also. I never cared much for pearls, but I'm happy he's taken an interest. We've always sold a fair number of freshwater pearls around Valentine's Day and graduation, but with Arthur's knowledge and his Japanese connections, we now sell choice Mabé and Akoya pearls as well, usually at Christmas or for anniversaries.

In the last ten years, I've seen to it that Arthur became a member of the American Gem Trade Association. I've taken him to the gemology conventions with me, and I've passed on to him what my father taught me about the cuts and clarity of diamonds and other gems. Arthur has an unfailingly good eye for quality and value.

I've hired a lot of salespeople in the last thirty years, but Arthur Manigo is one of the best. About twenty years ago, I hired his cousin Annette, as a favor to Arthur, but she's no Arthur. Annette was good enough with customers, I suppose, until a few years ago, when she became rather bossy. She ignored every one of Celia's suggestions for designing the display windows and started telling her how to run the store, saying we ought to improve our layaway system and carry more colorful jewelry, "for folks who have other places to go to besides the country club." Annette was snippy with customers, too. She dropped the Ma'am and Missus and called them by their first names. She left Miss Hampton waiting at the counter for *ten* minutes, and when she came back, she told her, "We don't carry sizes for fingers *that* fat." It took Celia an hour to calm Miss Hampton. The morning Annette quit she didn't even come in. She *phoned* to say she wasn't coming to work that morning and, by the way, she was *never* coming back. I couldn't understand it. We paid her a more-than-fair wage and we gave her all the holidays off—including the Jewish holidays, two days for Rosh Hashanah, one for Yom Kippur, and two for Passover. And she didn't even have the courtesy to give us notice or tell us to our face.

"Have we done anything to offend your cousin?" I asked Arthur after Annette hung up.

"I don't believe so," he said.

"If we did, we'd like an opportunity to apologize to her and correct it."

Arthur raised one eyebrow and shook his head.

"That was Annette on the phone just now," I said. "She quit. Did you know this was coming?"

"No, Mister Jacob. I did not."

"Do you have any idea why she would do this to us?"

He shook his head.

"None at all? There must be something."

"Annette has her own ways," he said. "I don't always understand her, but I respect her ways."

I expected Arthur would ask his cousin why she left us and come tell me. I questioned him about it several times, but he wouldn't say what kind of trouble Annette was having. Celia thinks Annette was going through the Change and that's why she started acting so hostile and unlike herself. She's probably right. Women aren't my department.

Arthur is a different matter. I trained Arthur and I've always been partial to him. He's always been a customer favorite, too. If a woman or a gentleman comes in, black or white, teenage or elderly, Arthur knows just how to treat them. If they like to be left alone to explore the merchandise themselves, he keeps the perfect distance. If they like to be fussed over, he fusses. And he's respectful. All the customers notice that.

Last winter, after Celia and I came back from our Caribbean cruise, Arthur started acting strange. He cut his hours at the store so he could take a nursing course at Sangaree. Nursing, of all things! When he came back full-time this spring, he seemed depressed. He wasn't excited about the new Hadro line and he didn't engage customers in his usual way. He was attentive enough; he just wasn't *himself*. I overheard him tell Myrtis, the new black salesgirl Celia is breaking in, that he was unhappy because he felt he had never done anything with his life.

I tried to cheer him up. "Look how far you've come!" I told him. "From inventory clerk to helping me run the store to establishing and overseeing the classiest gift department in the entire southeast!"

"I'm forty-eight," he said, "and what have I accomplished?"

"I'm worried about you, Arthur," I told him. "Is there anything we can do to help? You know you can come to Celia and me for anything. We'd be more than happy to help, with anything you need."

We take good care of Arthur. He's like a son to us. All of our sons moved away—Atlanta, Palo Alto, Denver—but with Arthur here, Celia and I feel like we still have a *family* business.

"You've been very good to me, Mister Jacob," he said.

Celia thought Arthur might be worried about putting his son and daughter through college and that he would feel better if we offered to pay him a sales commission on top of his hourly wage. When we told Sid Karesh we were thinking about this, he told us flat out not to do it.

"He'll tell Levi," he said, "and then *he'll* get ideas, and I can't afford to pay Levi any more than I am right now."

Sid has never been as concerned as Celia and I have to show courtesy to his employees and gratitude for their loyalty. He's had a huge turnover in help over the years. Karesh's Department Store is quite a different operation from Yblansky's. After talking it over, Celia and I went ahead and gave Arthur the commission.

That satisfied him for a while. He perked up around the store, chatted with the customers the way he used to, busied himself with touching up the displays when business was slow. He and his wife, Lillie, went to Bermuda for their twenty-fifth anniversary. Arthur lost a little weight, and he looked better than ever. When they came back, Celia gave Lillie a fabulous pearl necklace—eighteen inches of first quality Akoyas—and I gave Arthur a diamond pinky ring I had designed and made myself. They were so pleased.

It wasn't long before Arthur started moping again and his sales dropped. Celia decided she should have a heart-to-heart with Lillie, so she took her to the country club for lunch. Lillie told her Arthur was thinking about taking a job at the nursing home Sarah Smalls had opened, Apostolic Home. Smalls, a member of their church, had offered Arthur a good position, promising to help him finish his L.P.N. degree, if that's what he wanted.

Celia delicately suggested that nursing home work could be, well, an unpleasant job.

That didn't faze Lillie. She said Arthur knew it was a dirty job. Smalls had told him you see a lot of nasty things in her business, but that the physical was the least of it. "It's not what comes out of a person's wounds and other openings that dirties you," she told him.

Apparently Smalls also convinced Arthur he had a gift for ministering and for healing, like Elisha, and that he shouldn't bury his talents. She promised him that if he wanted to go to Interdenominational Theological Seminary in Atlanta to study the Bible and ministry, she'd find a way to send him, and when he came back, he could be the minister for her nursing home.

When Celia asked if Arthur wasn't too old to go to seminary, Lillie said, "He doesn't want to waste his life, Miss Celia"—just like that.

Celia was hurt, naturally, but she didn't let on.

"Arthur wants to *do* something with his days," Lillie explained. "Something that has *meaning*. He wants to make a *difference* in the world."

Celia reminded Lillie that Arthur had already made an important contribution, being the first black hired in merchandising in Coosawaw County and serving for so many years as a role model for the younger men, including his own son, someone they looked up to and learned from.

"Has he?" Lillie asked. "I wonder." Looking at Celia she said, very distinctly, "Sometimes what's good for a person isn't what's right."

Celia didn't know what to say to that.

About a week later, Arthur asked to take a leave of absence for a month. I told him to take all the time he needed. But as his mentor, I felt duty-bound to remind him that though Sarah Smalls's business might be the most successful black-owned venture in Coosaw County right now, it was brand-new and hadn't proven itself yet, and I did just that. Arthur and Lillie aren't kids anymore. They have to think about what would happen if Smalls's nursing home can't make a go of it, or if Sarah Smalls's New York husband decides to move her back up North and make her close the business. Arthur would be left without a job. When he and Lillie retire, they don't want to have to clean houses and rake yards to make ends meet. They don't want to hang a sign outside their house that says "FUNERAL PARLOR," "TERMITE CONTROL," and "WE GOT RED BAIT."

Arthur disregarded my cautions. "Better a handful of quietness," he said, "than two hands full of toil and a striving after wind." Those are his exact words: "Better a handful of quietness than two hands full of toil and a striving after wind."

Celia doesn't have a clue what he meant by that. Nor do I. Arthur said it was something he had been reading in the Bible, Ecclesiastes, but neither Celia nor I have ever heard it. We can't figure it out. It sounds crazy. It makes you wonder if Arthur's mental function has been affected by his depression. I've heard depression can cause confusion.

Celia and I have gone over and over this, and neither of us can understand it. How can Arthur be so blind to all he's accomplished here at Yblansky's, the respect he's earned for himself from everybody in the community, black *and* white, for his courage in taking this job and his loyal service in it? If he wants to be a minister, fine, let him volunteer in his church. But don't throw away his good life to do it.

"Don't you have to have a *call* to be a minister of God?" I asked Arthur yesterday when I called to see how he was doing. "I don't know much about Christianity, but it seems to me you need a *call* to be a minister. You can't just decide you're going to do God's work. God has to call you. Not Sarah Smalls or anybody else, but *God*. Otherwise, it won't work out. Isn't that right?"

"That's right," he said.

"And you have a call?"

"I'm listening," he said.

I called Arthur to the store this morning and told him Celia and I were prepared to double his pay and his commission, starting immediately. I told him that if he came back now, in a few years we would be ready to talk about selling the store to him for a *very . . . good . . . price*. He said thank you, but he wasn't ready. He had to pray over it. He would let us know at the end of his leave of absence.

Celia is convinced that Arthur won't come back, that he's going to quit for good. She's already worrying about whether we'll be able to replace him and if we'll have to close the store. "We need somebody we can depend on," she says. "Without Arthur, we can't take time off, and I'm ready to ease into retirement. I want to visit my grandchildren. I want to go to Paris, China, Hong Kong."

Don't worry, I tell her. Arthur's just going through a midlife crisis. He's not going to turn his back on all that we've done for him. He knows what he has here with us. I'll suggest he go see Doctor Reuben, and I'll mention to Doctor Reuben that he's been depressed and maybe he needs an antidepressant to help him over the hump. I've been like a father to Arthur. Sarah Smalls can't give him that. We're part of Arthur's life. We're like *family* to him. He'll be back.

THOSE WHO SHINE
LIKE THE STARS

R ain or shine, hot or cold, drunk or sober, every Friday night without fail, Sheldon Rosen locked up the
shop at six o'clock sharp and drove directly to the synagogue to welcome the Sabbath. In less than two minutes, he could guide his '83
Cutlass the five blocks to the shul and park it under the live oak out
front. In another three minutes, he could kick open the swollen
door, screw on the *yahrzeit* lights, pour the wine, and ascend the
beemo to pray. Davening the *ma'areev* service, including making
kiddush, adding the prayer for David, and washing the sticky wine
out of the cup in the tiny kitchen afterward, took him twelve minutes. The weeks Jacob Yblansky showed up, it took nineteen, and
on those nights, Sheldon's wife, Nancy, and his mother, Edyth, waiting for him at home, would wonder why he was taking so long.
"Killing roaches at the shul," he would say, grabbing his Rob Roy on
the way to the den to listen to Beethoven's Ninth. "What else?"

The shul was in ruins. The second you stepped into the foyer,
you were swaddled in dank decay and a cold darkness that persisted
no matter what wattage bulb burned in the overhead lights. It made

you unsure of yourself, like a tourist who dutifully enters an ancient crypt on a sunny day and stumbles through it, waiting in vain for the eyes to adjust. In the sanctuary, desiccated roaches studded the carpet; those still living dragged themselves down the aisle and up the step to the *beemo* after laying their eggs among the musty books, yarmulkes, and prayer shawls heaped here and there among the pews. The windows flanking the pews hadn't been opened in years. There was no use trying; they were sure to be corroded in place by now. On the *beemo,* mildew bloomed on the paneled walls and the wooden reader's desk. Brown stains covered the ivory quilted satin lining of the ark, where spiders nested among the scrolls. The Eternal Light suspended above the ark turned off and on spasmodically; not one of the electricians Sheldon brought in had been able to repair the short in the connection. The *yahrzeit* light for George I. Love wouldn't come on at all, no matter how many times Sheldon replaced the bulb. Divine retribution, Sheldon thought, for the attorney's bloated self-satisfaction, though how a hollow man like George Aaron Kantrowitz could be so full of himself as to give himself a name like that, have it legally recorded, and force people to call him by that name and that name only was a mystery greater than the parting of the Red Sea. George had always made a loud show of how much pro bono work he did for the Negroes and the poor, but as far as Sheldon could see, he had never cared for anybody but himself. The only time George—Aaron Kantrowitz *or* I. Love—had come to the shul was for its dedication in 1952 and then only because he had insisted on being the one to give the speech, which appeared in full the next day in the *Gazette*.

The fortieth anniversary of the shul's dedication was coming up in May, as Sheldon's wife and mother kept reminding him, but there would be no celebration. Except for Sheldon and Jacob, no one had davened in the shul for ages. The Sonenshines, the Kareshes, and the Doroshows had come for High Holiday services until six years ago, but after the last retired rabbi Sheldon hired garbled the prayers, wandered through his sermon, and pissed all over the floor in the anteroom to the sanctuary—a bladder condition, he claimed—even they hadn't come back. On rainy days, the rabbi's stench still crept under the locked door of the anteroom onto the *beemo,* reminding Sheldon what the world, Jew and goy alike, thought of Pinesboro Jews. The new Jew, a doctor who had moved to town five years ago to start his own practice, was no different from the rest of them. Shortly after Jake Reuben had moved to Pinesboro, Nancy and Edyth urged Sheldon to invite him to Friday night services. Sheldon didn't trust Reuben. Every time he heard Reuben's skill praised in town, he would mutter to himself, "My David's just as smart as he is. When David becomes a doctor of philosophy, he'll teach all the doctors what's what." Still, a few months after the doctor first arrived, Sheldon made a point of inviting him to daven with him and Jacob Yblansky. But the Harvard graduate said he and his family had already joined a congregation in Charleston. He preferred, Sheldon knew, to drive an hour there and back so that he could pray with other doctors and without roach carcasses crackling under his feet. Let him go, Sheldon thought. It's not the company you keep when you pray, but the prayers that matter.

Friday evening services in the Pinesboro shul had been empty for almost a decade, unless you counted the times pairs of Mormon boys sat in the back or Evangelicals sneaked in and littered the foyer with tracts while Sheldon and Jacob were davening on the *beemo.* There was no point in reading the tracts before he tossed them out: They always said the same thing: "Behold, the days come, saith the Lord, that I will make a new covenant with the house of Israel, not according to the covenant that I made with their fathers. The Church of Jesus Christ is the NEW Israel, the TRUE Israel." That was a joke. Pinesboro Jews couldn't even be bothered to be the old Israel, the false Israel, for a few minutes on Friday evening. If only those

Mormons and Evangelicals could see that. The Klingmans were too busy going to oyster roasts and the country club. The Levys had health problems. Solly and Yetta Kurtz had their own reasons for not coming—*Borukh Hashem*. One spring Matt Purdy, the convert, had ducked in a few Fridays on his way home from work, but he moved to Savannah that summer and within months he was dead, stabbed because he wouldn't hand over his gold Star-of-David. That pockmarked Christian boy, Cody Morgan, had come every week for a while, slumped morosely in the back corner, never making a sound, but he disappeared, too. Suicide, someone said. Slashed his wrists in his mother's powder room. Made such a mess she was forced to redecorate.

None of the Jewish kids ever came. Most of them had moved away, even the Yblansky boys. One of the Karesh boys, Larry, had stayed, but he joined the Episcopalian church to cement his chances of being elected county administrator. What could you expect? His mother, Min Karesh, had attended the Presbyterian church every Sunday morning with the ladies from her bridge club and taken communion "for social reasons." Alan Klingman had married a Baptist in town and was raising his kids Christian. That was no loss. Those kids were bound to be as vacant as he was. Brian Levy was an active member at an independent church where they played drums and danced for Jesus. His sister, Susan, was still a Jew, but she liked working with teenagers and led the youth group at the Methodist church, which met on Friday night. The only time Susan had been to the shul since her brother's bar mitzvah was the evening a year ago, when she hauled her youth group up on the *beemo*, took a scroll out of the ark, uncovered it, and rolled it out naked in front of them. Sheldon walked in on them while they were all leaning on it with their dirty elbows, rubbing it between their greasy fingers, and practically drooling on it. Susan, who couldn't tell a dalet from a resh and for whom the scroll was as arcane as the Egyptian Book of the Dead, stood in the middle of her worshippers, basking in their awe of secrets concealed from the goyim and her power to reveal them. Behind the group, the ark gaped wide at the offense. Shaking, Sheldon stumbled onto the *beemo* and chased them all out. Then he rolled the scroll, dressed it, kissed it, and returned it gently to the ark.

At least Sheldon's kids knew enough to treat the Torah with respect. But they were gone, or near gone. His oldest, Laurie, was leaving in a few weeks, the minute she finished high school. Though two years younger, David was already away at the university, on the same scholarship Sheldon had won years before. Nobody younger than David was left—not one Jewish kid under sixteen in the whole of Coosawaw County. All the young people got out of Pinesboro if they could. There were no opportunities.

Except for Jacob Yblansky. Jacob still had his opportunities. He had turned his father's jewelry shop into Yblansky's Gem and Gift Emporium, selling Waterford crystal, Rosenthal china, and Lladro porcelain, custom-cut diamonds, and one-of-a kind settings to customers who drove from Beaufort and Charleston for fittings. Nobody in Pinesboro could afford to shop there. Not that they would want to. Most of Jacob's help were blacks. Worse, Jacob bragged about it. He loved to tell the story of how he was the first one to hire a black in Pinesboro, Arthur Manigo in 1968. He claimed his mother had called to tell him hiring that kind was sinful and he had told her, "I run the store now, Mother, not you."

Jacob could turn anything to his favor. On the desk where he did his silver engraving and custom fittings, he kept a shoe box of photographs he had taken at Bergen-Belsen. When he met a new customer he especially wanted to impress, like Reuben, he would bring out the box and show off the ovens, the piles of dead, the specters at the fence welcoming him and the other American liberators. Before he was forced to move his store to a side street, Sheldon could look out the window of his store and watch Jacob across Lucas Street, pointing and nodding, playing at humility and sorrow. The trouble was, they all believed Jacob. Jacob was only eight years older than Sheldon and hadn't done nearly as well in school, yet the town, Jew and Gentile alike, treated him as if he were Moses. When Nathan Gold, the Hollywood producer, had his secretary call the Pinesboro town council to get the number of the local rabbi to conduct the seder he was throwing at his plantation, the mayor gave him Jacob's number. Sheldon had had to listen to that story from Jacob for months. How Gold had consulted him about all the preparations, how he had flown in from L.A. on his private jet and had the food flown in from New York. How marvelous the plantation was—designed by Frank Lloyd Wright—with stables of Arabian horses for Gold's guests, early Disney prints in most of the rooms, a painting in the den of Paul Newman riding a tractor through a cornfield, and Gold's famous collection of communist sculptures in the camellia gardens. How Bruce Willis and Demi Moore had shown up and been so gracious to him and Celia. How Gold's girlfriend was wearing a Versace dress and nothing else—not even shoes! How Jacob's choice of the armed-services Haggadah, the one he had brought back with him after the war, had been such a hit: long enough to provide a good show, but short enough not to tax Hollywood *sitzfleisch*. How the ritual meal, as Jacob had led it, was old-fashioned enough for Jews who didn't know anything about Judaism and wanted their romantic longings about it confirmed, but modern enough for Jews who wanted their Judaism moral or political, free of embarrassing trappings. How Jacob had conducted the seder in English but with a sufficient number of Hebrew blessings sprinkled in to give it an authentic flavor, clearly historical yet exotic enough for the Gentiles who expected Judaism to be obsolete but fascinating. The funniest thing, Jacob never failed to add, was that Gold had arranged for everything for the seder perfectly—the kosher shank bone and horseradish and *charoses* and matzos—but when it was time for the meal to be served, tuxedoed waiters danced in carrying sparkling silver trays of wedding challahs.

"Bread at Passover?" Sheldon had blurted out the first time he heard the story. "The most God-forsaken Jew knows better than that."

"Nathan said the only thing he remembered about Passover," Jacob said, "was that his grandmother used to get constipated from eating all those matzos."

"The guy's as funny as he is smart."

"You should have seen it!" Jacob said. "It was like something out of a Fred Astaire movie. I thought Celia would die laughing. I had to kick her under the table to keep her from spilling the beans and embarrassing Gold."

"Did you eat it?" Sheldon asked.

He didn't need to ask whether Celia had. "I'm a Southern Jew," she was fond of announcing, with a cock of her red head and a giggle far too young for her age. "I never ask what's in the barbecue." Jacob was more careful. He had to uphold his father's reputation as the leader of the Jewish community, which he had to accomplish without calling too much attention to himself as a Jew. One of the duties he took seriously as a leading citizen of Pinesboro was putting the Gentiles at ease.

"When in Rome," Jacob said, shrugging. A satisfied smile conquered his face. "That was a night to remember!"

A night to remember. That was just like Jacob, turning a moral lapse into a tale of triumph to amuse others. If Jacob were in prison for the most heinous crime in the world, he would still believe he was superior to everyone else around him, the only one worthy of attention, like Joseph in Pharaoh's dungeon, just waiting for them to come take him out and dress him in finery so that he could rule the land in style.

What did Jacob know that he, Sheldon, didn't? Jacob had forgotten all the Hebrew he had ever learned, except for *Mazel tov,*

Gut Shabbos, and *Borukh attaw Adonoy.* He stumbled through the easiest parts of the Friday evening service, making so many mistakes Sheldon didn't know whether to wince or laugh. Sheldon was the one who knew the prayers and the melodies. He had taught them to his children, too. David, who was studying Hebrew at the university in addition to all his required courses, already read better than most rabbis. Even Laurie, as much as she labored over it and as hesitant as her pronunciation was, could outread Jacob. But when Jacob showed up at the shul on Friday nights, he assumed he and he alone would lead.

And he would stop at nothing to keep Sheldon from usurping his position. Once, after Jacob had started his sloppy rendition of the opening prayer, *Mah tovu*—"How goodly are thy tents, O Jacob"—slaughtering every word but *Ya'akov,* Sheldon took over the chant. But before he could finish the prayer the way it was supposed to be done, Jacob switched to English, raced to the end of the prayer, and drowned Sheldon out with "May this our Sabbath worship bring peace to our hearts and strengthen our desire to live in peace with all our fellowmen. O-mayn." Another time, Jacob stole from Sheldon the honor of making kiddush. Jacob arrived late that Friday night, after Sheldon had already made it through most of the prayers without him. He strutted in just as Sheldon started making kiddush. Standing behind the reader's desk on the *beemo,* Sheldon was holding aloft the kiddush cup, which he had filled to brimming, the wine running over with *Shabbos* joy, as tradition demanded. When Jacob made kiddush, he filled the cup only half full, to save the shul's money, he said, and to prevent stains on the blue velvet covering on the reader's desk, though the real reason, Sheldon knew, was fear of ruining his white cuffs and the sleeves of his designer wool suits. Sheldon didn't get past *Borukh attaw Adonoy* before Jacob was next to him on the *beemo,* pulling the dripping cup out of his hand, and saying softly, "That's enough, Sheldon. You're drunk. Go sit down. I'll finish."

That wasn't all. Sheldon was the one who saw to it that the shul's heat pump worked, the one who let in the exterminator once a month, met the roofer when there were leaks, got after the blacks who raked the yard, found a dance teacher to rent the social hall to, called the plumber when the little ballerinas plugged the toilets. He shared the maintenance bills with Jacob fifty-fifty, too. Yet Jacob got all the credit, just because he had been old enough to go fight the Nazis and because he was a Yblansky. Old man Isadore Yblansky had been the same, lording it over Sheldon's father because he was a member of city council and a close friend of a venerable U.S. senator.

Sheldon would have gotten out of Pinesboro and been done with the Yblanskys long ago—he almost had—if his father hadn't died suddenly the day before Sheldon graduated from Vanderbilt. His mother needed someone to run the shop, and his sister had already married and moved to Montgomery. Sheldon had accepted a fellowship for graduate studies in organic chemistry at Duke University, worlds away in North Carolina, and he had been forced to turn it down. "Just for a few years," his mother had said. "Until I get on my feet. Then you can do whatever you want. There's plenty of time for someone as smart as you." But by the end of three years, he had married Nancy and they had started a family. And he hadn't kept up with the literature or the personalities in his field. Going back to school was impossible. His mother had grown more dependent on him, too. He had learned better than she how to run an auto supply business so that it made a decent income. If he left, the business would fail, and how would he support her then? Even if he did get his degree and found a teaching job, how much would he be able to make?

His mother knew how hard it was for him to work under her. "When I retire," she would say, "the store will be yours. You can make all the decisions yourself." But Edyth turned sixty-five, seventy, seventy-five, eighty, and never missed a day behind the front counter checking the books and waiting on customers. Once, she went to her daughter's in Montgomery for the High Holidays and left Sheldon in charge. Sheldon had hoped these visits would become regular and longer, perhaps extending into a permanent move. But his mother broke her hip the day before Yom Kippur and had to spend four weeks recuperating in a Montgomery hospital before she could be transported home. "You can't imagine how awful it was to be stuck in a place like that, Sheldon," she said when he picked her up. "My roommate was colored and her people came every night and prayed around her bed, makin' such a hellish racket crying for Jesus that I couldn't sleep. When I informed the nurse, she told me, 'Instead of complainin', you should ask them to pray for you, too. You'll get out of here sooner.' Can you imagine? They wouldn't *dare* say that to me in the Coosawaw hospital!"

Sheldon's mother wasn't blind. She could see how unhappy he was. From time to time she would say, "Why don't you go to one of those academic conferences? Or continue your research independently? You could study at night, write a book. You should write a book, Sheldon. You're the smartest person I know."

At first he believed her. Friends from school sent him notices of meetings and conferences, and he would pore over the list of presentations in his chair at night. Or he would be invited to join a research team or contribute an article to a journal, and he would stay up late making elaborate notes for the projects. But there was no one in Pinesboro to talk to about things that mattered, so his ideas dimmed and his mind grew slack, until he became convinced he was no longer fitted in any way to the academic life. At thirty-five, already bald and stooped, he abandoned his project on Illudin M and started daydreaming about getting away to the annual Small Business Owners' convention for a weekend so that he could golf in peace. On his forty-fifth birthday, he gave his professional library to David's college.

David would get out. All Laurie wanted to do was bitch about not getting invited to Cotillion because she was Jewish and scheme to get her name on the list the next year. She had no head for books, no head for business, no head for anything. David was different. Only sixteen and already finishing his freshman year, in all honors classes and getting all A's. He studied so hard he hadn't yet made it home for a weekend or any of the vacations, though he kept promising he was coming. Next year he was planning to study in Israel and wouldn't be able to make it home at all. Sheldon would close the shop for two weeks—let Edyth rant, how could she say no to the Holy Land?—and go visit. He and David had always been devoted to each other. They could talk, and argue, about anything with no loss of respect. In Jerusalem, the two of them would walk the streets of the old city together, watch the sun fall golden on the stone hills at sunset, and fill their lungs with desert air—not Lowcountry air that choked you with its soddenness, but air that was clear and clean, that opened the world, made space in it so that you could move freely. Maybe David would do his graduate work at the Hebrew University and become a professor there, write classics in his field and travel the world speaking at conferences. "Can you believe he's from a small town in South Carolina?" they would whisper in the audience. His genius would be world-renowned. This was no fantasy. David was the brightest kid who had ever come up through the Pinesboro schools. Everybody said so. No one could remember another student who came close to matching his gifts. Though anxiety-ridden, David Rosen was brilliant, endowed with such an abundance of talent, his teachers said, that he could do whatever he chose to do.

His son—*Borukh Hashem*—had a blazing future ahead of him. Sheldon's job was to make sure that nothing, *nothing,* kept David from that future, not girlfriends, not marriage, not family obligations, not Edyth's expectations, not Nancy's worries, not even his own hopes for his son. Even though you weren't supposed to petition God for favors of any kind on Shabbat, every Friday night, immediately after he made kiddush, Sheldon added a silent request for his David.

The Friday night before David was to come home for Passover—his first time back since he had left for school—Sheldon prepared the kiddush cup with greater care than usual. He polished it until his fingers burned. He washed and rinsed it thoroughly so that no chemical taste would embitter the wine. To avoid marring the perfectly shined silver with finger marks, he carried the cup to the *beemo* wrapped in a clean dish towel. He placed it in the exact center of the small silver tray that lay at the front of the reading desk and filled the cup with wine. The sweet, viscous liquid nearly reached the brim. He poured in a bit more, to fill it completely, but he miscalculated. The wine spilled over the rim. It ran down the sides and collected on the tray below. Jacob would snort in annoyance at the waste, the mess. But to Sheldon it was beautiful: It looked as if the gleaming cup were emerging from a ruby sea.

Jacob arrived and began chanting *Mah tovu,* How goodly are thy tents, as he donned his yarmulke in the foyer. Still chanting, he grabbed a siddur, flipped to the right page, and strode up the aisle. On the *beemo,* he delivered a quick nod to Sheldon before planting himself before the ark. No doubt eager to be on his way to yet another memorable occasion, he raced through the *Borkhu* and all the blessings of the *Shema.* He sprinted through the *Hatzi Kaddish.* During the *Amidah,* Sheldon had to interrupt him to remind him, once again, not to forget to say *Masheev haruakh umoreed hagashem,* You cause the wind to blow and the rain to fall. Almost six months had passed since *Sukkos,* and still Jacob couldn't remember to add the five lousy words that were supposed to be recited between *Sukkos* and Passover. Just as they were resuming the *Amidah,* the outside door groaned open.

Jacob and Sheldon traded glances. What kind of nosy goy this time? How they found the place was beyond Sheldon. By design, the shul was on an unfrequented side street, and there was no sign outside and not a single identifying Jewish marker on the building. With its red brick and red wooden door, it could have been a Lutheran church or Nazarene hall.

Feet scraped across the mat in the foyer. At the back of the sanctuary a man appeared. He looked about twenty and gave the impression of vibrant health. His tanned skin, stretched flawlessly over his strong-jawed, smiling face, seemed to glow. His hair, pulled back neatly in a ponytail, was silken black and so glossy that patches of light from the ceiling fixtures were reflected in it. He was wearing white jeans with a white dress shirt open at the neck, revealing a firm, powerful throat, and in his right hand he held a sheaf of papers.

"May I help you?" Jacob asked.

"'At the end of days,'" the man proclaimed, his voice sure and resonant, "'the Lord shall save the tents of Judah first.'"

"Another asshole missionary," Sheldon muttered.

"Shh!" Jacob said.

"'And I will pour upon the house of David,'" the man said, louder now, "'and upon the inhabitants of Jerusalem, the spirit of grace and of supplications: and they shall look upon me whom they have pierced, and they shall mourn for him, as one mourneth for his only son, and shall be in bitterness for him, as one that is in bitterness for his firstborn.'"

He paused for a moment, gauging the effect of the prophet's words, and said, "This prophecy has been fulfilled. The time has come for the house of David to confess to the Lord Jesus Christ and your crimes against him."

"Who are you?" Jacob asked. "Do I know your family?"

"I am Daniel."

"Daniel?" Jacob said, stretching out the name so the man would volunteer his last name and he could place him.

"Daniel twelve. 'At that time shall Michael stand up, the great prince which standeth for the children of your people.'" He drew himself up. He stood over six feet tall, his broad shoulders and narrow waist like that of a swimmer. "'And there shall be a time of trouble, such as never was since there was a nation even to that same time; and at that time thy people shall be delivered, every one whose name shall be found written in the book. And many of them that sleep in the dust of the earth shall awake, some to everlasting life and some to shame and everlasting contempt. And they that be wise shall shine as the brightness of the firmament; and they that turn many to righteousness as the stars for ever and ever.'"

"I'm sorry," Jacob said, closing his prayer book, "but we've finished here. We were just on our way home. If you'd like to leave your literature with us, you may."

The man strode down the aisle and handed the sheets up to Jacob, motioning for Sheldon to look on with him and read. They were covered with home-typed quotations from the prophets, and from Tacitus, Suetonius, Arthurus, and the Babylonia Talmud as well. Sheldon's eyes fell on a passage from Ezekiel: "Go ye aftwr him thru the city and smite; let not your eyue spare, neuther have ye pity; slay utterly old and youngm both maids, and little chilren, and women: but come not near any man upon whom is my markl; and begin at my sanctuary."

"Very interesting," Jacob said, handing the pages back. "But you have the wrong place. Try the Pentecostal church a few blocks over. I'm sure they'll be happy to discuss these matters with you."

"Time to go, Sheldon," Jacob ordered, picking up the kiddush cup and tray from the reading desk, careful to wrap his fingers over the Star of David engraved on the cup and to hold the dripping cup over the tray so he would not spill on the carpet.

As Jacob stepped down from the *beemo* into the center aisle, the man grabbed for the cup. Jacob jerked it out of his reach, spilling on the white cuff of his shirt, his Perry Ellis suit, and the carpeted step.

The man withdrew his arm.

"Let me share the cup of the covenant with you," he said, staring at Jacob.

"That's not possible," Jacob said.

"We're brothers. One vine, two branches."

"I'm sorry," Jacob said. "Nothing personal, you understand."

"You're rejecting me?" the man asked.

"Absolutely not," Jacob said. "It's simply a matter of timing. The blessing's over, it's time to go. No different tonight from any other night."

Why didn't he just tell him, Sheldon wondered, that it wasn't what the trespasser thought it was; it wasn't a cup of blood, a cup of suffering and death for a select fraternity, but a cup of joy, and that this was much harder to swallow, because you knew it would never be yours.

The man leaned toward Jacob and studied his forehead. "Do you bear the mark of the Lord?"

"Yeah," Sheldon muttered from the *beemo*. "Guess where."

"I have no idea what you're talking about, sir," Jacob said. "As I told you, we're finished here."

"Your own scriptures prophesy the coming of Jesus Christ," the man said. He shuffled through the pages of quotations and, pointing to one, read, "Isaiah nine: 'For unto us a child is born, unto us a son is given: and his name shall be called Wonderful, Counselor, the mighty God, the everlasting Father, The Prince of Peace.' Or look here, Isaiah fifty-three." He thrust the page at Jacob. "'He is despised and rejected of men; a man of sorrows and acquainted with grief . . . Surely he hath borne our griefs, and carried our sorrows . . . but he was wounded for our transgressions, he was bruised for our iniquities . . . yet he opened not his mouth, like a lamb that is led to the slaughter.' It's here in the Word of God, your very own Bible testifies to it. Do you deny it?'"

"This is a house of worship," Jacob explained in his benevolent patriarch's voice, "not a public forum. We're locking up now. I'll have to ask you to leave. If you'd like to leave your literature with us, you may."

"Do *you* deny it?" the man asked Sheldon.

"This is neither the time nor the place for religious discussion," Jacob said more loudly. "Again, I'll have to ask you to be a gentleman and leave the premises."

The man folded the quotations lengthwise in half, firming the crease with his thumb and forefingers several times while he looked intently from Jacob to Sheldon and back again.

"That's your answer then."

He slapped the bundle against his left hand, turned, and walked out. Within seconds an engine roared alive and a car took off down the street.

"Thank the Lord," Jacob said, blowing out his breath. "I thought we'd have to call Posey Kinard over here to explain those prophetic texts to him. No one can argue like a Baptist minister."

Jacob stepped back on the *beemo*. He held the kiddush cup in the air, blitzed through the blessing, took a sip, and offered it to Sheldon. When Sheldon handed it back after wetting his lips with it, Jacob set the cup on the reading desk. "We can wash this later. Let's go. Celia'll be worried. We're having dinner with the Beeches."

"I'll wash it out," Sheldon said. "Won't take but a minute."

"Be sure to turn out the lights when you leave. Last week Posey told me when he drove by on Saturday the outside light had been left on. I came over on my lunch hour and turned it off."

When Jacob's Lincoln Town Car pulled out, Sheldon picked up the kiddush cup and walked to the kitchen. In the social hall, the light reflected off the floor-to-ceiling mirrors the dance teacher had installed, surrounding him with Sheldon Rosens. Each dark figure mocked him. They stood around him like a chorus of scoffers, the shadows of who he might have been, walling him in.

A knot of anger hardened in his chest. The pressure choked his breath, made him dizzy.

He flung the wine at the mockers. Drops ran down the mirror. Still they glared at him, staring through a veil of blood.

Shaking, Sheldon walked into the kitchen and turned on the light. Sickening green walls lit up around him. Setting the cup on the counter, he knelt to open the cupboard next to the oven. He reached behind the matzo ball soup pot and wrapped his fingers lovingly around the smooth handle of his half-gallon Johnnie Walker Black. Not bothering to take out a water glass, he poured the kiddush cup full and slung the scotch down his throat. The comforting bite of the whiskey was arrested by the sweet drops of wine left at the bottom of the cup. He shook his head in wonder. Everywhere he turned, the world conspired to constrain him. As he was refilling the cup, the outside door opened. He downed the scotch and started to recap the bottle. If he slid the bottle inside the soup pot and quickly began washing the cup at the sink, Jacob would never know. Before the cap was tightly fastened, he stopped. The hell with the Yblanskys! What business was it of Jacob's whether he enjoyed a drink before going home to Nancy and Edyth on Friday nights? Celia's mother didn't live with *them*. And who was Jacob Yblansky to judge? He put away two or three stiff drinks every time he and Celia went to the club. Why should he be afraid of Jacob? The man was nothing but a blowhard. An idiot, too, so sure that the new doctor would be joining them soon for services, just because *he* had invited him, when Sheldon knew that a man like Reuben, Harvard educated and world traveled, would never darken the door of the Pinesboro shul. Reuben was smart enough to know that Pinesboro was a black hole into which everyone fell if he stayed long enough. The doctor would stay a few years, just long enough to establish himself as a smart doctor with a reputation for compassion and to build up a thriving practice. Then he'd sell the practice for a bundle and leave, never to look back.

Sheldon unscrewed the whiskey cap. In his rush, he lost control of it, and it clattered across the counter and fell to the floor. He poured until the kiddush cup was brimming. *"L'chaim,"* he said, raising the cup, and as he did so, in the window over the sink, he saw the reflection.

Still holding the cup aloft, scotch dribbling down his hand and arm, he turned round to face him.

It was the Great Prince. He was smiling and pointing a rifle at Sheldon's heart.

"'Therefore say unto the house of Israel,'" the Great Prince declaimed, "'thus saith the Lord God; I do not this for your sakes, O house of Israel, but for mine holy name's sake, which ye have profaned among the heathen, whither ye went.'"

"Drink?" Sheldon asked, offering the cup to him. Golden liquid spilled over the side and dropped to the floor. The room was fragrant with its smoky scent.

Without taking his eyes off Sheldon, the Great Prince leaned toward the cup and sniffed it. He stood straight again, shoulders squared. His tawny face was relaxed and open, fawn-colored eyes glittering, a sad smile lifting one side of his mouth. He was a handsome man. He had taken off his dress shirt and was wearing a spotless, brilliant white T-shirt that stretched over the muscles of his chest and revealed his powerful arms. He looked to Sheldon like one of Michelangelo's angels, strong, his powers unlimited, glorious.

"I ask you now," the Great Prince said, "will you turn to righteousness and shine like the stars, for ever and ever?"

Sheldon saw the midnight heavens alive with stars, myriads of stars, some steady, some coruscating, some constant, some streaking madly through space, all blazing with life, unbound. And he was among them, so close he felt their light, still new, not spent with years of travel, enlarging him; their heat spreading through him, expanding him until he knew no limits but fit free in the every-changing pattern of spaciousness, and he was radiant. He was the star, not Jacob, who was now so many light years away on earth in Pinesboro. And in the instant he realized this he knew that it no longer mattered: Now there was endless room for him to burn with possibility.

He gulped the rest of the whiskey, tipping the cup high to drain the last drops.

"'The soul that sinneth, it shall die.'"

The shot was clean. It burst upon his chest brightly, and as it did, Sheldon burst into prayer, "Let my David go."

EPIPHANY

Did I just call this number? I'm sorry, I just do things. I say things, too—by accident, I can't help it. Forgive me. I won't keep you but a minute. You don't know me, but I know your husband. Has he talked about me? Doris Bishop? The one who writes poetry? I'm always getting inspirations. Tonight I was starin' at the dogwood tree in my back yard and the leaves were shinin' in the moonlight like tongues of fire and they were tellin' me somethin' but I couldn't understand what they were sayin' so I called you because your husband says you been to school about the Bible and you know things. I heard you and your husband were movin' out of town and I wanted to tell you it wasn't my fault, don't move on account of me. I'm a fat old lady. Give me a pot of butter beans cooked up with fatback and neck bones, and I'll skip the steak I cook up for Mister Bishop. Before my accident, I thought it was my pituitary gland makin' me fat, but your husband says no, that can't be. Don't worry, Mrs. Reuben, I'm not after your husband. It was my prayer group who told me to go see him, about that funny feelin' in my chest. It's always heavy in there, like that Bryde's whale that stranded itself up the Ashepoo River last winter, down by Bennett's Point, and had to be pulled out with a tractor.

They never found out what made that whale die. I already went to the healin' waters up in Blackwell to cure that feelin' in my chest. They got four springs of water bubblin' up from the ground in the woods there in Blackwell, and nobody taking money for it so you can drink as much as you need without worrying yourself. They got one spring for high blood, one for joints, one for your eyes, and one for your heart and everything else. I drank most of a gallon of the heart water right there and took another one home with me to sip at night, but that funny feelin' just kept on. The ladies heard me prayin' about it and told me, "What's wrong with you? You expect God to come down here and help you? God helps those who help themselves. Go see the doctor." That's how I got to see your husband. I'm not after him. Doctor Reuben's a good doctor and a good Christian, too, a real kind man, but his looks don't interest me. I'm sorry, but they don't. He's too short for me and his forehead's too broad. He should clip his mustache, too. I'm glad *you* like him. My daddy ran around, and I respect every woman's right to her husband. Southern women know how to keep their men. Feed, flatter, and fuck—that's what my mother taught me. I told Doctor Reuben that yesterday when I went to see him about that feelin' round my heart and he asked did Mister Bishop and me get along all right. I told Doctor Reuben, too, that before I married Mister Bishop, I wanted to be a nurse, but I was always havin' that hard time of month, you know, bleedin' all the time, like some ladies do, so it didn't work out. I heard you need breast milk when you're young and then you won't get crazy later. Your husband didn't know about that. Have you heard that? You and your husband are Jewish, aren't you? I know what it's like not to have no friends. Let me ask you somethin', since you're not from around here and you know things. Did you ever hear that if you sit under a fig tree on Epiphany that Jesus will talk to you? My mother sat under Miss McCubbin's fig tree every Epiphany, and Jesus talked to her. Told her all sort of things, where to find Miss Brown's lost child, how many jars of okra to can, to walk to Edisto Beach with a cross on her back, to go to Billy Harrelson to have her uterus tied. Do you think Jesus'll talk to me if I go there and sit under that fig tree tomorrow? If Mister Bishop finds out I'm sittin' there, he'll come after me and carry me to Charter Hospital again, put me in with those gibbery people, make me eat cold slop and answer all those dimwit doctors' questions about my nerves and the stories I see in my mind. Still, I want to know about those dogs. If you had a question in your mind about your husband, wouldn't you want to know? You think it's better not to know some things? I don't know. Those dogs came after me on a Wednesday evenin' when I was comin' home from church. I know people say Mister Bishop let 'em run free that night on purpose. I'm not *that* dumb. But Mister Bishop says he can't for the life of him figure how his dogs got out of the pen—the Nesbitt boys down the street, maybe. Mister Bishop *loves* those dogs. They've been with him longer than I have. He's always careful to lock 'em up, especially since we had that trouble last year with the family next door that moved away on account of them dogs. They said our dogs ate their terrier, but dogs don't eat what they kill, do they? That's not natural. The police told us if there was any more trouble, we'd have to put the dogs down, we wouldn't have a choice about it. Why would Mister Bishop have let 'em out to get me, when he knew that meant trouble? It was my neighbor Lloyd Smoak who heard the dogs in our backyard that evenin' I was comin' home from church. Those dogs were raisin' the devil and they wouldn't quit. Lloyd came out to see if they had a raccoon trapped and saw me lyin' on the ground, half dead. He kicked those dogs off me and fired his gun in the ground right by 'em so they run off and then he yelled for Mister Bishop to come out. It took Mister Bishop a long time to come out. Too long, Lloyd says. Mister Bishop says he was nappin' in his chair with the TV on real loud. Lloyd had to pound on the door with the butt of his rifle a bunch of times to wake him. I was about bled out by the time they got me to the emergency room. I stayed in the hospital two months. I was sure in a fix. Mister Bishop visited me every week. Came with a candy bar or a sack of boiled peanuts, just for me. I know it was hard for him to shoot those dogs, and I cried for his loneliness. I know what it's like not to have no friends. Your husband says more surgery might ease the scarrin' and the nerve pain, but there's no money and Mister Bishop says it don't matter to him how I look. Those dogs chewed up my arms and my face and my chest pretty bad, but I don't mind. It's the Spirit that counts. The Spirit gives you the revelations you need. Do you think I should go sit under Miss McCubbin's fig tree tomorrow? Pastor George says you don't force the hand of God. He says some things God don't mean for us to know, that life's a mystery and we have to trust God and forgive men. God's the only one can punish men, he says, and He does it in His own way and in His own time, like the prophet Isaiah says: "For, behold, the Lord cometh out of his place to punish the inhabitants of the earth for their iniquity; the earth also shall disclose her blood, and shall no more cover her slain." Sometimes I think I'd like to see the earth disclose her blood, open up her womb and let all the bloody secrets she keeps hidden there spill out for everyone to see—every murder, every wallop, every shove, every mutilation of the spirit. But I know that's not Christian of me. Pastor George is right: The iniquity of this world is *God's* business, not mine. I've got enough troubles. I hope you're not movin' on account of me, Mrs. Reuben. I don't want anythin' to do with your husband or anybody else's. I have my own. You don't have to worry about me. Goodbye, then.

*Even the resurrection of the
dead is a long journey.*
— YEHUDA AMICHAI

STRANGERS
AND SOJOURNERS

Ialways make your twenty-eight miles, Sonny. If I
don't, my sugar'll go sky high and I'll get meshuga
and Marcie will come home and fuss at me again, tell me I have to
move into one of those places where they take care of you. I don't
need anyone to take care of me. I need to *ride*. This little bit of rain
isn't going to stop me. I've ridden through thunder and lightning,
you know I have. I rode through those first winds before Hugo and
through all the mess in the streets afterwards. I've ridden when my
chest was aching and my head was pressured up with sinus infection and my tush felt like the devil's pincushion. I've ridden with
sweat pouring down my cheeks and all in my eyes so I couldn't see.
I've ridden through everything there is. Just thirteen miles more
now, thirty-nine loops. If I have to take a quick break to run in and
put on another layer of Vaseline and Pond's, I will, but I'm making

those twenty-eight miles. Not one loop short. At first Doctor Calloway agreed riding every day was good for me. "Can't hurt," he said. What does he know? It *hurts!* Inside my legs, way up where it's private, I'm rubbed raw as ground meat. Wendell's already taken me to see the doctor twice this week because of the chafing. It's so bad I can hardly stand to sit down when I'm through riding. When Doctor Calloway looked at the raw inside of my thighs yesterday, he said, "If you want to chase your tail all day, do it in your car like normal people. You'll live longer."

What about that woman driving behind that logging truck on the Beaufort road last year? I asked him. On her way to pick up dance costumes for her kids. Chain snapped and logs spilled all over the road. She rammed right into them. Gone, just like that. A husband and three children left behind.

"Get one of those gel seats and stop bothering me!" he said. "I've got patients waiting with real problems."

That seat cost thirty-five dollars, and it didn't work any better than those inflatable doughnuts I had to sit on for my piles when I was pregnant. This split seat with a hole for my parts I'm trying tonight irritates me, too. As soon as I finish my final loop, I'm going to send it back to Marcie and tell her to get her money back. She wastes too much. And she's too bossy. Why should I quit Doctor Calloway and see that doctor from up North just because she tells me to?

"Reuben's Jewish and he's up-to-date," she says. "Remember when you took me to see Calloway when I was sixteen and he gave me a pessary to flip my 'tipped womb' right side up? Come on, Mom, pessaries went out in the nineteenth century."

What does Marcie know? She lives in California. And if she thinks Jews are the only ones with heads, why doesn't she marry one? Some of Doctor Calloway's ways may be a little old-fashioned and there's no denying he's rude—he told Wendell to go to hell when she complained about the side effects of that blood pressure medicine he gave her—but he's never been a drunk or a pill user. And who knows how long a man like Reuben will stay in a place like this? How does Marcie know he's not going to make his money off people here and run home with it? Wendell heard he's moving to Atlanta or Israel, somewhere where they have Jews. Where would I be then? Doctor Calloway's taken care of our family since we were first married, and he'll take care of us 'til we're all buried and gone. Loyalty heals over a lot of things. Marcie could stand to learn that. She doesn't even bother to light you a *yahrzeit* candle, and they're only seventy-nine cents at the Piggly Wiggly!

"You tell me, Mom," she yells at me, "how it's going to help Daddy if I go praise the name of God with a bunch of old men every morning for a year? I'm going to save his soul with a little hot wax?"

She knows I didn't say Kaddish for you, Sonny, and that I don't light a candle to remember the day you died. I don't have to: I ride. Twenty-eight miles every day. May 3, 1991. Five for the month plus three gives you the eight, and you put the nine and one together to get the ten, and then you add those to the other nine and one to get another ten, and you end up with twenty-eight miles you have to ride to make it come out right. I started the day after the funeral, three loops to every mile, setting out down our street and riding past the tennis courts, the Yblanskys', the Ulmers', over past Barnwell's little pond, and back down our street. Marcie and the rabbi from Charleston told me to take it easy, but I wasn't going to sit like a lady when you needed me. I got up before sunrise, put on your blue work pants, your yellow seersucker shirt, and your brimmed Dacron hat with the maroon ribbon band, and set out. The heat near killed me. It was already *shvitz* by seven o'clock. I was dizzy by the third mile, and no matter how much water I spritzed on my face or how many frozen Jell-O cubes I sucked, the dizziness wouldn't go away. I kept on, though, in honor of your memory. I rode from six to nine, took a rest, and then went out again from three to six. That schedule would have worked as fine as your morning and afternoon prayers if those Bilton boys on Magnolia Court hadn't thrown rocks at me every afternoon, and if those three boxers on the cul-de-sac hadn't torn my shoe off one morning, and if the school bus hadn't knocked me down and buried gravel in my elbow and hip. It took Tuke Drain a week to fix my bike, even though it doesn't have any gears, and I had to pay for the rental bike and the repair even though it wasn't my fault. The bus driver brought witnesses to testify before the judge that I always rode right in the middle of the street, weaving and wobbling, talking to myself and ignoring everything around me. They said I wouldn't budge when people honked and yelled to get by me. Those people were just pretending I was the one holding 'em back, because they were mad their lives weren't going anywhere, but the judge ruled that I couldn't ride the bus route during the day anymore.

It's better riding in the dark. It's cooler between midnight and six, and I see more. Last month, about the nineteenth mile, as I was making the fifty-sixth loop past the Ulmer house—Terry would roll over in his grave if he saw the mess those renters have made of his house and his prize camellias—I saw two police cars parked out front. I stopped and straddled my bike, careful not to bump my tender area—if I wear a pair of those terry shorts inside my pants, it doesn't hurt so bad. A policeman and a parole officer came out leading a skinny kid in boxers and handcuffs between them. He was looking down at the ground, kind of smiling but kind of sad, like a little boy who's had fun doing his mischief and is glad he did it but knows it's going to make his mama madder if he doesn't put on a face that says he's sorry. What are the people who love him going to do now? I wondered. Here they've been pulling for him to turn his life around and get beyond his troubles, and he does this. What are they going to do now, give his soul up for lost?

　　　　　　　STRANGERS AND SOJOURNERS

That boy reminded me of the Hale girl a couple of streets over. I guess the family didn't know she was having troubles. Wendell says everybody else in town knew. The girl started roaming the neighborhood when she was thirteen, ringing doorbells and asking could she come in and use the bathroom. She came to my door once, but I don't let anybody in since you're gone. Wendell let her in twice. "When someone's got to go," she says, "she's got to *go*. You don't stand in the way of nature." She said both times the girl stayed in the bathroom so long she got curious. She thought maybe she was having her time and didn't know what to do. After the girl came out and thanked her, polite as she could be, and left, Wendell checked the bathroom. It was clean as a whip and smelled fresh as ever. She heard the girl went around the whole neighborhood that way, stealing drugs, anything she could get. That's how she died. Took somebody's pills, didn't even know what they were, got drunk and headed out to Edisto Beach in the dark of night to see her boyfriend. She missed a turn on the island and the car went into the marsh and she drowned. Sixteen years old. Her parents had to be called home from their vacation to bury her. Their only child gone, just like that. *Melissa Hale.*

There's so many gone. Last year, a little boy was run over by his granddaddy when the man was backing out of the garage, and all those Indian kids died in that fire in Creeltown. The year before that, the shop teacher at Pinesboro High and his helper got killed when a hay gate broke loose and all the bales fell on them. Broke one's spine and crushed the other's chest. The helper was still breathing when they uncovered him, but he died before EMS could get him to the hospital. Only thirty-one and forty-six. *Dean Crosby* and *Peden Lovett.* Had a big funeral for the two of them out by Edisto Beach. Wendell said she heard they released balloons at the end, after their families scattered their ashes in the waves. All colors, floating in the sky. Not Christian, she says. Not Jewish either, I say. Gone just the same.

I knew the Lowcountry was a dangerous place the minute you brought me here, but you wouldn't hear of it. You were always after me not to be so crazy worried. Quit your fussing, you told me after Ben died. Thirty-eight years old and healthy as a man can be, went fishing in the Ashepoo one sunny morning and drowned. But I should quit fussing. Sarah never got over Ben's going that way. Looks like their daughter, Susan, won't either—Marcie's age and with a good job teaching math at the middle school, but she drifts around town in rumply jeans and a greasy old ponytail and no makeup or boyfriend, smoking, smoking, smoking. Wendell says she throws her money away buying vanilla cokes and bologna sandwiches for the young people who hang out at the drugstore. You should be here, Sonny, to tell that girl to settle down and stop playing the wandering Jew. *Ben Levy.* Gone.

If you had been here three years ago, when that crazy man shot Sheldon in the synagogue, right in the kitchen where we used to fry latkes and serve the Passover chicken and farfel muffins, you wouldn't tell me to stop fussing. Nobody's prayed in the shul since. Jacob will have to sell it before long, and God knows what kind of a bargain he'll make. Wendell says one of those independent gospel churches has already made an offer. There was hardly anyone at Sheldon's funeral. Jacob mooshed his way through *el malei racha-mim* and the Burial Kaddish, and he didn't even give us a chance to throw dirt in the grave. *Sheldon Rosen.* He's gone.

Same thing with snakes. Every night I have to watch for copperheads on the road, especially alongside the clumps of pampas grass in my middle loops. Their eyes shine up in my headlight. I have to maneuver around them, or they'll rise up and strike my heels when I run over them. You always told me nobody ever died from a snakebite around here—as long as you lived, you had never seen it, that's what you told me. But last summer, that Green Pond man got bit in the arm cleaning out the rake of his tractor when he was harvesting peanuts. He chased the snake down to get a good look at it, and it bit him again. It was a rattler. He lived four months in the hospital. First his arm sloughed off and then he died. The papers were full of it, because if he had known that there's a universal anti-venom now and the doctors don't have to know what kind of snake bit you, he'd be alive today.

So many gone. When it's dark and still, Wendell and all those other meddlers in their beds, there's room for all the missing ones. That's why it's better to ride when it's dark. Twenty-eight miles goes fast when you're with the ones you miss. Only seven miles left now already. Your cousin Solly's gone. Yetta, too. She didn't last six months after Solly died. Her niece came and dragged her to a home up in New York State, and that was it, she died. *Solly Kurtz. Yetta Kurtz.* Same thing with Ruby and Dave Ferris, the ones I used to buy my eggs and country butter and collards from. Ruby had stomach cancer, but she cooked Dave's food and kept that trailer spotless and her garden as neat as a pin until the day she died. Dave couldn't live without her. They found him dead on the couch about a year later. Bony as a skeleton, Wendell said, and with Ruby's gold cross around his neck. *Ruby Ferris. Dave Ferris.*

When I was riding your miles in the daylight, I never heard the names. They come in the dark, when everything is resting and you can hear the earth breathing, breathing out the names. You know I can't tell Marcie about it. She'll tell them I have never got over the tragedy and move me to a home in California where they make you watch game shows all day and force you to eat mushy, gray food, and she'll visit me once a week just to tell me I look good when I don't. Marcie's welcome to her theories, PTSD or PDST or PSDT, if that's what gives *her* comfort, but she's not going to take *my* way from *me*. I can't tell Wendell about the names, either. She'll gossip it all over town. What does Wendell Daniels know? She lays in bed all day reading books and talking on the phone. Only gets out for the dinner her maid cooks. She says she's got all kind of ailments that keep her in bed, but she's just lazy.

When Adailgus died, Wendell had to look a long time before she got herself another maid who would cook her dinner for her before she went home for the night. The younger women all want to get paid forty dollars a day for a little light housework, not ironing or washing or doing deep cleaning. I told Wendell she never paid Adailgus enough and that she couldn't expect a woman to put her own children and grandchildren after her employer's dinner. I told her she's going to have a hard time keeping someone this time and she's going to have to pay a lot more, but she says no. She's always arguing with me. She *still* argues with me about Marcie's birthday. She *insists* it's April 2, not April 3. *I'm* her mother, I say. I think I'd know.

"Doctor Calloway had you so drugged up," she says, "you didn't know an English pea from a Crowder pea."

Yesterday morning, Wendell called me at noon, woke me up, just to ask, "Are you going to invite me to your funeral?"

"No!" I told her. "You'll just start an argument with me."

Wendell's still got Robert, but she misses Adailgus. She'll never replace her. *Adailgus Nettles. She's mine.*

Why should I tell Wendell about hearing the names? She'd just tell me I didn't. You'd like to tell me that, too, wouldn't you? Don't go blabbing that around, Dinah, you'd like to say, unless you want people to think you've lost your marbles for good. Don't be meshuga, Sonny. I know God's not going to speak to me, Dinah Sonenshine, not out of a bush or a whirlwind or Miss Barnwell's open mailbox; I know I'm not Moses—I'm not *that* good of a Jew yet. So stop worrying, you've got enough troubles. But I know what I've heard riding in the dark, and you and six million rabbis aren't going to tell me I didn't hear it.

It's not like any voice you've ever heard, when the earth starts breathing out the names of the missing. It's a softness rising up from the ground, making space in the earth so worlds can live where no flea could fit before, and then that great spaciousness rises and fills all the air, until the shrubs and the trees are spilling over with it, until all the space around you is full with it, crowding your ears so you feel the names brushing against them. Each name riffles over you in its own way: some tickly, some hard and almost painful, some sharp. Some are names you know better than your own; some, names you never heard before; and some, names you can barely make out but you recognize in your bones just the same. And after every name you hear, *He's mine,* or *She's mine.* And every once in a while, after a string of names, you hear, *They're mine, mine.* And then there's a silence, a breath, before the names start again.

Don't you tell me it's just the names of the ones who get sick or old that get called, or the names of the ones who get killed by somebody else. That's not right, I don't care *what* Wendell says. Wendell's not even Catholic, she's Methodist, so what does she know about mortal sin? And I know Sam Cohen's got his brains and his piety and his principles, his own troubles and his own way of crying, and I love him to death, you know I do, there's not a more generous man alive, but I don't care a fig for what he thinks about dying and burying. He and Elyse wouldn't come to your funeral or shivah, for the same reason they wouldn't go to Jonathan's— because "the rabbis teach" that those who take their own lives may not be buried with the faithful of Israel and they may not be mourned. When Marcie called to tell him the time of your funeral, he told her, "Being a Jew means choosing life. That's why the rabbis teach that 'I will seek your blood for your souls' applies to the one who destroys his soul. I can't change that, Marcie, even for Sonny. I wish I could, but I can't."

The rabbis teach, the rabbis teach. Can't those rabbis teach Sam Cohen to act human to his own son and his best friend?

I thought Sam might have changed by now—you know how grief can turn you inside out—but he goes on in his way. He's just a little quieter about it these days. I remember how he yelled when you tried to persuade him to sit shiva for Jonathan. He and Elyse had just gotten the news that Jonathan had thrown himself over a cliff on the northern coast of Maine, on Yom Kippur, and we went over to comfort them. You thought you could reach Sam in the tearing of his heart. But he couldn't be reached. "Our son has been dead to us from the moment he declared to us he was *to'evah* and had no intention of ceasing to be an abomination," he yelled. "We already sat shiva for him."

"Sit shiva again," you urged him. "For *Elyse's* sake."

"Even if I wanted to," Sam said, "it would be impossible. You know what is written in the Talmud: 'One who takes his own life is worse than a murderer. Suicides do not receive a share in the world to come.'"

"At least say Kaddish for him then," you begged him, "to atone for his sin, so his soul won't be lost forever. Isn't it also written, 'The world stands on *g'milut chasidim,* acts of mercy'? He was a *boy*, Sam, a boy in a dark time who couldn't see his way out. He didn't know what he was doing. Who of us does?"

But Sam wouldn't listen. He still won't. He won't allow Jonathan's name to be spoken in his presence, even today. Elyse visits the grave, but she has to do it in secret, so Sam won't find out.

Even if it's true what Sam says about the Talmud, that was a long time ago, and those rabbis he likes so much didn't live in the Lowcountry. What do the rabbis know about Jonathan Cohen's trials and griefs? They weren't born gay. They didn't have to see their last loved one in the world die of AIDS. They didn't have the door shut in their face by their parents when they came home for Rosh Hashanah. Maybe some of those rabbis chose to be martyrs, but that's different. What do those rabbis know about you and your life, Sonny? You all wrapped up in your tallith and tefillin those last months, shaking like a leaf about to fall, praying over and over, *"We long for the name by which You are called"*?

Sonny, listen to me. I hear the names of the ones who kill themselves, too. They just get slipped in with the others, nice as you please. You know Pug gave himself an injection of morphine because he couldn't take one more day of his patients' pain, and I heard *his* name one night. *Pug Padgett.* I heard the name of that young woman on Camellia Avenue, too, the one who took pills because her husband left her. *Patty Hayes.* And Joe Rider, who had to retire from the police department because he couldn't remember how to write out speeding tickets anymore—he took his shotgun and killed himself a year after you, and I heard *his* name. *Joe Rider.* And I heard the name of that poor Morgan boy, whose mother blames herself for what he did. *Cody Morgan.*

I heard Jonathan Cohen's name, too. If I were as smart as you, Sonny, I'd go to Sam's house right now and prove to him he's wrong about Jews and God and choosing life. I'd tell him what I heard in the dark. I've heard Jonathan Cohen's name, Sonny, as clear as anyone could hope, in this world or the world to come or any other world you want to dispute about. *Jonathan Cohen.* And don't tell me knives are different—neat as a *shochet* you were.

Only six miles to go now. Eighteen loops. Eighteen dollars you gave to the Jewish National Fund to plant trees every spring, eighteen dollars every Passover to sell our *chametz* to the rabbi in Charleston, eighteen for *tzedakah,* eighteen for a bar mitzvah, eighteen to honor your parents' *yahrzeits.* "For life," you would say, doing that spindly dance of yours and singing, *"Chai, chai, v'kayam,* lives, lives, forever."

The last eighteen loops are the easiest. That's when my rhythm carries me. I can't even feel my thighs right now. I'm riding free. Nothing interfering with my listening. When I first started hearing the names, I thought it was spirits calling out for help and I had to do something for those poor people, talk to them, ask what they wanted, put them at rest. But that's not it. It's the *earth* calling the names. It takes up our dead bodies and makes them live, sings out their names into the darkness, every night a new song. All we have to do is listen. *Libby Doroshow. She's mine. Slappey Jones. He's mine. Israel Nettles. He's mine. Batula Patel. She's mine. They're mine, mine.*

The earth belongs to God. We're strangers and sojourners here. *You* used to tell me that. When we're born, you told me, God sings a song over the earth, calling each creature into life by name, singing it into this world. That could be. I haven't heard that creating song myself, but I believe it could be. The part you left out, Sonny, is the part I know for sure. When we die, the earth sings an answering song, each night gathering up the names of the lives buried there and making them into a song it sings to God, so God won't forget our beauty here. That song is singing every night, all around us. I've *heard* it. I hear it now. I listen every night, Sonny. I'm waiting to hear your name. If I keep riding, I'll hear it. If I have to ride for forty more years, I *will* hear your name. And when I hear it, when I hear the dark call *Sonny Sonenshine, He's mine,* I'll know the earth and God have taken you up and you're not a stranger anymore; you're the song.